River's Edge

By

Rolland Love

River's Edge
By Rolland Love

All rights reserved. Copyright © 2018

This novel is based on Rolland Love's experiences growing up in the Ozark Mountains; however, it is a work of fiction. Names, characters, places, brands, media, and incidents are either the product of the author's imagination or are used fictitiously. The author acknowledges the trademarked status and trademark owners of various products referenced in this work.

Cover Design by Paul Middleton
Shadow Dancer Images

Reviews

Amazon Kindle – Featured Author Review – Rolland Love "Love's writing transfigures his Ozark Mountains stories into a series of fantastic tales Huck Finn and Tom Sawyer could have only dreamed of and his style is compared to Mark Twain."

"To understand Overland Park writer Rolland Love, think Mark Twain. Love's stories are enjoyed by all ages." Nick Kowalczyk, The Kansas City Star.

Introduction

Blue Hole and its sequel, River's Edge, are two mystery suspense novels set in the Ozark Mountains. These adventure stories are enjoyable for all ages.

The story River's Edge recounts a camping trip with my grandsons, Nick and Jake, and my brother Dub.

The location is the Blue Hole, on an Ozark Mountains stream where greyish-black snapping turtles bask on piles of driftwood, where cottonmouth water moccasin snakes slither across the surface of the river and fishermen stalk the elusive smallmouth bass. Turkey buzzards soar on thermals above towering limestone bluffs and cold spring water with the scent of ancient earth pours from the mouths of caves.

In this idyllic setting, I never imagined we would relive the horror of a murder committed at the Blue Hole the last time Dub and I were there in 1949, or that I would confront the bitterness between kinfolk buried in the deep cool spring fed river valley of my youth.

Chapter One

The journey began as a celestial call from a spring-fed river. The power of water brought me home. All I had to do was patch up a long-standing feud with my brother, stop thinking about the murders, and not give another thought to the old man who mysteriously appeared behind our tent in the middle of the night the last time we camped at the Blue Hole. I was that close to having the three best days of my life.

I left Kansas City with my grandsons Jake and Nick at sun up and at noon we arrived in Lewiston, a sleepy little river town deep in the Ozark Mountains. I stopped the car on the wooden bridge my Grandfather helped build in the early 1900s and hung my head out the window. I looked down at a pile of sun-bleached driftwood that had washed up against a concrete and stone support pillar. Basking in the late morning sun on a log close to the water was a greyish-black snapping turtle. Aware of our presence, the turtle stretched its neck out and raised his head.

"Wow, that's a big snapper," I said. Jake, the nine-year-old opened the back door and jumped out for a look. "Turtles are prehistoric, you know."

"Yeah," Nick, the twelve year old said as he stepped outside the car to check it out for himself. "They've been around 200 million years."

"How do you know?" Jake asked.

"Saw it on TV. Read a story on the Internet." Nick grabbed Jake's hand and held it up in the air. "They got jaws powerful enough to bite off a finger, too."

Jake jerked his hand away and gave Nick a shove. "That true, Papa?" he asked.

"It's true. They're tough, mean and fast. Mess with 'em and they'll bite ya."

"That one's the size of a steering wheel," Jake said. "How big do they get?"

"Fifty pounds or better," I said.

Jake ran his fingers through his silky black hair and brushed it away from his forehead. "That's bigger than me. I hope one doesn't crawl into our camp tonight."

When Nick and I laughed, the turtle slid off the log into the water and disappeared under the pile of driftwood.

I squinted my eyes against the bright sun and gazed up the river at what looked like flecks of gold dancing on the surface of the rippling water. I took a deep breath and smiled. I had forgotten how sweet and fresh the air smells on a spring-fed Ozark river. I looked up and watched a half dozen turkey vultures circle overhead in the wide blue sky—big black birds the Ozark locals called buzzards.

"My friends and I used to dive off of this bridge," I said.

Nick tilted his head to one side and looked at me with questioning brown eyes. "Doesn't look deep enough to me."

I turned my head to the right and plain as day, I saw myself as a boy about Nick's age standing on the bridge railing, waving at my friends who waited in the water below for me to take the plunge. I had a golden tan from a summer of outdoor fun; my blonde sun-streaked hair was blowing in the wind. I had forgotten how much Nick and I looked alike when I was his age.

"What did you say?" I asked when I looked around and saw Nick staring at me.

RIVER'S EDGE

"I said was the water doesn't look deep enough. What were you looking at, Papa?" Nick asked as he leaned over the edge of the railing and looked down at the water.

"Thinking about something, that's all. The water was a lot deeper in the old days. Mother Nature filled in the hole with gravel. Any luck?" I yelled at a couple of kids under the bridge where an uprooted Cottonwood tree had washed against the bank and created a haven for fish.

"Got some goggle-eyes," the taller of the two boys, who wore a straw hat, yelled back.

"Caught myself a nice Smallmouth bass," the kid wearing bib overalls and no shirt shouted as he held up a stringer with a half dozen fish flopping their tails back and forth.

"Nice mess of fish," I called down to the young fishermen. We waved goodbye and got back in the car.

"Can we catch some fish like that, Papa?" Jake asked.

"Sure, only ours will be bigger."

I stopped at the end of the bridge and stared at a list of men's names chiseled into a limestone rock.

"What are you looking at now?" Nick wanted to know.

"Your great-grandpa helped build this bridge." I pointed at the cornerstone. "There's his name at the top of a list of men who worked on the project. Tom Benson."

"Looks like it's been here forever," Jake said. "I can hardly read some of the names."

"Forever is about right. I used to ride across the bridge with Grandpa Tom in a hay wagon pulled by two black Belgian workhorses."

"How old were you?" Nick asked.

"Not quiet as old as Jake. Probably seven."

As I drove down the main street of Lewiston I noticed there was a vacant lot where the church once stood. All that remained was a gravedigger's shed at the entrance to the cemetery.

I thought about the Halloween night I walked the tree-lined road that wove its way in and out of the tombstones. Sycamore trees that swayed back and forth in the light of a full moon looked like a congregation of ghosts. Halfway though I heard a noise that sounded like someone had scraped a knife blade across a whetstone to sharpen it up for some serious cutting. I ran so fast I fell down on the gravel road and cut my knee. When I got to the gate where my friends who dared me to take the spooky walk were waiting, I was shaking all over. It did not bother me that they laughed and laughed; I figured someday I would get revenge and eventually I did.

Now, I stopped the black Lincoln in front of my younger brother Dwayne's house and turned off the key. Since he was nine years old, he had been "Dub" to everyone who knew him. He and his wife, Molly, walked out onto the front porch of their impressive-looking two-story log home and waved.

Even though he seemed healthy and fit, Dub's curly blond hair had turned white since I saw him last. Molly still had the trim figure of a teenager. She wore a long, blue cotton dress, and the color of the sky. They waved again and smiled as they started down the front steps. Instead of waving back, I looked down at a package lying on the floorboard. I had picked it up the day before at the post office. It had my brother's return address on it, so I left it in the car, unopened. Since I had not spoken to him more than a half-dozen times over the past thirty years, I could not imagine the contents being anything but bad news.

"You getting out, Papa?" Jake asked. He opened the back door and petted a black and tan coonhound that had poked his skinny head inside the car.

"Sure." I had a knot in my stomach as I watched Dub and Molly walk across the yard. They smiled at one another and laughed, as if everything were okay between Dub and me.

"Get out. Stay awhile," Molly said. "Got homemade lemonade for you thirsty travellers. Glad you came. It's been a long time."

I got out of the car and stood beside the front fender. Dub walked up to me and I shook his hand. The last time I looked into his pale blue eyes, harsh words had been spoken. "How yak doing', Tommy?"

"I'm okay," I said with all the confidence I could muster

"I'm glad. Real glad."

My mind flooded with memories at the sound of Dub's voice. Hard to believe with all the good times we had as boys that something went wrong between us. On the trip down I thought about what I would say when we came face to face. Mulled over a couple of things in my mind that seemed right, but the healing words never made it to my lips. The only time Dub and I had been together during the past fifty years centered on death: the funerals of our parents and grandparents. We talked on the phone when we sold our folks' farm and grandpa's homestead. The conversations were mostly about business. Sadly we knew very little about each other's lives or families.

I had called Dub a few days earlier, after a five-year silence. I was bringing my two grandsons down to camp at the Blue Hole. He told me that the road to the river was rough and rocky, then offered to loan me his Jeep. I took it as a sign he might want to patch things up between us.

I walked beside Molly as we started toward the house and Dub followed along behind, talking to Nick and Jake. The boy's finally bolted and ran across the yard, jumped up and grabbed the low hanging branch of a maple tree. They laughed as they swung back and forth like a couple of monkeys. I remembered what it was like to always be on the move, climbing trees, fishing and swimming in the river. I felt guilty about not making more of an effort to put a stop to a sad situation. It had robbed Dub and me of so many good times.

I looked up at the vaulted ceiling as we walked into the living room. Six hand-hewn support beams the size of railroad ties ran across the open space from wall to wall. I stared at a deer head hanging over a large stone fireplace. I remembered the day Dub shot the ten-point buck with a lever-action 30-30 Winchester that belonged to our Grandfather. Who should get the rifle after our Grandfather died was one of the things we got into a disagreement about. *What a stupid thing to do,* I thought. Why should I have cared who got the damned thing? At the time we had the heated discussion, I lived in the city and did not even hunt. I looked intently at the dark, glass eyes and remembered the dead animals that hung on the walls of Grandpa Tom's river cabin.

"What happened to the church?" I asked. "Only thing left is the grave-digger's shed."

"Good question," Dub said. "One night it just burned to the ground. People talk, you know. Some said it got lightening struck. Other's thought it was the work of the Devil. All I know is there wasn't a cloud in the sky the night it happened. Chalk it up to another unsolved mystery during a full moon."

"What kind of unsolved mysteries?" Nick asked. "Somebody get killed or something?"

When Dub looked at me and frowned, I changed the subject. "I'll tell you about it later," I said to Nick.

"Nice place y'all got here, Molly." I found myself slipping back into a slow, down-home manner of speaking. My Ozark roots, which were still ingrained, had been buried in citified ways for many years and were now branching out.

"Thanks," Dub said. "Built it ourselves. Cut the logs off Grandpa Tom's farm place. Saw ya lookin' at the deer head. Remember the day I shot it and we hauled it out of the woods?"

"Like yesterday. Biggest rack anybody around these parts had ever seen before."

"Or since," Dub added with a smile.

The boys stood under the deer head and looked up through the antlers into a background of red Cedar boards that covered the ceiling. A skylight in the middle of the room looked out toward the heavens.

"Do you still hunt deer, Uncle Dub?" Nick asked.

"Dub hunts and fishes all the time," Molly said. "We eat a lot of wild game. Fact is I still have jerky from the last deer he shot. You boys like jerky?"

Nick looked at Jake and smiled. "Yeah, sure. I like jerky. Don't you, Jake?"

Jake wrinkled up his nose and did not comment one-way or the other.

"I'll gather up a sack full. You can take it on your camping trip." Molly turned around and walked toward the kitchen.

"You still messin' with computers?" Dub asked.

I was surprised he remembered. I had only mentioned it in passing many years earlier. "Actually, I sold my company last year," I said.

"Papa used to travel all over the world," Nick said. "He even went to China.

"I travelled a lot in the past, but I've slowed down," I said.

Dub looked at me and folded his arms. "Sounds like you've had an exciting life."

"I've done well, but there's been a price to pay. So what have you been up to?" I asked. I tried not to sound overly friendly. Did not want it to seem like I was trying to build back in a few minutes what had been lost for many years.

Dub lowered his head and looked up at me through bushy white eyebrows. "I farm some. Put up hay and harvest a little corn. Run a small herd of Black Angus cattle. Hunt and fish my fair share. Do some preachin' now too. Got a little country church down by Buck Holler turnoff. Been the pastor goin' on five years."

Dub looked deep into my eyes and waited for a reaction. It was obvious the part about him being a minister had taken me by surprise. As a youngster he was the most mischievous boy in town. If anyone had been voted most likely to end up being a troublemaker, it would have been Dub.

Molly broke the silence when she walked into the room. "Dub's good at capturing the ear of sinners. Come hear him on Sunday. He may say something worth thinking about on the drive back to Kansas City."

I gave her a startled look. I smiled and agreed to listen to Dub preach before we headed home. I figured I could take anything he had to say so long as he didn't dwell on repentance and bang his fist on the pulpit when he looked at me.

Dub always could get people to do about anything," I said. "Too bad there are not more like him to deliver the message."

"Don't worry about me trying to convince you to get baptized in the river on Sunday, Tommy. I'm not one to push the Lord's will on people. Folks come around in due time one way or the other."

I laughed nervously and was glad Jake changed the subject.

"What happened to your foot?" Jake asked. Everyone looked down at a bandage wrapped around Dub's foot and ankle.

Dub looked at me and laughed lightly. "You may not believe this, Tommy. I got myself snake-bit."

"Lordy, how'd that happen?" I asked.

"It was dark. I was giggin' frogs. I stepped out of the boat onto a gravel bar. A cottonmouth moccasin bit me on the ankle."

"Did it hurt bad?" Nick asked as he hunkered down for a closer look. "Did you almost die?"

"It hurt real bad and I got sick as sin. I did think I would die. But I'm still here."

"That's awful," I said, thinking at least we had one thing in common. Too bad it had to be snake bit.

"I thought about you after the snake struck me, Tommy. Figured you lived through it, so I would too."

"Can I see the snakebite, Uncle Dub?" Jake said.

"Sure." Dub reached down and removed the bandage. "It was all swollen up for awhile, black and blue. Now I'm pretty much cured."

Except for two small holes that looked like Dub had been stabbed with a lead pencil, his foot seemed to be okay. I remembered the day I was bit. The big cottonmouth moccasin buried his fangs in my flesh and hung onto my leg pumping in poison until I finally shook him loose. I shivered and looked away.

"I think Dub left the bandage on longer to get attention," Molly said. "But the sympathy's about to play out."

Everyone but Dub laughed.

Dub looked down and wiggled his toes. "Hey, you don't get bit often. You've got to make the most of it when you do."

"You've got a couple of fine looking grandsons," Molly said.

"Thank you," I said as I looked around the log cabin and wondered if my travels and hard work in pursuit of the almighty dollar was worth the effort. No doubt I had missed the laid-back times once I moved from Lewiston to the city. Many times I ached for the serenity of the cool, clear spring-fed Ozark River.

"So you're headed for the Blue Hole, your favorite camping spot," Molly said. "You're welcome to spend the night. I'll fry some ham and eggs for breakfast. You can get an early start with a full belly."

"Don't think so," I said, much quicker and sounding harder than I should have. I softened my words. "Thanks for the invitation, Molly. Like I told Dub on the phone yesterday, the boys and me are camping two nights at the Blue Hole. We'll come back here on Saturday to tour the town. Get up Sunday and go to church with y'all. Head back to Kansas City around noon."

Dub looked at me and grinned. "I can go along if you want. You're not used to driving these roads. The Buck Holler hill is rough and steep. It can be dangerous."

I shook my head. I knew sure as the world he would make a run at going with us. I figured his approach would be a little subtler.

"Well, I don't know. I . . . I've driven down the steep hill before with no trouble. Doubt it's changed much," I stammered and wished I were already on my way. I felt bad turning Dub down on his offer, but not enough to say I wanted him to go along. "The boys and me had this trip planned for some time. Fact is, by the time we set up camp it will be close to dark. We best get down the road."

I looked at Jake and Nick and wondered which one of them would ask why Uncle Dub could not go with us to camp at the Blue Hole. Neither said a word. I wished they had. Like the endless number of seasons that had slipped away since Dub and I were best friends as boys, another opportunity to patch up our feud had passed us by. It seemed we were destined to spend our remaining days like two lost souls standing at the river's edge watching the water flow by until time ran out. The brother that remained would wallow in sadness and wonder why he had been such a fool.

Chapter Two

    The boys and I got our gear from the trunk of my black Lincoln and we climbed into Dub's red Jeep wrangler with an open top and a metal roll bar. We headed south of town for a ten-mile drive over a rough gravel road. We were on the final leg of our trip to one of the best camping spots and swimming holes in the country, at least it used to be. I had not been there in fifty years and my anticipation about going back to the Blue Hole had been building for some time. It was fun driving Dub's Jeep down the country road on a warm August day. The air was filled with the smell of honeysuckle, purple and yellow wild flowers that grew in the ditch lines waved in the breeze. I looked at the boys and smiled, I felt blessed to be alive.

    "How much longer until we get to the river?" Jake asked.

    "Not long," I said, wondering what he and Nick thought about me not bringing Dub along. I would talk to them about the situation between Dub and I when the time seemed right. It was hard to explain something that you do not understand yourself. Our disagreements had been over silly things, like who would get Grandpa's 30-30 lever action rifle and how much we should get for the sale of our parents' farm. I, of course, wanted to ask more for it than Dub did. As it turned out, what he had in mind in the first place was a fair price.

    "Is this it?" Nick asked when I stopped the Jeep at the top of the hill that led to the river and rose up in the seat to look over the top of the windshield at the steep grade in front of us.

"We're close. All we've got to do now is drive down this hill," I said, not remembering so many rocks sticking up in the roadbed. I sat down and looked out the driver's side into a deep hollow covered with large boulders, Dogwood and Cedar trees. There was only a foot or so to spare before the wheels dropped off the edge of the road. The slope was steep and a couple hundred feet from top to bottom.

"Seems like we're awful close to the edge," Jake said as he leaned over and looked around at the steep slope to the side and in front of us.

Instead of answering him, I took a deep breath and eased the front bumper a few feet closer to the top of the hill. Anxious to get to the river, Nick said, "Go on down, Papa. I'm ready to go swimming."

My heart quickened when I took my foot off the brake and there was no turning back. My first rush of fear came when I heard a piece loose gravel zing out from under the knobby front tire, strike an oak tree sapling and ricochet back into my open side door with a thud. The front bumper dug up a rock that tumbled and scraped its way along the undercarriage, violently tearing at the floorboard as though it might burst through at any Moment. It rolled out from under the rear bumper, taking the muffler along with it, and a loud roar filled the cab. A cloud of dust boiled up behind us, a foul smell of exhaust fumes permeated the air.

"Are we okay, Papa?" Jake's voice quivered.

When I looked over my shoulder and forced a smile, the Jeep tipped up on two wheels, Momentarily hanging in midair. Jake whimpered and Nick groaned loudly. I gripped the steering wheel so hard my hands felt numb. The Jeep fell back onto the ground with a heavy jolt. My heart pounded. Sweat burned my eyes. My brain shifted into overdrive. If ever nerves could scream, mine would surely have shattered the windshield.

From the corner of my eye I saw the pale look of fear on Nick's face. He was obviously scared too, but covered it well with a twelve-year olds stubborn bravado. I had to remain calm. I had to act as if everything was under control.

"We've got it now!" I yelled above the roar as I looked at Nick again, then back at Jake through a cloud of reddish brown dust. "Everything's going to be okay."

"Do we really got it now, Papa?" Jake yelled back. "Will we be okay?"

"We'll be at the bottom of the hill soon!" I shouted as I pumped the brake pedal to make ready for the last sharp curve.

The boys grabbed the overhead roll bar and hung on for dear life. *I've gone too far this time*, I thought. I wished I had never started down the hill—what was I thinking? God help me if I turn the Jeep over with the boys inside! I imagined us tumbling off the side of the road and crashing onto the rocky ledge below.

I tapped the brake pedal once again. I had to be careful not to apply too much pressure and lock up the wheels, which would cause us to slide down the hill out of control.

Finally we came around the last bend and I saw the river a hundred yards up ahead.

The racing engine and grinding gears quieted down as I eased the back wheels of the Jeep off the hill and onto the flat gravel road. After a wild and frantic ride, we had arrived at a place called Buck Hollow.

"We made it, guys," I said with a half-hearted smile. "Did you have any doubt?"

Nick shook his head. "That was tight. Good thing you can control this Jeep."

I heaved a sigh of relief. I leaned back in the seat and thought about how lucky we were to have survived. I was proud of myself for being able to maneuver through the potentially deadly situation while remaining calm, or at least give that appearance. I was even prouder that Nick recognized I did a good job.

How could I know the road would be in such bad shape? Loggers used it all the time when I was a kid. Of course, that was over fifty years ago. A lot of heavy weather had come and gone since those days.

"Sorry about the rough ride, boys." I grabbed a blue bandanna off the dashboard and wiped the sweat from my eyes.

Nick patted me on the shoulder. "It's okay, Papa. I was freaked when the Jeep got up on two wheels. But I'm okay now. It was like a ride at Worlds of Fun, only for real."

Jake laughed nervously and wiped the sweat from under his chin with the back of his hand. "Actually, now that it's over, it was a lot of fun."

"I had it under control all the way," I said, still feeling nauseous with a stomach full of quivers. "You saw me bring the Jeep back to the ground. That takes a lot of skill."

I looked across the river and listened to the sound of fast-moving water splashing up against the base of a limestone bluff. A half dozen buzzards circled overhead like big black gliders in airborne freedom. I remembered an experience Dub and I had where a flock of buzzards were feeding on a dead deer. It would be one of the many tales I would tell the boys before we headed back home.

The smell of Sycamore trees and fresh clean air helped clear my senses of the lingering exhaust fumes. I was on my way to recovery—much quicker than I figured I would be.

"What are you thinking about, Papa?" Jake asked as I stared at the tall bluff across the river.

"I was thinking about the rope swing we had tied to the limb of a Sycamore tree at the Blue Hole."

RIVER'S EDGE

"Will the swing still be there?" Nick asked.

"I don't know. If it's not, we'll tie on a new rope."

"Cool," Nick said. He looked back at Jake, who was bouncing up and down in the seat, and they laughed.

It seemed like only yesterday that Dub and I ran up and down the riverbank, free spirits having the time of our life. I looked out the side window at myself in the mirror. Even though grey hair and wrinkles told a different story, inside I felt like I was still Nick's age and I never grew up. I squinted my eyes and smiled back at the reflection. I could not have asked for more than to spend three days on the river with my two favorite boys.

"Let's get goin' Papa. You said we needed to set up camp before dark," Nick said and Jake agreed.

"You got it boys. We're on our way." I fired up the engine, shifted into low gear and we headed toward our destination.

We drove across a spring branch, eased our way around a fallen oak tree and came to a stop when the gravel road ended a hundred feet or so up river from the Blue Hole. In front of us was a large Cottonwood tree with dried brown leaves and sun-bleached driftwood piled up against the massive trunk—a result of Mother Nature's housecleaning during the last flood.

"We're here," I announced as I shut off the engine. "But hold tight. I've got something important to say before you get out of the Jeep."

"What?" Nick grabbed the door handle ready to let the fun begin.

I pointed up ahead. "See that Cottonwood tree? I've seen plenty of snakes in those havens. Be sure you're careful not to take a blind step."

"What's a blind step, Papa?" Jake asked and settled back down in the seat.

"Taking a step without looking where your foot will land. That's a blind step. Snakes consider driftwood piles and weed beds part of their home. A cottonmouth moccasin doesn't take kindly to people walking into his living room. If you crowd 'em they'll bite you. This would put a damper on our trip. If an old river rat like Uncle Dub can get bit, anybody can." I spoke slowly and deliberately, since I was talking to young boys who thought they were invincible.

Jake looked at me and frowned. "I'm afraid to get out now."

"I don't mean to scare you—I'm just saying look where you plant your bare foot. If you see a dark brown snake, back off. A cottonmouth moccasin has a mean streak wide as the river. They fear neither man nor beast."

"Why are they called cottonmouth moccasins?" Jake asked, his voice barely above a whisper.

"When they open their mouth, it's as white as cotton inside. That's where they got the name."

I looked back at Jake and he was staring at me with eyes the size of quarters. "Maybe I should put on my shoes."

"You don't have to do that, Jake. Just be careful. When Dub and I were kids, we never wore shoes all summer long."

"Okay, we will," Nick, said as he and Jake followed me out the driver's side. Standing almost on top of one another they looked all around before taking another step.

"Is this the place where Uncle Dub got bit?" Jake asked.

"Not sure. I didn't hear him tell where it happened." *I should have asked him where the snake attack took place*, I thought.

"How old were you when you moved away, Papa?" Nick asked.

I looked across the gravel bar at the river. "Seventeen. I was seventeen years old when I left the country."

"Why haven't you brought us here before?" Jake asked.

"Yeah," Nick said. "You've talked about this place forever."

"Because of some strange things that happened. I'll tell you more later." I walked away, figuring I would wait until we were sitting around the campfire and the mood was right. What I had to say was an important lesson to be learned and I needed the boy's serious attention.

I looked up the river and saw a rope swing tied to the limb of a Sycamore tree. I heard the gurgling sound of spring water running from the mouth of the Cave. Nothing had changed in all the years I had been gone.

"Look." Nick pointed at a flock of buzzard's overhead. "You said they only eat dead stuff. So why are they circling us?"

I chuckled. "Maybe they've got nothing better to do than wait."

When we walked to the back of the Jeep, Nick picked up the tent and proclaimed he would be responsible for the set up. Jake and I gathered the rest of our gear and headed down the gravel bar toward our camping spot. There, alongside the spring branch, Nick pitched the tent in less than five minutes, and we were set for the next two nights.

"How does that look?" Nick said.

"Couldn't be any better," I said. "You really did learn something in the Boy Scouts."

"Kack, kack, kack," the harsh rattling call of a bluish-grey and white Kingfisher winging its way downier caught my attention and I followed the bird in flight. A rush of cool air from the mouth of the cave felt good on my sweat-soaked T-shirt. I cupped my hands and scooped up some cold spring water and splashed it in my face. I stared at the rope swing hanging over the deep pool of water and wondered how many ropes had been replaced in the past fifty years? Even during dog days when most of the river warmed up, the cold spring water from the cave and a towering limestone bluff that shaded the Blue Hole until mid-morning kept the deep pool of cool water.

"What kind of bird made all that noise?" Jake asked.

"It was a Kingfisher. One of my favorite birds on the river," I said.

Memories of the last trip were etched in my mind. I felt like a kid again, standing on the gravel bar barefoot in the hot August sun. It was as if I had been in a time warp and it was still the summer of 1950. I looked at Jake and Nick and savored their freedom, not a care in the world and even more I envied their age of innocence. Never giving a thought that someday they too would grow old.

The boys turned around and walked away, tossing a Frisbee Nick had pulled out of his backpack. I stepped off the gravel bar onto a rock ledge to look at a hand-painted sign nailed to the trunk of a Sycamore tree. In red letters painted on a grey oak plank someone had scribbled the message: "Hundreds of Snakes. KEEP OUT!"

Obviously, the work of some boys who wanted to scare away intruders—something my friends and I might have done years ago. We never wanted people snooping around and disturbing the private setting of our favorite swimming hole. I walked over to the sign, pulled it off the tree and tossed it behind a clump of Cedars. I had preached at Jake and Nick enough to watch out for snakes. There was nothing to be gained from them seeing a sign about hundreds of snakes all around, even if it was just a prank.

I walked over to the place where we would build our campfire and sat down on a big sycamore log, two- feet in diameter and ten foot long. In a few hours a full moon would rise above the towering bluff and fill our campsite with white light. The sounds of crickets chirping, Whippoorwills calling and the jug-o-rum of bellowing Bullfrogs would fill the air. Nick and Jake came over and sat down on the log, one on each side of me. I gave the boys each a pat on the knee and felt like the luckiest guy in the world.

"What kind of log is this, Papa? It's a big one," Jake said.

"An old white oak, probably lived a hundred years or better. Nice it came to a stop right here during the last rise of the river, so we could have a nice seat at the campfire," I said.

"What's the first thing you remember, Papa?" Nick asked.

"Not sure. Let me think back a ways."

"Was it catching a fish?" Jake asked, knowing I spent a lot of time trying.

"Good guess. Actually, it was getting into trouble for not doing what my Dad told me to do."

"How old were you?" Nick asked.

"About three years old. I walked into the garden and stepped on a ripe tomato. I laughed as the red juice squished up between my toes. Dad picked me up and carried me to a picnic table in the backyard. He told me to stay put. A few minutes later I waddled back into the garden again, stomped on another tomato and laughed even louder."

"Did you get a spanking?"

"Funny you asked, Jake. Yep, the second time Dad swatted my behind. I cried and my dog Trouser licked away the tears. That was the only time Dad ever spanked me. Even when I accidentally broke a kitchen window with a baseball twice in the same day. Even still, when I look at a tomato, sometimes I think about what happened. As it turned out, we had more tomatoes than we could eat that year."

"How can you remember so far back?" Jake said. "That was ancient times."

"I remember a lot from when I was a kid. You'll probably get tired of hearing about it by the time we head back to Kansas City."

"No I won't, Papa," Jake said. "I never get tired of your stories."

"What about you, Nick?" I asked.

"If I haven't heard them before." Nick picked up a rock and skipped it across the water. "Some of the really good ones would be okay, I guess."

"I'll try to tell the best of the lot," I said as I watched the ripples from the rock spread across the surface of the water and come to rest at the river's edge.

"I know one story I don't want to hear again," Nick said. "Can you guess which one?"

I smiled. "No, but if I start to tell it you can stop me." I figured it was either the one about the dead opossum that walked away, or the time I got bit by a snake.

"Okay, I will." Nick jumped up off the log and waded barefoot into the water where the spring branch that flowed from the mouth of the Cave ran into the river.

"Oh! Oh!" Nick yelled as he ran out of the water up onto the gravel bar.

I laughed. "Cold enough for ya?"

"It's like ice water! I never felt nothing so cold!"

Jake jumped off the log and waded into the spring branch up to his knees. In the time it took for Nick and me to look at one another and smile, Jake turned around and high-tailed it back to the bank. "My legs are frozen!" he yelled, his lips trembling.

Still laughing about how quickly Jake got in and out of the cold water, I looked up when I heard a loud screech and saw a pair of red-tail hawks circling overhead, soaring effortlessly on the thermal updraft.

"When I was a kid I'd lay in the yard and watch red-tailed hawks for hours. They mate for life, so the same pair would return each year. Sometimes they would fly around each other and turn cartwheels in the air. Even free fall hundreds of feet and recover just before hitting the ground."

"How come those two aren't doing all that stuff?" Jake asked.

"They only act like that in the springtime when they're mating."

Nick and Jake looked at me without saying a word. I figured the subject of mating had raised some questions, but they were too embarrassed to ask and I was not well enough informed on the sensitive subject to launch off on a diatribe about the mating habits of hawks.

"I'd like to see hawks doing that sometime," Nick said and Jake agreed that it would be a cool thing to watch.

"Next spring we can drive to the country and see them do their dance. I had something really weird happen to me once after watching a couple of red tail hawks. Hardly anybody knows about it so if I tell, you've got to promise it stays between us fellas."

The boys quickly agreed that my secret was safe with them for the rest of their lives.

"I had been watching the hawk dance off and on for a couple of days wishing I could fly. So I made some wings out of cardboard, jumped off the roof of the barn and broke my leg."

I figured there would be a barrage of questions, starting with how old was I, what did my Mom and Dad say and other stuff. Instead, Jake just frowned and Nick simply said, "I wouldn't want anybody to know either, Papa."

"Yeah, well that's why I haven't told anybody before," I said in disbelief because so little interest was shown in what was a really daring thing to do.

"I'm going to check out what's up there." Nick jumped off the log and started up the spring branch toward the cave with Jake close behind. The boys stopped when they reached the spot where a crumbling dam made out of concrete and limestone rocks ran from one side of the spring branch to the other. From there the boys climbed up to the top of a big boulder in front of the cave.

"Wow, this is incredible," Nick, yelled.

"Come look at what we've found, Papa," Jake said.

I smiled, knowing what an unusual site it was seeing the cave and a deep pool of crystal clear spring water for the first time. As I hurried along, my footsteps fell silent on a layer of spongy green moss that was shaded by Willow trees growing along the water's edge. "What do you think of this place?" I asked as I climbed up the boulder and stood behind Jake as he stared at the astonishing work of Mother Nature.

"I've never seen anything like it in my whole life," Jake said as he pointed at the mouth of the cave, a dark hole in the side of the bluff the size of a small house.

"I used to be afraid of this cave when I was young. I never walked up here by myself until I was at least ten years old," I said.

"How come?" Nick asked.

"I thought there might be something living down deep down in the bowels of the cavern that might like to feed on the flesh of a tender young boy."

I realized that was the wrong thing to say when Jake looked at me and wrinkled up his nose, so I changed the subject.

"After I was older and not afraid of what might be living in the cave anymore, I used to think it would be a good place to hide if I ever ran away from home. Plenty of cool water to drink and the air would be the same sixty-degree temperature all year long. I figured I'd get along just dandy living on fish, squirrels, watercress and wild berries."

"Why would you want to run away?" Nick asked.

"I wouldn't when I was a kid. I might be tempted now to get away from the rat race. I'll let you know when I'm ready to go. If you want to come along you're both welcome."

"What's the deal on the dam?" Nick asked.

"Now that's an interesting story."

"Anything you don't have a story about, Papa?"

I patted Jake on the top of his head. "Not I can think of offhand," I said. "Let's climb down and I'll tell you the history of the dam. It's a good one."

Standing in front of the crumbling limestone remains that held back the deep pool of spring water, I pointed at a rock with the date 1896 chiseled into the face and started my story.

"More than a hundred years ago a man named Bob Madison and his two sons built this dam." I stopped when I heard a noise off to my right that sounded like the snap of a dead limb. It could have been a squirrel chewing on a hickory nut or a wild hog running through the brush. More likely it was the announcement of the Madison's spirits. As in the past, there was a strange feeling like something had thinned out the air. The first time it happened I thought it was just my imagination. Later on there was no doubt about what it was and now, all these many years later, the same closed-in feeling has come back. It only lasted for a couple of minutes and then went away.

"What are you looking at, Papa? Did you go to sleep?" Nick asked, being cute like twelve-year-old boys have been known to do.

I looked at Nick and squinted my eyes but did not say anything.

"So why'd they build a dam here?" Jake asked as he walked out into the spring branch, stood there for about five seconds and hurried back to the bank complaining that the water was so cold.

Before I could answer, Nick turned around and started to walk toward camp. "Why do we even care? I'm going skip rocks."

"Why care?" I said, louder than need be. "You'll care plenty when you find out how the Madison's died. Fact is, what I've got to say might just save your life."

Chapter Three

Nick looked at me and narrowed his eyes. "Come on, Papa. Quit trying to scare us. Let's go cook hotdogs."

"We've got time. It'll be plenty light even after dark."

"How can that be?" Nick asked.

"Once the full moon rises above the top of the bluff. It will be almost light as day. Sometimes people do strange things during a full moon. You boys ever heard that before?"

Jake brushed off my reference to a full moon as if it were not worth talking about. "What about the Madison's?" He asked.

"So, you want to hear more about the Madison's." I paused and looked around. "They dammed up the spring branch to power a water wheel, which would turn a grinding stone and crush corn into meal."

"It takes dirt to grow corn," Nick said. "There's nothing' around here but hills and hollers and gravel."

"That's true," I said, wondering how Nick knew to call the valleys between Ozark Mountain ridges hollers, a term normally used only by local residents. "However, the Madison's had a good plan."

"Like what?" Jake said.

"Farmers would haul wagon loads of corn to Rocky Ford- that's a crossing ten miles upriver - float it downstream on flat-bottom barges to the Blue Hole. After it was ground up they'd float the meal down to Ashbury, from there it would be shipped by rail to St. Louis and Little Rock."

Nick grunted. "Sounds like a wild idea."

"Wild ideas are what created the nice things you have, Nick. People thought Ben Franklin was off his rocker when he tied a key to a kite and discovered electricity. You'd miss not having electric lights and your computer I bet?"

Nick cocked his head to one side and stared at me. "Where did you hear the Madison story?"

"Grandpa Tom knew old man Madison. He told me. No way he'd make up such a story."

"Just wondered. So what happened in the end?" Nick said.

"Grandpa Tom said their idea would have worked. Except a month or so after the dam got built, the Madison's died."

"All of them?" Nick said.

I nodded my head. "All three."

"What happened?" Jake blurted out. "Did they die right here, Papa?"

Before I could say anything, I heard a noise in the brush that this time sounded like the crack of a whip.

Nick looked at me and his eyes got big. "What was that?"

"Could have been a limb snapped. More likely it was the ghost of the Madison's. I'm sure they don't like us tromping around in their space. Stepping on their ghost toes."

"Come on, Papa. You're trying to scare us," Nick said.

"Can't think of any reason I'd do that, Nick. Once it gets dark, you'll scare your own self enough. You won't need any help from me."

"So what happened?" Jake asked. "What killed them all?"

"Tick fever. Common ol' deer ticks killed the whole bunch. You boys best check yourself good before you go to bed."

"You serious?" Nick looked at his arms and legs and brushed a brown speck of dirt off his knee.

"As a heart attack. That's why I told the story. There's some things to watch out for on the river and that's one."

Jake shuddered. "I don't feel very safe."

"You're safe as can be. All I'm saying is check for ticks, especially in places where the sun don't shine. Don't reach into a driftwood pile. Don't put your barefoot where you haven't already looked. Do those things and you'll be fine?

A spray of gravel flew into the water as Nick kicked the ground. Minnows darted over to investigate. "If I've already been tick-bit. What good will it do?" he whined.

"None," I said grimly. "That's why I said keep your eyes open. Catch the little creatures while they're crawling around."

"Darn you, Papa," Nick growled. "I hated that story—true or not."

Jake pulled the front of his bathing suit away from his belly and looked down. "Not all ticks cause tick fever do they, Papa?"

"That's right. Fact is, most don't. I'm just saying an ounce of prevention is worth a pound of cure."

I looked across the river at the ridge covered with Cedar trees and remembered what I saw the last time Dub and I camped at the Blue Hole. A white headed old man with a long beard stood in a beam of light. As usual, Dub thought I was trying to fool him. That was until later that night when the mysterious old man showed up behind our tent, where a fire burned brightly. I looked down and there were goose bumps on my arms.

"What are you looking at, Papa?" Jake asked.

I turned around. "Nothing. How about we gather some wood? We want a blazing fire, don't we, boys?"

"Yeah, a really big one," Jake, said.

"You look pale, Papa. Are you sick? Please don't say you saw a ghost."

"I'm fine as a fiddle," I said to Nick as I started to walk down the riverbank and the boys followed close behind.

Dub used to think I was trying to fool him. Now Nick did the same thing. I had been known to pull a trick or two but, not enough anybody needed to guard against becoming a victim.

I stopped in front of a driftwood pile and looked at the sun-bleached limbs and dry leaves that were stacked up at the base of a Cottonwood tree. A survivor of Mother Nature's abuse for a century, the giant tree would soon be dead. Erosion had exposed the roots; during the next flood the power of rushing water would rip the tree out of the ground. Downstream, it would come to rest against a bluff or a rocky bank and provide shelter for the fish and other river creatures. One day the last of the trunk would rot away. The gentle giant would be consumed by the earth from which it came and a sapling would sprout and take its place.

"Lots of wood here," Jake said, not making any sudden moves.

"Enough to burn 'til we go to bed." I took a step so the three of us were side by side.

"Who's going to pick up the first piece?" I asked. My heart raced as I stared at the driftwood pile. The sting of a cottonmouth moccasin's sharp fangs as they sank into my flesh was something I would always remember.

"Let's make some noise. Throw rocks and yell—that would scare the snakes away, wouldn't it, Papa?" Jake said as he reached down and grabbed a handful of gravel.

My mind flashed back fifty years. I saw Dub and me standing side by side on the riverbank when we were kids. He yelled and kicked gravel in front of him toward the driftwood pile. Only back then, it was after dark and we were both so afraid we were numb.

"Are you scared, Papa?" Jake asked when I did not answer him, catching me off-guard.

I looked at him and thought about what Doc Barnes, the old country doctor in Lewiston, told me after I got snake bit. He said I had to face my fears. If I didn't, I may be scared for the rest of my life. I did what he said and it worked.

"Tell you what, boys, people scare themselves for no good reason except fear itself."

"Don't try to fool us with words, Papa," Nick said.

I tossed my head back and got a little defensive. "Have I done that so far? I didn't mean to if I did."

Nick frowned. "I don't know. I guess not."

Once again I thought about how much Nick was like Dub when he was a kid- both thought I was trying to fool them much of the time.

"Tell you what, Nick. I won't make up a story and play like it's for real, okay? I may stretch the truth some but that's what storytellers do."

"Okay, Papa. If you say it's so, I'll believe it. But I'm pretty grown-up now. Not easy to fool like when I was ten years old." Jake looked at Nick and frowned. "I didn't mean you, Jake. I was talking about other kids."

Jake reached down and picked up a rock the size of a baseball and threw it at the driftwood pile. Nick and I laughed. Nothing stirred. To my amazement, Jake bravely walked up within wood-picking range and stopped. When Nick and I stepped up beside him, Jake reached into the woodpile and grabbed a limb the size of a baseball bat and he tossed it onto the gravel bar behind us.

"What made you so brave all of a sudden?" I asked.

"I've always been brave." Jake reached down and grabbed another stick. "Just don't talk about it like some people."

Nick and I smiled at one another as we picked up an armload of wood.

"When Dub and I camped here last time a tree frog jumped out of a driftwood pile. The thing scared me so bad I wet my pants," I said.

"Did Uncle Dub laugh?" Jake asked.

"No, he didn't. It was dark and there was too much spooky stuff going on for us to think anything was very funny."

Jake snickered. "Can't believe you told Uncle Dub you wet your pants. I wouldn't tell anybody."

"I only did it because I was so happy to be alive. I said if he ever told anyone I'd be mad forever."

"What kind of spooky stuff was going on?" Nick asked.

"I'll tell you later. Let's dump the wood and seine some minnows. We'll go down river and catch some fish for dinner."

The sound of gravel crunched under foot as we walked toward camp with and armload of firewood.

"What we doing tomorrow?" Nick asked.

"We've got great adventures," I said as we dumped the wood. "One thing is we're going upriver a quarter mile to explore Leatherwood Cave. Last time your Uncle Dub and I were there we found a dead man."

"Did you really, Papa?" Nick said. "What happened?"

"It's a gruesome story. I'm afraid to tell it so close to bedtime. You'll have nightmares."

"You keep saying you'll tell us things later. I hope we don't run out of time. We might miss some stories."

"We won't run out of time. I'll make sure of that, Jake."

Nick pointed at the mouth of the cave and said, "Why don't we explore this one? Why go so far away?"

"You can only go inside maybe fifty feet because it's filled with water. Leatherwood Cave has a lot of crawl space and deep caverns. It would take days to explore.

Jake looked at me wide-eyed. "Will there be bats flying around?"

"Sure there will be bats," Nick said. "Mr. Hodges, our science teacher said bats carry rabies."

I patted Jake on the shoulder. "Nothing to worry about. You'd stand a better chance of being fluttered to death by bat wings than be bit. Don't bother them and they won't bother you."

"Let's see what all might bite us: There are killer snakes and ticks, snapping turtles that can bite off a finger, and now there are bats. Anything else?" he asked.

Nick sounded so cocky I wanted to give him a swift kick in the butt.

"Nope, that's all," I said calmly. "Just do what I said, you'll be fine. If people were bit on a regular basis there wouldn't be anyone left alive in this part of the country. Look at your uncle Dub, he hunts and fishes about every day and in sixty-odd years, he's only been snake bit once. He's had gobs of ticks on him and been around bats all his life. Probably been snapped at by a hundred turtles."

"Anyway that's all you've heard about," Nick said.

"I'm sure that's right." I looked at the sun setting behind the treetops and figured we had a couple hours of daylight left at best.

"So what are we going to do now?" Nick asked.

"Let's seine a few minnows. Then we'll head down river and fish the swift chute. I've caught some good-sized bass there in my day. Dad caught a five-pound Smallmouth there once. It was the most excited I ever saw him.

"Good idea." Jake hurried over and pulled the minnow seine from a green duffle bag.

"Let me have one end and we'll stretch it out." I grabbed the corners of the three-foot by twelve-foot brown mesh seine. I walked to the edge of the ripple and laid it down on the gravel bar.

"Let's hurry, I want to catch a big bass for dinner." Jake jumped up and down, grinning from ear to ear.

"What are you seeing?" I asked Nick when I saw him staring at the bluff.

"How old were you first time you jumped off the high ledge, Papa? Looks like a long way down."

"About your age, I guess. I need help over here," I said. "You boys take the axe and cut a couple of poles to tie on each end of the seine. We'll catch the bait we need to catch some fish."

Nick walked over and picked up the axe. He looked up the river at a patch of Willow trees growing along the edge of the water. "How long you want 'em to be?" He asked.

"Six foot should be about right. Be careful, that axe is sharp."

God forbid one of the boys accidentally cut off his toe, or something worse, I thought as I stretched the seine out on the gravel bar. I looked at the face of the bluff and wondered if Nick would climb sixty feet above the water to the ledge and jump off. A person's imagination runs wild once they get up there. Silly things, like what if I hit the water so hard I knock myself out and drown?

"Kack, kack, kack," I smiled when the call of a Kingfisher echoed off the bluff as the bird dipped and dived its way down river. As a kid when we floated the river, a Kingfisher would spend the entire day flying downstream in front of us. The bird would light in a tree a few hundred feet up ahead, wait for us to catch up and head down the river again as if it were assigned to be our sentry. My Uncle Ira said if you heard the call of a Kingfisher before the fog lifted off the water early morning, you would have good luck that day. Some folks made fun of him because he put so much stock in old-time sayings. All I know is, nobody in the Ozarks knew more about the ways of Mother Nature than Uncle Ira.

"Look at these!" Jake yelled as he held up one of the poles Nick had cut and positioned it back over his shoulder as if he was going to use it for a spear.

"Those poles look perfect!" I shouted as the boys headed down the gravel bar toward me. I waved my hands in the air. "Nick, don't run with the axe in your hand."

Proud of their accomplishment, the boys threw the two broomstick-sized poles down on the gravel bar. I tied one onto each end of the seine and we were ready to make a sweep.

Jake made a circle with his arms. "There was a turtle on a log big around as my tire swing."

With me on one end and the boys on the other, we picked up the seine and walked upriver, the long brown net stretched out between us. I looked back over my shoulder when I spotted a school of minnows swimming along the edge of the current on the far side of the riffle. "There's a school." I pointed to the right. "See 'em, boys?"

"Yeah I see 'em!" Nick said as I waded into the fast-moving water that was about two feet deep and lowered my end of the seine. Nick grabbed the other pole, wadded into the water and Jake followed along close behind.

"I don't see 'em," Jake said. "Where are they?"

"Right up in front of us. Follow me." We walked slowly up the river and pulled the seine against the current. I leaned forward to keep my balance. "They're Red Fin Shiners, my favorite Smallmouth bait." I bent over so the bottom of my pole would dig into the gravel. I moved faster and the boys followed my lead.

"Dig your pole into the gravel. The sinkers need to drag the bottom. Don't want the minnows to swim underneath the seine."

"Must be a hundred. Boy they're fast!" Nick said. He was so excited his voice quivered.

"Slow down," I said when I saw a shiner jump over the top. "You're walking too fast. Look, the water's running over the middle of the seine."

"How's that, Papa?" Nick said as three wooden floats in the middle popped to the surface.

"We've got a bunch trapped. Don't lose 'em. Stand still. I'll swing toward the bank." I moved my end around quickly and we surrounded the school before they could dart out in front of the seine. When I reached the gravel bar, Nick brought his end around and we dragged our catch up onto the bank.

"If we don't catch fish we can eat minnows," Jake said, so excited he was jumping up and down. "We'll make minnow soup."

I watched the minnows flip flop on the gravel bar. Their silver sides glistened in the fading sunlight as it streaked through the tops of the trees. I remembered the first time I helped Dad and Uncle Ira. I let half of the school swim under the seine because I raised my end too high. I patted Jake and Nick on the back. "Good job guys! We'll keep a dozen and throw the rest back. We can get more tomorrow if need be."

"We've got a Crawdad." Nick grabbed the reddish-brown creature behind the pinchers with his thumb and forefinger. He held it out in front of him for a few seconds to check it out, then tossed it in the minnow bucket. "Whoa, hold on. What's the brown squiggly thing?"

"A hellgrammite. They're good Smallmouth bait too."

"Look's like a flat worm with pinchers on its head," Jake said. "Where do hellgrammites come from?"

"Do you really want to know?" I said.

"If it's not a dragged out story," Nick said.

"Okay, I'll make it short. A Hellgrammite is the larva of the Dobsonfly. After mating near the shore, the female dobsonfly lays her eggs on plants overhanging the water and they drop into the water. Once the larva, called a 'hellgrammite', hatches, it eats small aquatic animals including other hellgrammites. They're usually found under rocks. Sometimes when you seine, the sinkers stir up one or two and they are caught in the net. If a person didn't know better they might think they are looking at a Centipede."

Nick shook his head. "I'd hate to hear the long version."

"Look at this." Jake raised the hellgrammite out of the water, its jaws clamped to a stick in his hand. "I bet I know more about Hellgrammites than anyone in my class."

"How about you, Nick?" I asked.

Nick looked at me and grinned. "I learned something, I guess."

"Okay, let's each try a different bait. Nick, take the Crawdad. Jake, try a red fin minnow. I'll go with the hellgrammite."

The same excitement of catching a big Smallmouth bass that I had when I was a kid was still there. My heart pounded in anticipation as we walked down the gravel bar toward the fast-moving water. I figured we would catch a couple for dinner, build a fire and fry them up crispy brown. Roast a few marshmallows for desert. We would turn in early to get a good night's sleep and be ready for an exciting day tomorrow.

I grabbed Jake by the arm when we got close to the hot spot and I motioned at Nick to hunker down.

"Bait up," I whispered. "Don't want to get to close. We'll spook the fish." I set the minnow bucket down on the gravel bar and grabbed the hellgrammite. The squirming creature wrapped its thin brown body around my finger. I slid the sharp point of the hook through the thick collar behind its head.

I helped Jake bait his hook with a feisty red fin minnow that we hooked behind the dorsal fin. Nick grabbed the Crawdad and threaded the barb through its tail. We were set to go. "Follow my lead," I said and the three of us duck-walked along the gravel bar until we were within fifteen feet of the river's edge.

I gave Jake a nod and he cast his minnow into the swift clear water. Nick followed with a cast that landed his bait upstream of a huge boulder. I waited until their lines drifted downstream and sailed my hellgrammite through the air. It dropped in close to a rock ledge where a Willow tree shaded the water and a clump of green ferns hung down from a limestone ledge.

"Nice cast, boys. They'll think someone brought them a picnic dinner."

The words were barely out of my mouth when Jake's rod tip dipped down and his line began to move up stream.

"Set the hook," I said.

"I've hooked a big one," Jake shouted when he pulled back on the rod and felt a tug.

He tried to reel in some line but he could not turn the fish as it swam across the river toward the rock ledge. He slipped on the loose gravel, fell down and scraped his elbow on a rock. His rod tip flew up in the air. The line stretched tight and the fish came up out of the water in a sparkling explosion. The minnow dangled from the corner of its mouth. Golden brown sides glistened in the sunlight as a Smallmouth bass shook his head from side to side and tail walked across the shadowy surface of the water.

"It's a hog," Nick yelled. "Don't lose 'em."

"Keep the rod tip down, Jake. Don't let him jump again, he'll throw the hook," I yelled. I was amazed how well he handled the fish. His only previous fishing experience had been catching a few Perch in a park pond using bacon for bait.

Jake followed my instructions and stopped the fish from jumping. As line peeled off the spool it sounded like a mad bumblebee.

"I've got 'em, Papa." Jake worked the fish toward the bank in a tug of war. A nine-year-old boy with excitement pulsing through his veins verses a powerful Smallmouth bass whose life depended on getting free.

"Maybe the biggest one I've ever seen," I said. I hurried to Jake's side in case he needed help at the last minute to land the fish.

In an instant, the thing that makes fish stories happen, happened. When the bass saw us standing on the riverbank, he swished his powerful tail and made another run for freedom. He stripped out more line and headed for a boulder in the middle of the river. My heart sank when I heard a loud snap. The six-pound test monofilament line floated through the air toward us like a spider web drifting in the wind.

"Damn it," I said. "That was a nice fish."

"I'm sorry, Papa," Jake said.

"You did good. I couldn't have done any better." I patted Jake on the shoulder. "We'll catch more fish, maybe even a bigger one."

I stood up and shaded my eyes, hoping to catch a last glimpse of the old mossback, but he was gone. I walked to the edge of the water, cupped my hands together and splashed some water in my face. "You know another way to look at it, Jake?"

"No, what?" Jake's lip quivered and he sounded as if he was about to cry.

"A fighter like that deserves to be free."

"Yeah, I guess. It would of been great to say I caught a bass so big."

"I bet you'll dream about the fish tonight," Nick said. "He'll be jumping out of the water over and over. Only you know what? You'll be dragging him up on the gravel bar."

Jake looked at Nick and smiled. "I hope you're right."

"We've stirred the fishing hole up pretty good," I said as I reeled in my hellgrammite. I walked down the riverbank and made one last cast into the swirling current. "I don't think we'll do any good now."

"I don't even care," Jake said. "I've had my fun."

"Let's go set our lines in the Blue Hole. I've caught some nice fish there too. I even caught an eel one time. Talk about a fight, those slick devils give you all you can stand."

"They look like snakes, don't they, Papa?" Jake said.

"They do and they have sharp teeth. They're tasty. You skin them like a catfish. Not many left in the river anymore, I don't imagine."

"What'll we have for dinner if we don't catch fish?" Nick asked.

"Hot dogs. We've got lots of good hot dogs."

Nick laughed. "If we don't catch anything, when I'm eating my hot dog, I'll close my eyes and play like I'm eating a fish."

We picked up the minnow bucket and our rod and reels. With the sound of gravel crunching under foot as we headed back to camp, the fresh clean smell of the river air and a red tail hawk circling overhead in the clear blue sky, there could not have been a better end to a better day.

Chapter Four

When we walked into camp, Nick looked at me and said, "Tell you what I'd like to do next. Let's go look for arrowheads."

"Now there's a good idea," I said.

"Have you ever found any, Papa?" Jake asked.

"Your Uncle Dub has found more than me. I never spent as much time looking. He found a stone axe once in perfect condition."

"Whoa. A stone axe. That's what I want," Nick said. "I'll do me some choppin'."

Jake grinned. "Yeah, let's go do it."

"Do fish talk to each another?" Jake asked.

"Maybe, "I said.

"If they do, the fish I almost caught will have some story to tell."

We all laughed and picked up the pace as we headed for our next adventure.

"How big was my fish, Papa?"

"I'd say close to five pounds."

"Look!" Jake pointed across the river at a tree on the top of the ridge. A flock of half-dozen buzzards were Perched on the dead limbs, watching us. "I thought they only ate dead stuff. Why do they keep hanging around us?"

"Maybe they know something we don't?" I thought about the time Dub and I walked up on a flock of about twenty-five of the nasty things eating on a dead deer.

Jake looked at me and cocked his head to one side. "Like what would they know?"

"Could be they're after a dead deer or a range cow, or maybe a beaver. Buzzards have a keen sense of smell. They can find dead things like they have radar. They're also very curious."

"So if they've smelled a bunch of bad stuff, then they've had a good day." Nick laughed.

"They make me nervous circling around and sitting in dead trees watching us." Jake picked up a rock and threw it in the direction of the buzzards.

"Not much we can do about it," I said.

"Guess not. You think the bass might bite again?" Jake asked as he walked up beside me.

"You never know. We can try again in the morning. The minnows will stay alive. We'll need to tie the lid shut to keep out the raccoons."

"Are you serious?" Nick said. "Could a raccoon open the lid on a minnow bucket?"

"You bet. A raccoon can get into anything not welded shut. They're smart little critters; really good with their hands."

We stopped across the river from camp and watched the buzzards as they flapped their powerful black wings and climbed toward the sky. "Lots of stuff to learn about in the wild," Jake said.

"Get going," Jake yelled and waved his hands. "Crazy buzzards. Nothing's dead around here."

As we walked across the river, I noticed the rope swing moving back and forth as if someone had swung off of the rock ledge, but the surface of the water was like glass. There was no wind to make the rope move. The air was dead still.

"What are you looking at, Papa?" Jake asked.

"Nothing," I said as I set the minnow bucket down on the gravel bar and laid my rod down beside it. *Nothing but everything*, I thought.

RIVER'S EDGE

I felt cool air from the mouth of the cave as I walked toward the Blue Hole and I shivered. I looked back over my shoulder to see if the boys were watching and there stood Jake. He stared at me a few seconds, then turned and walked toward the tent. I waved at him and smiled.

When I looked down at the water, I saw the face of the dead man that Dub and I found. Maybe the rope was moving back and forth because the dead man's ghost had swung off the ledge. Then he slipped into the water without creating a ripple. It seemed crazy to think that way, but not really. A lot of strange things happened when we were there last.

Not only did we find a dead man in the Blue Hole, we found another body in Leatherwood Cave, then Buzzard Thompson drowned in the river and a mysterious old man appeared in the middle of the night behind our tent. Too much spooky stuff happened in only two days. After my snakebite, Doc Barnes told me the only cure for my nightmares was to face my fears. "Go to the source you are afraid of and stare it down," he said. His theory seemed to work okay at the time, but apparently I was not completely cured. Why else would I be reliving the horror of the two dead men we found?

"Smell something funny, Papa?" Jake asked, sniffing the air.

"What does it smell like?" I asked, taking a deep breath.

"Rotten eggs or something dead." Jake looked up at the buzzards circling overhead. "I bet they smell it."

"You smell anything, Nick?" I asked.

"I smell something. Don't know what it is though. Maybe like something burning. Could be Jake letting pooters again." Nick laughed and sniffed the air like a hound dog. Jake started after Nick and chased him around the gravel bar until Jake finally fell down and gave up.

"What should I do with the seine and minnow bucket," Nick asked.

"Stretch the seine out on the gravel bar to dry. Tie the minnow bucket to one of these Willow trees so it hangs in the water. Remember the raccoons. Tie down the lid." When I looked around Jake was staring at me.

"Did you know you've been talking to yourself, Papa?" Jake said.

"A lot of people talk to themselves," I said, sounding more defensive than I needed to be. "I see 'em all the time in their cars. They pretend to be singing when they get caught. You've seen 'em I bet, right Nick?"

"I see lots of people picking their nose," Nick said. "I don't know about singing"

Jake laughed and crawled inside the tent, taking his red plaid sleeping bag along with him.

"What are you doing? Going to bed in broad daylight."

Jake threw the tent flap back and poked his head outside. "Yeah right, Papa. I'm putting my bed in the middle. That's where I feel most safe."

"Did you hear that, Nick? Jake thinks he'll be safe sleeping in the middle. If something gets inside the tent, he'll probably be trampled when we scramble to get outside."

Nick laughed. Jake hissed like a snake. I turned around and looked down into the blue water again. The face of the dead man was gone from the watery grave, but the ashen image was etched in my brain. My destiny with the spirit world started fifty years earlier in the middle of the night when out of nowhere a mysterious old man with white hair appeared behind our tent. Under a full moon, a fire with glowing red coals appeared. In no longer that it took for the hoot of an owl to fade away down river, Dub's life and my life was changed forever. At the time I thought the old man had to be God. Later on in life I came to believe he might have actually been the Devil.

"Papa" Nick sounded too serious for comfort. "Come look at this that I've found."

I walked across the gravel bar toward him. "What is it?" I said.

"Looks like a bone."

"Let me see," Jake said as he walked up beside me. I bent down and scraped some of the sand and gravel away. Even though only part of it was exposed, there was no doubt it was a human leg bone, a Femur. I had scared the boys enough with the runaway ride down the steep hill, all the talk about snakes and ticks and snapping turtles that can bite off a finger. God forbid I tell them we made camp in a spot filled with body parts.

"I think it's a horse bone," I said as I watched Nick dig away more of the gravel. Crazy as it seemed, I wondered if it were possible the Femur belonged to the man known as the mystery killer when Dub and I were kids. The man suspected of kidnapping Doc Barnes, murdering Buzzard Thompson's family. Then killing the two men that Dub and I found, one in Leatherwood Cave and the other tied to a rope in the Blue Hole. It would be wild if it showed up now after all those years. Stranger things have happened, but not by much.

"How do you know it's a horse bone?" Jake asked.

Nick gave me a clinched tooth smile. "Yeah, Papa. How do you know it's not a people bone?"

"I'll tell you how: I grew up on a farm. We had lots of horses and some died. I've seen lots of bones. That's how I know."

My answer was met with a look of doubt as Nick raised his eyebrows and shook his head.

"Okay, I'll dig it up and use it as a club," Nick said. "This is really cool. I'll take it when we explore the cave tomorrow. I'll be like a caveman."

"You sure can. But it seems like we've got better things to do."

I could see us walking up the river toward the cave, Nick whacking away at rocks and trees with somebody's leg bone. Not that it was any big deal. Really whoever it belonged to would not feel anything. On the other hand, if his Mom found out, she may not take kindly to the idea. She was reluctant to let me take the boys on a camping trip into the heart of a wilderness. She had heard too many strange stories about things that went on in the Ozark Hills. It sounded a hair dangerous and somewhat uncivilized. When I promised that nothing too strange or out of the ordinary would take place, she agreed to let the boys go. Nick whacking his way down the trail with a leg bone would probably count against me.

What a crazy thing to have happen, Nick finding the bone. I figured I had a couple of options. I could tell the boys the story about the killer and how this could be the guy's leg bone, but I was afraid that might send a chill through them so close to bedtime. I would pay the price with one of them screaming in my ear. Jake already seemed a little on the edge. A sneaky, but safer thing would be to dig it up during the night and hide it in the Jeep then turn it over to the Sheriff when we got back to town.

"What better things do we have to do than dig up a horse bone?" Nick asked. "If that's what it really is."

"Well, we've got to lay the fire, for one thing. You boys want a roaring fire after dark, don't you?"

Jake yelled, "I want the biggest fire ever." Nick groaned.

"Next thing we should check out the blind fish that live inside the cave." I had been told that story many times and never seen a single one. But I had no doubt they were there. "We should also cast our bait into the water. We might hook another big fish while we go exploring."

"Okay," Nick said. "I'll dig the bone up later. What do we do first?"

"We'll stack up some twigs, like a tepee over a bed of dry leaves so the fire will catch easy. Once it gets going, we'll lay on a few bigger limbs, then a couple of logs. You're a Boy Scout, Nick. You know how it's done."

"I know how to build a fire." Jake took charge. He wadded up a piece of paper torn from a brown paper bag and gathered up a dozen small sticks. "We learned how in Cub Scouts. I like to build fires."

"It's good to have it ready. But we won't light it just yet. We want a roaring fire after dark. Come on, Nick, get us a couple of minnows from the bucket. Bring the poles and we'll set our lines."

Reluctantly, Nick went along with the plan. I would get him to go look for blindfish in the pool of water at the cave. That would keep him busy until it got dark. Afterwards we would light the fire. I figured he would be tired from a long day and turn in early. I would dig up the bone during the night and hide it under the seat in the Jeep. I would say an animal must have dug it up during the night and carried it away. There would be some suspicion, of course, but no proof. I did not like to be deceitful, but in an emergency, whatever needs to be done must be done.

"Here," Nick said. He handed me my rod and reel and one of the minnows. I hooked it through the lips and cast into the deep water close to the bluff.

"Need some help, Nick?" I asked. He seemed to be having trouble getting the minnow on the hook.

"No, I got it." He slid the hook through the belly of his minnow and cast within a few feet of where my bait landed.

Nick looked over my shoulder. "What now?"

"I'll cut a couple of branches to stick in the gravel bar. We'll rest the rods in the forks while we check out the cave," I said as I passed my rod to Nick. I unsnapped the leather holder attached to my belt and pulled out a knife with a deer horn handle. My Grandpa Tom gave it to me on my twelfth birthday. It was passed along to him by his father and was one of my most prized processions. I headed up river toward a patch of Willow trees where Nick tied up the minnow bucket. The metal scraping against the rocks as the bucket moved back and forth in the current made a tick, tick, tick sound like the sound of the Grandfather clock in Uncle Ira's house, ticking away life, one second at time.

"Why not lay the rods on the gravel bar" Nick said.

"Why," I said as I turned around. I tempered myself so as not to sound preachy. "Lay a reel on the gravel bar, sand gets in the gears. They wear out and malfunction faster. You'd be sorry if you were out in the middle of nowhere. Hook a big fish, but you can't turn the handles. Only takes a little time to care for your stuff. Remember, an ounce of prevention is worth a pound of cure."

I was surprised when Nick told me that an ounce of prevention made sense to him. Jake, on the other hand said he probably would not remember it since he did not know what it meant.

"Here they are," I said as I walked down the river toward camp. I paid it no mind when I passed within a few feet of the bone. I stopped at the river's edge and pushed the sticks down into the gravel bar.

"They look like upside down peace symbols," Nick said as we laid the rods between the forks and headed up the spring branch. More than at anything I wished we would catch a blindfish.

"Have you gone back inside this cave very far?" Nick asked as we climbed a bank covered with thick green moss that felt cool on our bare feet. We stood on top of a large boulder and looked down into the deep clear pool of spring water that backed up into the mouth of the cave.

"You can only go back inside about fifty feet. Even though the mouth of the cave is big, most of the cavern is under water."

"Have you fished here before?" Nick asked as he picked up a white rock the size of a quarter and tossed it into the water. We watched it flutter back and forth as it sank toward the bottom.

"Yes, I have fished here before. The story goes that blind fish live back in the darkness where the water is deep."

"Whoa, that's pretty far out, Papa. Have you ever caught one?" When I did not answer, Nick said, "Or ever seen one? Or know anybody that has?"

We looked around when Jake yelled for us to wait as he splashed up the middle of the spring branch toward us. He complained every step of the way about the cold water.

"No, I've never caught one. I saw a fish swimming around when I shined a light down into the water one time. I'm not sure if it was blind or not."

"What are you guys doing?" Jake asked as he climbed a moss-covered bank and crawled up on top of the big boulder beside us.

Nick looked up me and laughed. "Catching blind fish."

"I want to catch one," Jake said. "What do I use for bait, blind worms?"

"Blind worms are as good as anything." I laughed and rubbed Jake's silky black hair. I wished I had never brought up the subject of blind fish. The odds were we would not see or catch one for sure. One more thing Nick might think I made up.

"How about diving into the water from this rock?" Nick asked. "You ever done that, Papa?"

"Many times. When I hit the water I always wondered why I was crazy enough to do it again.

"How come?" Jake asked.

"It's too cold. It takes your breath away. Hell, I might have a heart attack if I tried it now. You've been wading in it and complaining. Think of plunging in your whole body."

"I'm going to do it," Nick said. "I'm going to jump. What about you Jake?"

"No way. You're crazy if you do it, Nick."

Without hesitation, Nick threw his hands up over his head and leaped from the top of the boulder into the water. When he bottomed out at about six feet under, he started flapping his arms up and down like a wild goose.

"Dammit! Holy crap!" Nick yelled when he reached the surface, churning the water like a thrashing machine as he swam for the bank.

"What's wrong?" I asked.

"Freezing! I'm freezing!" Nick climbed out of the water and lay down on a bed of pine needles that covered the bank. He rolled up into a ball and shivered. "My whole body's numb."

"Did I mention the water would be cold?" I laughed, remembering what it was like the first time I made the plunge. Like I had jumped into a tub of ice.

"That water's cold enough to cause hypothermia, isn't it, Papa?" Nick said.

"Probably fifty degrees. That's cold enough," I said.

"What's hypothermia?" Jake asked.

"Hypothermia is caused by extended exposure to cold. It happens when more heat is lost than the body can generate. You're okay if you don't stay in the water very long," I said. Jake looked at me and frowned.

Nick gave Jake a wicked smile. "Are you ready to jump in now?"

"No way. Why would I want to freeze like you did?"

RIVER'S EDGE

"Look at this beautiful place, boys." I raised my arms toward the heavens and turned around in a circle. A cluster of vines and green ferns hung from a rock ledge along the top of the cave. The sun that streaked through the tall Cottonwood trees cast a reddish-blue halo on the surface of the pool of spring water. "This was probably a family residence during ancient times, maybe even a shopping mall. The cave people would eat their meals, trade goods, made weapons and clothes here. They never ventured more than a few miles away to fish and kill wild game."

"I wonder if caveman kids traded stone collector cards," Jake said. "Maybe with pictures of animals and fish painted on them."

I smiled when Nick looked at me and rolled his eyes. For a nine-year-old, Jake had a very vivid imagination and the ability to reason like an engineer.

"How do you feel now, Nick?" I asked as he shielded his eyes from the sunlight with the flat of his hand. His lips were bluish-grey from the cold water.

"I'm getting warmer," Nick said. "I thought I'd never be warm again. My skin feels tingly. I've never been so cold. Try it, Jake. It'll really wake you up."

"Yeah right. I saw what it did to you, Nick. You were shivering like Deputy Dog on TV."

"Tell you what little brother. Let's jump in together. We'll make a big splash. I'll pull you out if you start to sink."

Even though Jake was game for anything within reason. He was also not afraid to back down when common sense prevailed.

"Okay," Jake said. "I'll do it if Papa will jump with us."

"Oh no you don't," I said. "I jumped into that cold spring water my last time fifty years ago."

I no more than got the words out of my mouth when a yellow jacket buzzed past my ear. I swatted at it and lost my balance. I grabbed Jake's arm and we fell into the water. Being a veteran of the cool pool, I popped up quickly and headed for the bank as fast as I could swim. Jake sputtered along behind.

"I'm freezing!" Jake yelled as he swam for shore. "Cold! It's cold! Let me get out!" He pulled himself up on the bank. Shivering and shaking, he said, "Did you do that on purpose, Papa?"

I assured him I had not, nor would I ever pull such a stunt. I rubbed his arms briskly. I smiled to myself because fate had caused us to go off the rock and into the water together. Something the two of us would never forget.

"I don't know about you two, but I'm glad I did it," Nick said as he looked down at Jake and me. "I feel wide awake as a wild animal."

We all laughed when Jake told Nick he might be a wild animal disguised as a boy.

"How much time do we have left before dark?" Jake asked.

I looked across the river at the sun setting and figured we had another hour of daylight at most. Certainly enough time for Nick to dig up the bone unless I came up with something more interesting and exciting to do.

"Tell you what we might do next, boys. Let's check our lines to make sure the minnows have not been stolen. Then we'll go up river and look for arrowheads. Like I said earlier, your Uncle Dub found quite a few and a nice stone axe years ago."

"How did you find the place where the Indians made the arrowheads? Jake asked.

"Years ago, my Uncle Ira showed me. It's a place where there's a lot of flint rock. Most arrowheads are made of flint. An arrowhead in good shape is worth more than most collector cards."

We climbed down off of the boulder and walked along the spring branch toward our campsite. Nick and Jake splashed on one another and yelled when the cold water hit their bare skin. When we walked toward the Blue Hole I saw my rod and reel lying on the gravel bar. I hurried over and picked it up. I jerked back on the rod to set the hook, in case a fish still had my bait in their mouth. When I reeled in the line, the minnow was gone. "Another case of a fish getting the best of a fisherman," I said.

"Shoot, that's too bad," Jake, said. "We could have had fish for dinner. Now we'll have to eat hot dogs."

"I don't care. I like hot dogs," Nick said as he tapped me on the shoulder. He put his finger up to his lips and motioned with his head that he wanted to tell me something in private.

I left Jake gazing at the water and walked away. I turned my head to one side and bent down so Nick could whisper in my ear.

"It's not a horse bone is it, Papa?" He caught me completely off guard. "You can tell me. I won't tell Jake."

One little white lie was bad enough. A second would fall in a category of a bad example that would come back to haunt me down the road. I hunkered down and looked into Nick's eyes. There was no doubt he had me nailed. I shook my head and whispered, "You're right. I'll tell you about it later, okay?"

"Did you say something, Papa?" Jake asked as he turned around.

"It was nothing important. I'll bait the hook. We'll go look for arrowheads before it gets dark. How does that sound?"

"Sounds good," Jake, said. "I'm buying a new bike if I find a new arrowhead. I want a new helmet and some leather gloves too. Let's get going."

"Where did you get the idea to wear leather gloves?" I asked.

"I saw it on TV. Trick riders use 'em so their hands don't get scraped up."

Jake looked up at a flock of ducks flying overhead and paid the leg bone no mind when we walked past. Nick paused long enough to knock some loose gravel away from the bone with the end of a stick.

"You're bad," I said as I rubbed his blonde head with my hand. He looked at me and grinned.

"Come on. Let's find some arrowheads," Jake said and we were off on another adventure. "I could use a new skateboard, too."

Chapter Five

We waded across the river at our campsite and headed up the gravel bar.

Jake pointed at a bed of weeds growing along the river's edge where a clump of Willows shaded the water. "That looks snaky," he said. "Lets throw some rocks."

Nick picked up a handful of gravel and scattered the pebbles in the weeds. "Get out snakes," he yelled. A brown and white snipe flushed out of the cover and took to the air. The bird squawked loudly as it flew up the river barely above the surface of the water in a zig, zag pattern.

I laughed.

"What's so funny?" Nick asked.

"Every time we leave camp you boys throw rocks to scare away the snakes. It must be working. We haven't seen any."

When we reached the head of a long ripple and rounded the bend, I saw a huge boulder out in the still pool of water up ahead.

"Look at that." I pointed at a spot on the face of the limestone bluff where the boulder had broken loose. "That's the most significant change I've ever seen take place on the river. It broke loose since I was here last."

"I bet it made a big splash," Jake said.

"What if a piece of the tall bluff broke loose at our camp site," Nick said. "We may get crushed."

"No need to worry. That rock's been there like it is for thousands of years." I tried to create trust by raising my voice. "Look up and down the river. You see all of that space? The odds of anything falling in the exact place you're standing would be about like winning the lottery."

"Now we got snakes, ticks, snapping turtles and falling rocks to worry about," Jake said.

I gave him a reassuring smile. "Come on, let's look for arrowheads before it gets dark. We've only got an hour." I headed toward the bluff where a spring flowed out of a crevice and splashed into the river.

"This doesn't look any different than the rest of the river," Nick said.

"It may not to you, but that's flint rock." I pointed at a layer of reddish-brown stone that was lighter in color than the rest of the bluff.

"How many arrowheads have you found here, Papa?" Jake asked.

"Like I said before, not many. Maybe a half-dozen. I've showed them to you haven't I?"

"No. I've never seen any arrowheads," Jake said.

"I have." Nick said. "So is this really where you found them?"

"I wouldn't tell you so if I hadn't. The first one I found, your Great-grandpa, Tom was with me. I was about Jake's age."

"So you just look around and hope you see one?" Jake asked.

"Get a stick and scratch around in the gravel. There's some good digging sticks." I pointed at a couple of poles the size of broomsticks that a beaver chewed off a Willow tree.

Jake picked them up and handed the longest one to Nick. The boys began to dig around in the gravel. I just happened to bring along a couple of the arrowheads I found years ago in the same spot. I pulled one out of my pocket and dropped it beside my foot. I walked to the edge of the water and dropped the second one.

"We're not going to find any arrowheads," Jake said after he had searched for about five minutes. "You sure this is the place you found some?"

"Hey, Dude. If it were easy, people would find arrowheads all over the place. Then there wouldn't be any. Keep looking, Jake."

"Hey, Dude, Papa." Nick mocked me in a whiny voice for using his native teenage lingo. "That was a long time ago. Maybe people found them all."

I looked at Nick and shook my head.

The boys walked over and sat down on a log. Nick looked up and watched a red tail hawk soaring high above us on the warm air currents. Jake pulled a Swiss army knife out of his pocket and began to whittle on a stick. I thought about how proud Dad would have been of Jake. He whittled enough during his lifetime to fill a dump pickup truck full of slivers, some of them so fine they looked like a lock of hair when they curled up and dropped to the ground.

"Have you boys given up the search?" I asked.

"Not me." Nick jumped up off the log, picked up his stick and began to scrape around in the gravel like someone hoeing weeds out of a garden. "Look at this." Nick held up a flat rock the size of a half dollar with a hole in the middle. "Do you think someone made this hole, or was it put there by nature?"

"I'd say nature. What's that by your foot? No, the other foot, by that clump of leaves."

"It's an arrowhead," Nick yelled excitedly. "I've found an arrowhead! How much is it worth, $500 dollars?"

"Let me see it up close," I said as Nick walked over and handed it to me, with Jake close behind.

"You might get two hundred dollars. Are you going to keep it or sell it? If you keep it, the value will go up every year. They're not making any more authentic arrowheads to speak of, you know."

"Why not me?" Jake said. "Why didn't I find one? I could use the money more than Nick. I need a new bike and my baseball glove's too little for my hand."

"Keep looking," I said as I handed the arrowhead back to Nick. "That's how people find things that are hard to find. They keep looking. We need to start down river before too long. It will be dark by the time we reach camp. If you don't find anything today there's always tomorrow."

"Yeah, right. How many times have I heard that?" Jake sounded really disappointed. "I may as well quit."

"Try over by the edge of the water. New rocks are exposed when there is a rise and fall of the river. Fact is, Jake, that's where I've had my best luck."

He dug around with his stick as if he were on a mission to unearth the river bottom. There was no doubt Jake had reached the low point of his day.

I walked to the edge of the water and picked up a flat rock, hunkered down and threw it side arm as hard as I could. It skipped across the surface of the water a dozen times. *When I was a kid I could get twenty skips or more before the rock sank to the bottom*, I thought.

I watched Jake as he got within a few of feet of the arrowhead. Nick was headed in the same direction. God forbid Jake did not find it first. I did not have any more arrowheads stashed away. I pointed at a flock of mallards winging their way upriver. "Look at the ducks," I said. While I had the boys' undivided attention, I kicked the arrowhead to within inches of Jake's big toe.

Jake screamed when he looked down and saw the reddish colored arrowhead by his foot. He picked it up and held it in the palm of his hand. He stared at it with a blank look on his face. Strangely enough, he did not ask how much I thought it was worth. There was not a word about the monetary value. It was as if for the first time Jake had found something that he might want to keep for a long time. Something he found on a trip with his old Papa.

As we headed down the river toward camp, both boys scoured the gravel bank as if they were looking for a needle in a haystack. The arrowhead find seemed to have given them a new perspective and sense of awareness about the great outdoors.

"We can come back tomorrow if you want too," I said, figuring they may find some arrowheads on their own.

When we reached our campsite and splashed across the river, I saw the rope swing moving from side to side again. I looked down at the bone sticking up out of the ground and I groaned.

"What's wrong Papa?" Jake asked.

This reminds me of something out of a Halloween experience, only more spooky because it is for real. That was what I might have said; instead I looked at Jake and smiled.

The Sycamore trees along the bank where the spring branch flowed from the cave cast shadows on the surface of the water as darkness closed in. I looked at my watch and saw that it was almost eight o'clock. In a couple of hours we would be in the tent asleep. In spite of almost having a wreck coming down the steep hill to the river, we'd had ourselves a good day.

I looked up when I thought I heard the rumble of thunder. I did not see a cloud in the sky. That would put a damper on things if it rained for the next two days. Especially if the river came up during the night, which it has been known to do. One time a rain up river brought a wall of water down that swept our camp gear and the tent down river with us inside. We were lucky to escape.

"What now, Papa," Jake said. "Is it time to light the fire? Can I strike the match?"

"Sure, go ahead." I reached in my pants pocket and pulled out a silver Zippo lighter that I used to start campfires on the river when I was a kid. "Don't burn yourself. The flame shoots up pretty good from these old box lighters." I walked over to the wood that was stacked up for our campfire and hunkered down. I flipped open the cap and put my thumb on the wheel to demonstrate to Jake how to light the wick. "To use it you turn this wheel."

Jake took the lighter, put his thumb on the flint wheel and flicked it hard. It flew out of his hand and landed on the gravel bar. Flames shot out of the top when he reached down to pick it up; he touched the metal casing and burned his fingers. He screamed, and fell backwards when he jerked his hand away. Not wanting to act like a little boy, he held back the tears that welled up in his eyes. I told him to put his hand in the cold spring water. He walked over and sat there for a long time.

Nick used a stick to flip the lid on the lighter shut and put out the flame. He picked up the lighter and started to toss it back and forth from one hand to the other until it cooled down. Jake told Nick he could light the fire because he was too hurt to care anymore.

I walked up the spring branch toward the mouth of the cave and pulled up a clump of cool, damp moss to use as a healing poultice.

Nick yelled at me to look at the dancing yellow flames created by the Cedar branches he had tossed on the fire. I took a deep breath and sucked in the sweet smell of the burning Cedar.

"Make sure you only use dry wood," I said as I pulled some fishing line out of my pocket and tied the wad of moss around Jake's finger. "How does that feel?" I asked.

Jake looked at his newly redecorated finger and frowned. "It looks pretty silly. I hope it works."

"Trust me it works. It's an old-time remedy," I said.

RIVER'S EDGE

Nick held up a stick. "How do I know if something's wet or dry? Why does it matter?"

"A stick is dead and dry if you can snap it in two easily. Green wood makes a lot of smoke when it's burned. I don't like a lot of smoke, because for some reason it comes my direction and makes my eyes water. You've heard the saying that smoke follows beauty?"

"If smoke followed beauty, it would follow me." Nick laughed as he raised his knee and snapped a dry stick in two.

The boys seemed to have settled in and enjoyed everything on the river. If they missed watching TV or sending email, I had not seen any sign of it. One of the worst parts for me had been seeing my brother again and feeling guilty about all the years that passed when we rarely spoke. Our kids did not even get to know one another because of our foolish feud. Whoever said sticks and stones can break your bones, but words can never harm you is a person who never got into a situation like ours. A ruckus among relatives can wreck more lives than the few people who are involved in the feud.

"I'm hungry, Papa," Nick said.

"Okay." I looked at Jake and Nick and hoped they would never be so stupid as Dub and I had been. "Let's roast some hot dogs?"

"My burnt finger can't hold onto a hot dog," Jake mumbled, feeling sorry for himself. "Look how big it is all wrapped up."

"Tell you what, Jake, Nick and I can help you out. He'll feed you the bun and I'll feed you the hot dog." I patted Jake on the shoulder and smiled.

Jake gave Nick the evil eye when he snickered.

I walked up the spring branch and cut three limbs off a Willow tree. I trimmed away the leaves and sharpened the end of each stick as I walked back into camp. "We can use these to cook marshmallows after we roast the dogs."

"Tell you what I'll do, Jake. Since your hand is messed up, when you're ready to eat. I'll cook your hotdog, then roast a marshmallow and poke the stick into the ground. You can eat it off without having to touch anything," Nick said.

"Where did you learn that trick?" I asked. I wondered how in all my camping and marshmallow roasting days, I never knew about the technique.

"Cub Scouts," Nick said.

"You guys might have to feed me the whole time we're camped here." Jake looked at me with sparkling dark eyes and smiled when I patted him on the shoulder. He was a great kid with such a good sense of humor.

I picked up a couple of hot dogs from the cooler and shoved them down onto the sharpened sticks. I grabbed a pack of buns and some mustard and headed for the big log close to the fire where the sound of gurgling water provided a peaceful backdrop.

When the boys plopped down, one on each side of me, I gave them a lesson in how to cook a hot dog that was edible, rather than end up a charred-gritty piece of meat. "The secret is to hold the dog in the center and up toward the top of the flames. Turn the stick slowly so the meat cooks evenly. This takes patience, boys." When the first dog was toasty brown, I pulled it off the stick and put it on a bun. I squirted a yellow strip of mustard down the middle. I offered it to Jake and he grabbed it with his good hand and wolfed it down in record time.

Nick pulled the dog off the other stick and chomped it in half in one bite. In seconds my perfectly cooked specimens were gone. When Jake asked for a marshmallow next, I started to tell him to eat another hot dog because it seemed more nutritious than a sugar treat. Then I figured, what the heck. We were on a camping trip. Plus, who actually knows what ingredients are in a hot dog.

I looked up when I walked over to the cooler to get the bag of marshmallows and stared at a reddish-orange glow in the western sky. A natural picture beautiful enough to take your breath away.

"What are you looking at, Papa?" Jake asked.

I pointed at the fading sunlight that shown through the tops of the trees, then turned around and walked back to the campfire.

I opened the top and handed Jake the bag. "Cook your marshmallows the way I did the hot dogs. Keep them at the top of the flames so they don't catch on fire. They'll have a brown crust and be better to eat than if they're charred black." In no time, Nick and Jake were huffing and puffing to blow out their flaming marshmallows.

"I like them better black," Jake said as he licked sticky pieces of black and white marshmallow from the corners of his mouth.

After the boys ate their fill, they began to pile wood onto the fire. There was a loud snap, crackle and pop as thick yellow flames leaped into the air. The heat forced the boys to back away and shield their faces with their hands. I moved further toward the end of the log to escape the heat and thick white smoke.

"That's the biggest fire I've ever seen," Jake said as he stepped back further.

"The only thing I've seen bigger was when a house burned down on our street," Nick said.

"Okay, let's not put on anymore wood. We'll save the rest for morning. We'll cover it up with a tarp when we go to bed tonight. There will be heavy dew tonight. What's left out in the open will get wet."

By the time darkness settled in, the roaring fire had calmed down. We moved in closer so we could poke at the pulsing red coals with our hot dog sticks and watch the sparks fly.

"That house was the biggest fire I've ever seen," Jake said. "I can see how it can get out of control."

"Yep, don't ever underestimate the power of fire or water," I said. "What got this fire roaring were the Cedar tree branches. They've got lots of tar in 'em."

"This is the last one. Okay Papa?" Jake could not resist throwing on one more limb. I smiled at him and remembered how when I was a kid, I loved to build a fire so big it would light up the sky. Actually, not much had changed. I enjoyed the blaze almost as much as the boys.

I stared at the pulsing bed of coals and thought about the estranged relationship between Dub and me. I needed to explain the situation to the boys but I did not know where to begin. What we argued about seemed so silly and simple now. I decided to sleep on it until the next day.

Jake poured some water from the canteen onto the wad of moss tied around his finger. "How long will it be until the moon comes up?" he asked.

"Not long. It'll be up before we go to bed. How does your finger feel?"

"It's better. Still stings a little, but it's not throbbing now. The moss medicine helped, Papa- even though it's kind of gross."

"There are lots of old time remedies that work as good as modern treatments. I keep seeing scientific people say this and that works better. Half the time they change their mind in the end. Like last week, I read after thirty years they can't prove eating fiber does a thing to prevent colon cancer. Hell, if I'd known that, I wouldn't have eaten so much rope."

It took a second for what I said about me eating rope to sink in. The response was much less than I had imagined. The boys simply looked at me and frowned. Then continued to poke at the fire without saying a word.

RIVER'S EDGE

"You know what I can't stop thinking about, Papa?" Jake said. "That big bass. How much did you say he weighed?"

"At least four pounds. Maybe even five. It was a nice fish. People don't forget about one like that very easy."

"I'll never hook a fish like that again," Jake said, shaking his head. "Never in my whole life."

"You don't know that, Jake. You might catch one tomorrow even bigger. You have to keep the faith. When you don't believe in bigger and better, you go backwards."

I looked up and saw the top of the silvery white moon rising above the towering bluff. It was a beautiful sight. "It will be almost as bright as day soon." I pointed at the moon with a backdrop of millions of twinkling stars.

"Look, there's the Little Dipper." Nick pointed up at the sky. "Hey, there's the Big Dipper,"

"You know what would be really neat?" Jake said. "To see a cow jump over the moon."

Nick laughed. "If I ever see that I'll know I've gone looney."

"The moon looks like it's made out of milk," Jake said as the glowing round ball continued to slowly work its way above the top of the bluff like a stalking white cat.

I picked up my hot dog stick and joined the boys, poking at the fire, watching red and yellow sparks shoot toward the sky and disappear into the night.

"Have you ever been bat bit?" Jake asked.

"No, I haven't," I said.

"Is it true they suck out your blood?"

"No, Jake. It's not true."

"Do they carry disease that can kill people? You know, rabies?"

63

"What was that noise?" Nick got up off the rock he was sitting on across from me and looked around. "Sounded like something slapped the top of the water."

"Could have a been a beaver. Maybe an owl swooped down and grabbed a fish," I said.

Jake looked at me across the shimmering heat waves that rose up from the fire. "Anything else about the bats?"

"That's all I know. Except like most wild creatures, if you mess with 'em, they may bite you. Don't mess with 'em, you won't get bit."

"That's one more thing to get bit by on this river," Jake said. He had obviously missed the point of my warning to let sleeping dogs, or in this case, leave sleeping bats alone. "What about the rabies?"

"Yes, Jake. Bats can carry rabies but it's not common. In the Ozarks there's mostly brown bats. They're not bloodsuckers like the Vampire bats in Mexico. Those bats suck blood from animals, but not normally from people. Bats are kind and loving creatures to each other. They've been known to risk their lives to share food with less fortunate roost-mates."

"Bats sound pretty cool," Nick said as he slapped a mosquito on the back of his hand.

"Yeah, one brown bat can eat over a thousand mosquito-sized insects every hour they're out hunting. I know it sounds wild, but it's true."

"Look." Nick pointed at a bat that dipped and darted its way through the air a few feet above our head. "It's like he heard you talking about him, Papa. He flew down to say hello."

We all laughed.

That would be like something I might have said, I thought as I leaned back into the shadows and studied Nick's darkly tanned face in the firelight. His blond hair that hung down over the tops of his ears and onto his forehead looked golden in the firelight.

"You got any more questions about bats?" I asked, hoping for at least one or two. Jake hunched up his shoulders and continued to poke at the fire.

Nick looked at me and shook his head. "I don't, for sure. But what about the bone?"

"What about it?" I said sharply, figuring he had sat there with that question on the tip of his tongue ever since I tried to convince him it belonged to a horse. "Best I can tell it's still in the same place."

"Can we dig it up first thing in the morning? I want to take it with me to Leatherwood Cave and use it as a club."

When I looked up at the top of the bluff again, I saw half of the moon shining down on us. I had forgotten that it came up so quickly. The bright white light glistened like sparkling diamonds on the surface of the rushing water in the ripple behind me as it flowed into the Blue Hole, where the water was still, dark and deep.

"Sure," I said, hoping when I got up in the night to dig it up myself that Nick did not catch me.

Nick stood up and looked at the bone sticking out of the gravel bar. "I could dig it up right now in just a few minutes." I rose up off the log and looked at him with raised eyebrows. "Okay, I'll wait until tomorrow."

"Good," I said. I hoped to regain some of the storytelling Momentum that I had going before the bone entered the picture. *But I can't talk about the murders*, I thought, figuring it best to wait until daylight before I told about something with very much blood and gore.

Nick cocked his head to one side and continued to study the bone a little more before he sat back down. He looked at me across the top of the flames and smiled. "I'll be up early to do some digging."

"So if there's not any more bat or bone questions, how about I tell a story?"

"What kind of story?" Jake asked. "If it's scary, I don't want to hear it. I don't want to be scared tonight."

"Is it true or made up. That's all I care about. If it's got made up parts, I don't want to hear it," Nick said.

"It's real all right. Fact is, not one bit is made up. Only problem, it may be too scary. After all you boys have been spooked about enough today. Snakes, Spiders, Ticks, Bats, Snapping Turtles and a runaway Jeep ride."

"Nothing's ever too scary for me, Papa" Nick said as he threw a pine knot onto the glowing coals. "Go on ahead, you'll probably scare yourself more than me."

"Does that happen? Do people get scared of their own story?" Jake asked.

"Who told you the story?" Nick asked before I could answer Jake. "Was it your Uncle Ira? He seemed to come up with some pretty wild tales. I wonder if they were always true?"

"Here's what you've got to remember about storytellers. They can't lie. If they do, they're just trying to deceive people and that's bad. Take Uncle Ira for instance. He would stretch the truth sometimes, but he'd never tell an outright fib. The story I'm talking about has nothing to do with my Uncle Ira making something up. I was there when it happened."

"Go ahead Papa, I'm ready." Jake looked over at Nick and grinned.

I watched black resin ooze from the pine knot as red and yellow flames lapped up the sides. I smiled when I heard the hoot of an owl downriver and glanced up when a bat fluttered past. With the boys

RIVER'S EDGE

sitting one on each side of me, the mood was right, the moon was bright and I was in a storyteller frame of mind.

Chapter Six

Okay, here we go," I said. "Stop me if you get scared. I don't want to cause any nightmares. A loud scream in my ear might cause me to overreact and bite a nose off."

"Yeah right, Papa," Nick said. "Go on with the story."

"How long is the story?" Jake asked.

"I don't know. Why do you care?"

"I might get sleepy before it's over."

"You can go to bed if you need to sleep. Anyway, here it is. Dub and I used to tag along on foxhunts with our Dad and Uncle Ira. We'd sit around a campfire and they'd tell stories while we listened to the hounds speak."

Jake laughed. "I didn't know hounds could talk? What did they say?"

"That's what you call it when hounds cry out. Dog's bark, but hounds are special. They speak. It's the music made when a pack is running a fox or another animal."

"Far out!" Nick said.

"Generally Dad and Uncle Ira stayed up all night. By about midnight, Dub and I would wrap up in blankets and curl up by the fire and sleep until morning."

"I could never stay awake all night," Jake said.

I laughed. "Neither could I when I was your age. So back to the story, one night Uncle Ira's hounds got on the trail of a fox down by the river. They cried that lonesome call hounds do when they get their running blood up. Then there was a scream. After that there was a deathly silence. It was as if everything within hearing distance was frozen. The pack came back to camp with their tails tucked between their legs. They whimpered like they had been scared half to death. That sorry sound coming from a whole pack of hounds at the same time made the hair stand up on the back of my neck."

"What happened?" Jake asked.

I poked the fire with my stick and looked up at the stars in the sky as sparks from the fire shot up beside me. "That's a good question? I don't know."

"Were you scared?" Jake asked.

"Clear down to the end of my toes."

"It was probably a bobcat," Nick said.

"Don't think so. A bobcat has a high-pitched scream. It sounded more like the cry of a woman. Like someone being chased."

Nick stood up and looked around as if he thought something might be trying to sneak up on us. "So, what happened next?"

"Uncle Ira talked to the hounds and tried to calm them down. It didn't do any good. They were shaking so badly the skin was about to crawl off of their bones."

"Was your Dad and Uncle Ira scared, too?" Jake asked.

"Everybody was scared. You bet. It was a strange situation. Unlike anything anyone had ever seen then, or since."

I stood up and looked toward the mouth of the cave when I thought I heard something that sounded like a cartridge being levered into the chamber of rifle.

"What's the matter, Papa?" Jake asked.

"I thought I heard something up by the cave."

"I didn't hear anything," Nick said. "Maybe you've scared your own self?"

Nick snickered. "Have you ever done that, Papa? Scared yourself?"

"Anybody that tells a good enough story has probably scared their own self," I said.

"What do you think the noise was, Papa?" Jake asked

I slapped at a buzzing mosquito to get it away from my ear. "Probably my imagination. Nothing to worry about. I'll go on with the story. Stop me if you get too scared."

"Can you tell it a little faster?" Jake said. "I'm getting sleepy, but I want to hear the rest."

"Anyway, the hounds were too scared to move. So Uncle Ira carried 'em to the pickup truck."

"How much does a hound weigh?" Nick asked.

"I don't know. Fifty pounds, I guess," I said as I watched Nick toss another pine tree branch on the fire. The long green needles crackled as they burst into flame and curled up into greyish-white ashes that rode off into the night on the shimmering heat waves. "Next time Dad and Uncle Ira wanted to fox hunt, even as much as those red bone hounds loved to run, they wouldn't leave the pen."

Jake leaned his head against my shoulder. "Sounds like so bad that the Devil might have done it."

"I don't know. Here's another crazy thing. The hound named Breaker who always ran out in front, she never came back with the rest of the pack. Uncle Ira even got Sheriff Johnson to search for her with his bloodhounds. But they came up with nothing, which was strange, since bloodhounds are keen enough to find a gnat on a bumble bee's butt."

Jake laughed. "A bumble bee's butt, that's funny."

"Look! A shooting star." I pointed above the top of the bluff where a streak of light raced across the sky.

"Where?" Nick jumped up and turned the wrong way toward the river.

Of course, Jake looked in the same direction as Nick and the star burned up before they saw the display.

Nick sat down on the rock and looked at me through the smoke rising above the dancing flames. "Funny you saw something we didn't," he said.

I threw my hands in the air. "I saw a shooting star. I wouldn't say I did, if I didn't. It helps to look in the same direction where the action is."

I remembered seeing a shooting star the night the old man appeared on the ridge across the river. Just like Nick did today, Dub missed seeing both of those events that night back then.

Jake looked at me and smiled when I sat back down on the log. "Go on, Papa. Finish the story."

"That's it. The story's over. Nobody found out what caused the hounds to get spooked. It just was something that happened during a strange time when lots of weird was going on."

"Seems like more scary stuff happens in this part of the country than anyplace I know about," Jake said.

I never thought of it that way, but Jake was right. There was a lot of spooky stuff that happened. The worst being, the night someone went on a shotgun rampage and killed Buzzard Thompson's family. At about the same time, Joe Peterson hanged himself in the barn. No way could I give the boys a detailed description of how poor old Joe looked when my friend Doodle and I found him swinging from a rafter. His bluish-black tongue hung out the corner of his mouth and blowflies swarmed around his head. What I could tell them about was when Ben Johnson got lightning struck. They would find it interesting that the jolt from the bolt blew off Ben's shoes. Since Ben was dynamiting fish at the time, which was illegal and immoral, that would be a good tale to tell that had a lesson to be learned.

A lightning bug flashed its neon colored tail in front of Jake's face and he snatched it out of the air. He opened his hand and we watched it fly away.

"The most lonely lightning bug is always the brightest," I said.

I pointed at the moon that had fully risen above the top of the bluff. "Another thing I remember about the night Uncle Ira's hounds got the wits scared out of them, there was a full moon that night too."

Jake held up a piece of jerky and Nick shook his head. "I'm too tired to chew."

Jake handed the jerky to me and I gnawed off a bite. "That's all the stories I've got tonight. Except for a short one that has a lesson to be learned. I was saving it for tomorrow, but I could tell it tonight. What do you think, Jake? Are you too sleepy?"

Jake shook his head. "What does a lesson to be learned mean?"

Nick stepped up to the plate with an answer. "You know. Like when something is used as an example. Like that makes a person want to do better." Nick sounded proud of himself for being able to decipher what I said and give Jake a good example.

"Is that right, Papa?" I nodded my head in agreement. With the sound of gurgling water and the howl of a coyote on a distant ridge, I started to tell the final story of the evening.

"There was a guy named Ben Johnson who got his tail end fried." I waited for a reaction to my cute remark. Jake looked at me and frowned and Nick poked at the fire. "He got struck by lightning. Fact is he was hit the next day after what happened with Uncle Ira's hounds. Bad luck runs in a pack sometimes."

"A lot of people get struck by lightning," Nick said. "That's not so weird."

"What makes this story different is weird, believe me. Old Ben was on the river dynamiting fish. A storm blew up and a bolt of lightning zapped him. The force was so powerful it blew off his

RIVER'S EDGE

shoes. The bottoms of his feet were brown like he'd stood on a bed of coals."

Nick slapped his leg and laughed. "Come on, Papa. How could anything blow off your shoes?"

"Go read about people that have been struck and you'll see. I'm surprised you haven't seen it on TV. You've seen about everything else. You'll see I'm right. Here's the important part. This, Jake, my friend, is where the lesson to be learned lives. It was Mother Nature's way of paying Ben back. Uncle Ira said it happened because using dynamite was a coward's way of fishing. Uncle Ira had strong feelings about poachers and people who broke the law."

"Is Ben still alive?" Jake asked.

"Probably not. He was about seventy back then, so he'd be about one hundred and twenty by now."

The boys laughed.

Nick leaned to one side and looked at the bone. "So what are we doing tomorrow?"

"We're going to fish and swim. Sail off on the rope swing and jump off the bluff. Explore Leatherwood Cave and who knows what all before the day's done."

"Let's look for arrowheads too." Jake pulled the arrowhead he found out of his pocket. He examined it closely in the firelight. "I hope I find another one tomorrow. Not only that, I hope I catch a big Smallmouth bass."

"We'll do it all. Tomorrow will be a great day for us. I bet your Mom and Dad have missed you guys. You'll have a lot to tell them when we get home."

"Katherine and Lauren will pester me," Jake said. "Girls want to know about every little thing."

"That seems about right to me." I looked up at the moon and thought about the missions I had planned before daybreak. The first thing was to dig up the leg bone and stash it away in the Jeep. The next involved the mysterious old man. I had a feeling that he would be back to visit me under the light of a full moon. I hoped he did, I had a question to ask him that had haunted me for the past fifty years.

"I'm going to bed before long, boys. We'll get up early and catch some fish. Hard to beat fried fish and scrambled eggs for breakfast."

"Can I make the first cast?" Jake asked.

"It's okay with me. Do you mind if Jake tries to catch a fish first, Nick?"

"I hope he does. He should. He's talked about it enough." Nick stood up and walked toward the Blue Hole when he heard something make a splash. "Looking down into the water is like looking into a silvery mirror."

I stood up and looked at the reflection of the moon on the surface of the water. It was strange how so many scary things had happened at such a peaceful place.

"You okay, Papa?" Jake asked.

"Yeah, sure. Just a little tired. Getting up early and driving six hours to get to Lewiston took its toll on me. So did the runaway ride down the hill, plus tromping up and down the riverbank as well. I'm glad, I will sleep the sleep of a tired body and a peaceful mind tonight."

Nick laughed. "The Jeep ride would have made a great video. I bet Mom would pass out if she saw it. Especially the part where the Jeep tipped up on its side and almost turned over."

I thought about making a plea for silence about that particular experience, then figured I would have a better chance of the boys not saying anything if I left well enough alone.

"The part I hated most was the dust," Jake said. "That and the smell like burning tires clogged up my nose."

"Nobody got hurt. That's the important thing. Maybe it's not worth talking about to anybody back home." The plea slipped out before I knew it was coming.

Nick looked at me and raised his eyebrows. "If we'd tumbled off the road. We may never have been found."

"Like I said, we came out okay. Nobody got hurt. So let's think about something else."

"Yeah, Nick. Let's think about the big fish I'll catch tomorrow."

"Jake's got the right idea. Tomorrow may be one of the most fun days of our entire lives.

Jake laid his hot dog stick down. Nick made an out of the way trip and circled the leg bone for one last look. I scooped up a bucket of water and tossed it on the bed of coals. The dying embers sizzled, a thick cloud of grey and white ash boiled up toward the sky and we headed for the tent.

Jake claimed his spot in the middle between Nick and me and settled in for what could prove to be an unusual evening.

"How's your burnt finger?" I asked. I patted Jake on the head when he gave me credit again for the moss poultice stopping the pain. I reached over and touched the green moist gob that was still wrapped around his finger.

"Can you tell one more story, Papa?" Jake said. "Nothing too scary. Okay?"

"Well let's see. How about the story of a dream I had when I was your age. It seemed so real I never forgot it. In the story I was a raindrop."

"That sounds like a good one." Jake laid his head on my shoulder and settled in for the last thing he would hear before drifting off to sleep.

"Sounds like a little kid story," Nick said.

"Tell you what, Mister Nick. If it's too young for you, stick this in your ears." I handed Nick a wad of cotton from an aspirin bottle and went on with my tale.

"I think I had the dream because my Dad and I got caught out in a rain storm. Lots of hail, some so big they broke the windshield on the pickup truck."

"Will we dig up the bone first thing in the morning?" Nick asked.

"Sure," I said and I went on with the story. "Anyway, the dream started with rolling dark storm clouds. There was a loud clap of thunder. A jagged web of lightning streaked down from the heavens and crashed into the earth."

"Did anyone get stuck by the lightning?" Jake asked.

I assured him no one was hit.

"In the dream, instead of being a person, I was a rain drop. Guess who my mother was?"

"Who?" Jake asked.

"Do you want to guess, Nick?" I asked.

"Sure. Could it be Mother Nature?"

"That's right, Mother Nature was my Mom. She had the body of a tree stump and the head of a deer."

Nick snickered. "That must have been scary."

"No, not at all. Raindrops aren't afraid of anything, except heat. As I fell to the earth through the swirling clouds, Mother Nature painted the sky with streaks of lightning to illuminate my path. My Mom told me I was a child of nature. She said I would remain alive so long as the sun did not burn me up. Instead of calling it evaporation, she called it zaporation."

I stopped and listened when I heard the noise again that sounded like a cartridge being levered into the chamber of a rifle. I started to ask the boys if they heard it, then decided not to stir things up since they had not said anything.

"Have you ever told anyone else this story?" Nick asked.

"I told your Uncle Dub the next day after I dreamed it. I also told my mother, Elsie."

"Did they think it sounded like something you made up?" Nick asked.

"It was a dream. People don't make up dreams."

"I just wondered. Go on ahead," Nick said.

"It was springtime. The early morning air smelled fresh and clean. There was a rainbow in a clear blue sky. Animals scurried from their hiding places where they escaped the rain and songbirds filled the forest with a joyful course. The river ran bank full and the once clear water had turned mud-based brown."

"So what were you doing all this time?"

"Funny you should ask, Nick. That was when I fell from the sky and landed on a Sycamore tree leaf. Remember, in the dream I was a rain droplet, no bigger than a drip. I was suspended between the sky above and the rain-swollen river below. As the sun rose higher in the sky, I felt the heat begin to draw the energy from my body. Too much heat and I would be turned into water vapor and drawn back up into the clouds. As critical seconds ticked by I felt my watery legs go weak. A crow that was Perched on a tree limb across the river cawed to ask if I was okay."

"So you talked to creatures in your dream?" Nick sounded as if he may be ready for the story to end.

"That's right," I said, bound and determined to finish with some Momentum. "A Kingfisher flying along the river cried out, telling the crow he would help me. So the Kingfisher flew close by the leaf that I was resting on and the breeze from his wings pushed me out of harm's way. I dropped into the river and was saved from the heat of the sun. From there I floated downstream to the ocean. It was the most beautiful trip you can imagine. When my real mother, Elsie, woke me up from the dream, it was pouring down rain. What do you think would make a person have such a dream?"

"I don't know, but you've put Jake to sleep," Nick said.

I eased Jake's head off my shoulder and gave him a kiss on the cheek. Nick said goodnight and turned over. Within minutes I heard his heavy breathing.

I stared into the darkness and listened to the high-pitched chorus of cicadas and tree frogs. A Whippoorwill called from down river and a Bullfrog bellowed back in the slough. I thought about what it would be like to visit Lewiston on Saturday. I wondered how many people I would see from the old days. I thought about the one room schoolhouse and the day I met my wife Lucy when we were six years old. I saw her freckled, tanned face and flowing, red hair. Her blue eyes sparkled when she smiled. The saddest places would be the cemetery and Grandpa Tom's river cabin. Lord only knows what Dub would say when he delivered his sermon on Sunday. Even though I tried to stay awake because I had to dig up the leg bone before morning, I drifted off to sleep.

Chapter Seven

When I awoke a couple of hours later, Jake had his head on Nick's shoulder and I could tell by the deep rhythmic breathing that both boys were sound asleep. I groaned when I started to get up and lay back down. My back was sore from sleeping on the gravel bar. I opened a bottle of aspirin, tossed a couple in my mouth and washed them down with a swig of water. A flood of moonlight filled the tent when I opened the flap. I crawled outside, stood up and listened carefully. Surely, the click I heard earlier in the evening that sounded like a cartridge being chambered into the magazine of a rifle was my imagination. What concerned me was that I heard it twice.

I walked toward the Blue Hole when I saw something swimming across the slivery surface of the water. *Probably a beaver or a muskrat,* I thought when the creature disappeared. I looked up the river toward the tick, tick sound of the metal minnow trap scraping against the rocks. Maybe that was what I heard instead of a cartridge being chambered. I pulled a camp shovel from the duffle bag beside the cooler and walked over where the bone was buried in the gravel bar. I looked around when I thought I heard something behind me. I figured one of the boys might have crawled out of the tent. What would I say if Nick caught me digging? I wanted the bone for myself? My heart pounded and sweat ran down into my eyes. I gritted my teeth when I pushed the metal blade of the shovel into the gravel. In the quiet darkness, the scraping sound was amplified in my ears.

I thought about the two men who were murdered the last time Dub and I camped there. What kind of strange event would it be, if fifty years later, I dug up the killer's leg bone? I pushed the blade of the shovel deeper into the gravel and leaned back on the handle. There was a loud sucking sound when I raised the bone to the surface and the hole filled with water.

When I reached down to pick up the bone, Jake cried out from inside the tent, "Where are you, Papa?"

I froze. The metal shovel clanked loudly as it fell onto the gravel bar. "I'm here," I said, making an extra effort to sound calm.

"Is it morning already? Nick asked.

"No, it's still night time." I hurried over to the tent, threw back the flap and stuck my head inside. "I'll be in shortly. Lay back down."

Jake blinked. "Looks like daylight."

I pointed at the sky. "It's the light of the moon. Go back to sleep. We've got a busy day tomorrow."

"Okay, Papa. Don't be long," Jake said.

"Okay I won't. It'll be morning quick as a wink."

Maybe it's wrong to dig up the bone and hide it, I thought. I would have to tell Nick an outright lie about what happened to it if I did. Nick already did not trust me to tell a story without exaggerating much of the time. Being caught in an act of deception would be double bad.

I decided to hide the bone under the back seat of the Jeep then turn it over to the Sheriff when we got back to town. Better yet, Dub could turn in the bone. His being a preacher and trusted member of the community, there would be no questions asked. I looked up and watched a cloud that was passing in front the moon, now hanging up above my head. I waited for a good long spell to make sure the boys did not crawl outside of the tent before I trudged off down the gravel bar. I held the bone out in front of my chest and examined it in the moonlight. I felt like a caveman getting ready to go on a hunting trip.

RIVER'S EDGE

I thought I saw someone standing in the shadows when I approached the Jeep and I stopped. I started to throw the bone at whatever it was under the Sycamore tree. My mind raced. Should I run to camp and get the revolver out of my backpack? If I did there would probably be a middle of the night gun battle. Another story to add to the list of scary things the boys had already experienced since they arrived at the river, which I hoped their Mom and Dad would never hear about.

With weak knees, I raised my shaking hand and was ready to smash whatever lurked in the darkness with the bone if I was attacked.

"It's okay, Tommy."

"What th' hell?" I yelled, almost falling down when I stumbled backwards. I thought I was seeing things when Dub walked out of the shadows and stuck out his hand.

"Didn't mean to scare you," Dub said. "I'd planned to sleep in my pickup truck until daylight. Get a fire goin' and have a pot of coffee ready time you got up. When I saw you diggin'. I had to see what you were up to. You okay? "

"I'm okay now. You won't believe what I found. Maybe the killer's leg bone."

Dub cleared his throat. "Could be the gruesome experience from last time we camped here got you out of whack?"

"Listen to what I'm tellin' you, Dub. I know lots of people have come and gone in the past fifty years. Still, I may have found the leg bone of the person that committed the murders when we were here last. I sneaked out in the middle of the night and dug up the bone because Nick wanted to use it as a club. His carrying around a chunk of someone's body and whacking things with it didn't seem right. So, I decided to dig it up, hide it in the Jeep and have you give it to the Sheriff when we got back to Lewiston."

"Are you serious? How could a body be buried here for all those years?"

"Stranger things have happened."

Dub took hold of the bone when I held it out in front of him and laughed nervously. "So the killer may have put his best leg forward tonight, so to speak."

"Funny, Dub. Here's something else really strange. The dead man we found in the Blue Hole. His ashen, grey face appeared before me today. A wide-open smile with no teeth. Also, for no good reason, the rope swing moved back and forth."

"Probably the wind?"

"Nope. There wasn't even a slight breeze."

Dub laid the bone down on the ground and put his hand on my shoulder. "Nothing was the same after our camping trip. You know that as well as I do."

"You got that right." We looked at one another for some time without saying another word. "You know what else? I almost turned the Jeep over coming down the steep hill."

"You've had a strange day, Tommy. At least nobody got hurt."

"Yeah, if you don't count shattered nerves. You're right, nobody got hurt and the boys for sure enjoyed the day."

"Hope you don't mind me showin' up. I thought it'd be good us bein' together on the river again."

"It'll be a nice surprise for the boys." *Plus, I won't have to explain my actions now, or feel guilty*, I thought as I picked up the bone, hid it under the back seat in the Jeep and we walked up the riverbank toward camp.

"Thought we might talk, if you're not headed to bed," Dub said as he hunkered down beside the campfire and laid some twigs and a pine tree branch on the smoldering coals. A burst of flame shot up and the pithy smell of pine tar filled the air.

"Nice job," I said as I sat down on the log and watched the flames and waited for Dub to speak.

"Fire is good," Dub said. "Stories aren't the same without a campfire."

"That's for sure. Water's good too," I said, thinking how silly I sounded.

Dub looked at me and smiled. "Yeah, water's good too."

"I should have asked you to camp with us in the first place. Don't know what I was thinking."

Dub looked at me and raised his eyebrows. "As you can see, I don't need an invitation. I just show up."

It was nice sitting with Dub again around a campfire. If would be even nicer once we cleared the air by talking about some of the things that drove us apart. I started to say something about Grandpa's lever-action rifle that we had the silly argument about. Then decided I would see what Dub had to say first. It seemed easier that way, probably because I felt guilty about the way things had happened. Hard feelings could have been avoided if I had not been so stubborn.

We watched the fire for a long time without saying a word, when I finally broke the silence, my voice cracked. "We had a great time when we were kids. Did some crazy things. Remember the day you rode the hay hook and crashed into the end of the barn. You knocked yourself out because you didn't let go of the metal tongs soon enough, remember?"

Dub grinned. "Funny you brought that up. I thought about the hay hook accident driving to the river tonight. Lots of stuff to do in those days and we laughed a bunch along the way."

A breeze came up and blew a cloud of thick white smoke my way. I stood up and looked at the dancing yellow flames reflecting on the surface of the deep, dark water. I thought about the good times that Dub and I had missed out because for no good reason, we decided not to be friends. So much laughter and so many memories were lost in all those years. I looked up at the moon and I wiped a tear from the corner of my eye with the back of my hand.

"Have you camped with your grandsons a lot?" Dub asked.

"A few times. Mainly to Cub Scout and Boy Scout outings. Until recently I was kept pretty busy working the business. I travelled outside of the country on business a lot, sometimes for a month at a time. I guess I was trying to make up for lost time taking this trip with the boys. That was part of the reason I didn't ask you to come camp with us. The boys will be glad to see you in the morning. They know you're more of a woodsman than I am."

"Makes sense I probably am more of a woodsman. I've spent a good deal more of my life in touch with nature than you have. Not that isn't a bad thing; it's just the way it turned out."

"Guess so. I've chased the almighty dollar and you've lived off the land." I looked up at the top of the bluff and remembered when my friend Doodle and I rolled a boulder half the size of a car off the edge. We lay down on the ground and hung out over the edge to watch the big splash.

"So today you saw the face of the dead man we found," Dub said as he walked up beside me. "I've seen him on occasions myself. I wonder if the old man will pay us a visit since we're back here together again after all these years."

"I don't know. We'll stick around and see," I said.

"It will forever be a mystery why we were the chosen to be exposed to his spirit or whatever he was when we saw him last."

We walked back over by the fire and sat down.

"Do you remember everything about what happened that night?" I asked.

"Sure I do. Why wouldn't I?" Dub sounded like he was a little nervous to talk about what happened.

"It would be easy not to remember everything since it was like we were in a trance."

"That's what it seemed like for sure," Dub said.

"I hope he does pay us another visit. I'm curious about what he has to say after fifty years?" *Maybe I should not be acting too cocky, considering we were dealing with something completely unknown?*

I remember Dub and I standing outside in the middle of the night staring at a bed of coals behind our tent. When they burst into flames, the Sycamore tree by the spring branch began to sway back and forth and in the light of the moon; its branches looked like a gathering of ghosts and the rope swing moved back and forth, just like it did today.

Next a great horned owl sailed across the river and the wind stopped dead still. The gurgling water in the spring branch and the sounds of the night creatures were silent. A flowering Dogwood tree grew up out of the pulsing red coals and up through its branches grew the image of a mysterious white headed old man, the same person I had seen on the ridge earlier.

A cloud moved across the sky that blacked out the light of the moon and there was total darkness. When the moon reappeared the old man was gone. It was as if Mother Nature herself had given a command and everything returned to normal. The moon shone brightly once again. The sounds of the cicadas and bullfrogs in the slough filled the air. A soft breeze rustled the leaves in the trees and the water in the spring branch began to flow.

"It was really weird the next morning," I said after a long period of silence. "There was no sign of a fire. No ashes or anything. I tried to convince you it was probably just a dream. Remember what you said?"

"I don't know exactly," Dub said. "But I'm sure it was something profound."

"You wanted to know how it could it have been a dream if the same thing happened to both of us at the same time?"

"Yeah, I remember now. All I know is something spiritual happened that directed how I should live my life. I never did anything about it for a number of years, but it was always on my mind. No doubt the experience pointed me in the direction to become a preacher. What about you? You never really said much about what happened."

"No doubt there was something spiritual took place. I became a better person and tried to do right by people, if that counts. Sometimes in business dealings it's hard to toe the line."

I had accumulated more money, lived in a bigger house and drove a fancier car. But even with all those earthly treasures, I felt hollow inside. Dub walked up in front of me and looked deep into my eyes.

"I'm like the old man now, Tommy," Dub said. "I was chosen that night to deliver a spiritual message. Given a blessing to never be afraid of anything on earth."

I was not sure if it was because of what Dub said, or the rush of cold air from the mouth of the cave that made me shiver, maybe a little of both. I stood up and shook Dub's hand. I was proud to know a man with such conviction and felt blessed that he was my brother.

"I'm going to bed," I said. "We'll talk more about it tomorrow." As usual, I did not want to face the reality that I needed to change my life, come to terms with the fact I was not going to live forever.

"I get up pretty early," Dub said. "I'll build a fire and put on a pot of coffee to boil. I set some limb lines when I first got to the river. We might have fish to eat for breakfast. By the way, you should have got a package from me last week? It was sort of a strange deal, the box had your name on it, but it was in care of me, at my address."

"I got it and it's in my car. I didn't open it. We'll do it when we get back to town." I felt a little weird having carried the package around so long unopened. No, I wasn't curious, just concerned about what might be inside.

"Kind of a strange thing for someone to do," Dub said as he patted me on the shoulder and headed down the gravel bar toward his pickup truck.

I crawled inside the tent where the boys were sound asleep and breathing deeply. As I lay on my back and stared into the darkness, I began to feel lonely and depressed thinking about the situation with Dub and me. The worst part being we played like it did not matter for so long. It was obvious that Dub was on a much more redeeming course than me. I felt like Marlon Brando when he yelled at Stella that he could have been a contender. My last thought before drifting off to sleep was that my weekend experience on the river with Dub and the boys would surely be a turnaround in my life.

When I woke up the next morning the boys were still sacked out even though it was past eight o'clock. Nick was snoring loudly. I eased my way to the front of the tent, poked my head outside and saw Dub hunkered down by the cook fire pouring himself a cup of coffee. I looked across the river when I heard the chattering cry of a Kingfisher and watched the bird fly, dip and dart along as it worked its way downstream.

"The Lord has blessed us with another beautiful day," Dub said when he looked up and saw me moving my head from side to side to get the crick out of my neck. He blew away the rising steam from the surface of the powerful black liquid, took a sip of coffee and smiled.

"How do you know?" I asked, feeling stiff from all my activity the day before and sleeping on the gravel bar.

"One reason it's a beautiful day is we're still alive and free of pain. At least me." Dub laughed. "For another, that Kingfisher's been up and down the river half-dozen times this morning. That's a good sign it will be a good day as well."

"Oh yeah," I said as I stood up and hobbled along barefooted toward the campfire, remembering how a Kingfisher always flew up ahead of us when we floated the river, lighting in a tree to wait until we got within a hundred yards or so and be off down the river again as if he was our sentry.

"Here's a cup of coffee. Be careful, it's hotter than hot." Dub passed me a blue tin cup with steam rising up off the thick black liquid. He sat the pot back down on the grill and moved a few coals toward the center of the fire with a stick.

"If you don't want to sleep in the pickup truck again tonight you can stay with us. We've got plenty of room and you're sure welcome. The boys would think it was great."

"Appreciate the offer. I just might. I did tell Molly I'd probably stay on the river until tomorrow. I figure you might need some help getting back up the hill."

"It should be easier going back up, a hell of a lot better than it was coming down. I came within inches of losing control of the Jeep, Dub. I really did."

"Sounds like an exciting way to start a camping trip."

"Stop it," Jake said as Nick threw the flap back and hurried out of the tent. He laughed as he hopped along barefoot.

"Oh Wow," Nick said when he saw Dub. "Where did you come from, Uncle Dub?"

I laughed when Dub said that he dropped in out of the sky. At that point, I would not have been surprised by anything he could do.

"Dub's going to stay with us until tomorrow. He may sleep in the tent with us tonight"

Nick stretched his arms above his head and looked up at the sky. He pointed at the buzzards circling overhead that were already on the job of watching us. "I hope he doesn't snore like you do, Papa."

"I can't promise that for sure. You may end up calling Tommy and me the snoring brothers." Dub and I laughed. Nick did not seem to think it was that funny.

"What are we doing today?" Jake asked as he walked up close to the fire and I warned him about stepping on hot coals. I grinned when I saw that he still had the gob of moss tied to his finger.

"We got more good stuff to do than we've got daylight to get it done. I bet your Uncle Dub will come up with a thing or two unusual that we can do as well."

"One thing we can do is check the limb lines I set last night," Dub said. "We might have a catfish or a bass that we can clean and eat for breakfast.

"That would be great. We'll roll the fish in cornmeal and deep-fry 'em crispy brown. We've got eggs and bread. I hope you have caught something," I said.

"We won't know 'til we check it out, will we fellas?" Dub jumped up off the log and the boys hurried over beside him, anxious to get started on the first adventure of the Lord-blessed day. All the activity and good cheer in the camp caused a red squirrel to chatter at us from a low hanging branch in a mulberry tree beside the mouth of the cave. I gulped the last of my coffee, set the cup down on a rock beside the fire and we started up the river with Dub in the lead, a position he had always assumed for as long as I could remember.

Chapter Eight

We walked barefoot on the sandy gravel bar along the riverbank to check out the limb lines Dub set the night before. The boys picked up a couple of flat rocks and skipped them across the water. Jake's best effort was six splashes and Nick had ten.

When we reached the long still hole of water above the ripple, one of the limb lines was bouncing up and down. Dub hurried out into the water and untied the line from the branch of a Willow tree.

"Oh my gosh!" I said when Dub pulled a big, brown creature out of the water onto the gravel bar. It was big around as his forearm.

"I can't believe it. How long has it been?" Dub was so excited his voice cracked.

"It's a snake," Jake screamed. He turned around to run and collided with Nick, knocking him down only a couple of feet away from an eel that squirmed and thrashed violently as it tried to get back into the water.

I reached down and picked up a handful of sand and rubbed it on the palms of my hands so I would be able to hold onto the slick skin. I grabbed the eel around the middle and held on tight. The tail curled around my arm as the powerful creature tried to wiggle free.

"First one I've caught since we were kids, Tommy. Might be a good sign?" Without hesitation Dub pulled a knife with a long sharp blade from the leather sheath on this belt and cut off the eel's head.

His quick violent action even shocked me. I could only imagine what the boys thought when the eel's head fell onto the gravel bar and stared back at us with its eyes wide open. A mouth full of sharp teeth moving up and down still trying to bite. Blood that pulsed from the body spurted onto and the sun-bleached gravel and turned everything around Dub's bare feet bright red. Even without a head, the eel's body continued to squirm back and forth. I began to feel sick and dropped it onto the ground. The boys stared at the carnage with their mouths open. I walked over and put my arms around their shoulders. I looked at Dub as he wiped the blood off his knife blade on his pant leg and shook my head.

"If it came to pass that Moses built another Ark I'm not sure he would allow you on board with the animals." I said.

"I bet they're not having this much fun at the mall today," Dub said as he put the knife back in the sheath.

"Why did you cut off the head?" Jake asked as Dub walked over to the eel and hunkered down for a closer look.

"An eel is strong and powerful. The only way to calm them down is to cut off their head." Dub picked the eel up by the tail, tossed it into the edge of the water and washed off the blood. He laid it stretched out on the bank while we walked up stream to check two other limb lines, neither of which had hooked anything.

The boys had a bunch of questions and by the time we walked back into camp, Nick and Jake knew more about catching, handling, cleaning and cooking a river eel than most kids would know in a life time. Not that eel trivia is that much in demand on a daily basis, but you never know when it might come in handy.

"I can't believe our good fortune can you, Tommy? How often do you get a chance to have eel and eggs for breakfast? Doesn't that sound great boys?"

There was a long delay and weird facial expressions before either of the boys said anything.

"Do we have some cereal I can eat?" Jake said. Nick agreed that would be just fine with him too.

"You can eat store-bought food if you want, but you'll never taste anything as good as fried eel," I said. I rummaged around in the camp box to get out the skillet and some plates in preparation for the delicacy.

"Try it, boys," Dub said as he pulled a pair of pliers out of his tackle box and got ready to skin the creature while I put more wood on the fire. "You like chicken, don't you? Eel taste a lot like that, only better."

"Does it really, Uncle Dub?" Jake asked as he walked over and stared at the carcass. He bent down and touched the cold slick skin with his finger. "Is this thing an animal or a snake?"

"It's not an animal or a snake. It's a fish. Another reason I cut the head off quickly is that eel have sharp teeth. I know because when I helped Uncle Ira clean one that he caught the thing bit me," Dub said.

"Do you have a mark?" Jake asked.

"Matter of fact I do, right here on my finger." Dub held out his right hand and pointed to a white scar on the underside of his index finger.

"How long ago did it happen?" Jake asked as he examined the scar.

"Fifty odd years ago, I guess. There were a lot of eel in the river back in the old days."

"It seems like everything happened fifty odd years ago," Nick said.

Dub and I looked at one another and frowned. No doubt we were both thinking how quickly the time had passed, time we had wasted.

"What happened to all the eel?" Jake said.

"A combination of things. More people moved into the area, so they were fished out. Same thing happened to the wild mink, people trapped or shot every last one of 'em."

"How big do eel get?" Nick asked as he rubbed the tip of his finger over the top of Dub's jagged scar.

"In rivers like the Missouri and the Mississippi, they get to be five or six feet long and weigh ten pounds or better. Females that is, males only get to be a couple pounds or so. This one would weight maybe five pounds. It's as big as any eel I've seen come out of the Oak River. Tell you what, one of you boys grab hold here at the neck and hang on tight while I skin it."

Reluctantly, Nick grabbed the eel and squeezed down on the bloody stump as Dub stripped the skin off the long snake-like body, after which he cut the eel up into a dozen pieces the size of an egg and rolled each one in flour. As flames lapped up around the sides of a black cast iron skillet, Dub dropped the white meat into the bubbling grease. Within minutes the delicacy had turned crispy brown. He scooped the fried eel out of the skillet onto a plate and handed it to me so I could divide up the meat.

"Things are lookin' good," Dub said as a second pot of coffee began to boil and bubble up into the glass dome.

"I'm telling you boys, this could be the best breakfast you'll ever eat. I remember the first time Uncle Ira fried eel for Dub and me. It was a taste I'll never forget." I placed an equal portion of meat on all four plates as Dub cracked a dozen eggs and began to scramble them in the skillet. The boys toasted a couple slices of homemade bread that Molly sent with Dub on hotdog sticks.

"I'm glad you came to camp with us, Uncle Dub," Jake said. "I'd never have eaten eel in my life."

"Yeah, me too," Dub said. "The best of times are spent campin' on the river with friends and family. I wouldn't trade it for anything, your Papa and I camped a lot when we were young."

When I scooped Jake's share of the scrambled eggs out of the skillet and onto his plate, he began to Crawdad a little. Not only about eating the meat, also about eating eggs that had been fried in eel grease.

"What if I don't like it?" he said. "Sometimes I've about puked when people tried to make me eat the wrong thing."

"Me too," Nick agreed quickly. "Like, I don't like broccoli. For sure I can't eat tofu."

"Tell you what, boys," Dub said as he forked a piece of eel meat and made an "um good" sound as he chewed and rolled his eyes around

"What is it?" Nick asked after Dub did not say anything else. "What do you want to tell us?"

"If you boys don't want the eel. We'll eat your share, won't we, Tommy?"

I smiled at Dub as he forked another bite and made an even louder "um good" sound that was like a bear growling.

Nick looked down at his plate and picked up a piece of eel with his fingers. He took a small bite, closed his eyes and began to chew slowly. He looked over at me after he swallowed the eel and smiled. "That's some of the best meat I've ever had."

That was all it took for Jake to dive in and within minutes, the boys had cleaned their plates.

"It really did taste a lot like chicken," Nick said.

"Only better," Jake added. "A lot better. More like smoked pork chops. Wonder if you'll ever catch another one?"

"I don't know, Jake. If I don't catch one for another fifty years, I'll be too old to chew." Dub and I laughed.

"Hey," Nick said as he pointed at a hole in the gravel bar. "What happened to the bone? It was right there yesterday."

I looked up at the mid-morning sun rising over the top of the bluff and tried to wish up a good answer. I drew a blank.

"I bet a dog carried it off," Jake said. I nodded my head in agreement.

"Wasn't any dog carried it off. Your Papa was afraid you'd get scared if he told you what happened. Maybe even want to go home early. You want me to tell 'em or will you, Tommy?" Dub said.

"Go on and tell it. Nothing could scare me that bad," Nick said and Jake agreed.

"Dub's right, I figured you boys would get spooked if I told you the story about what happened to Dub and me the last time we camped here. It's pretty long and involved, so I'll give you the big picture and we can talk about the details later."

"How could something that happened fifty odd years ago have anything to do with the bone?" Nick asked.

"It could have everything to do with the bone," I said as I sorted out where to start my story. No doubt, by the look on Nick and Jake's face, that I had their complete attention.

"Okay, here goes. It all started with the disappearance of Doc Barnes. He was an old country doctor who practiced medicine in Lewiston for many years. We came here to look for him because I kept seeing him in my dreams. Every time he would wave at me and say my name."

"How many times did you have the same dream?" Nick asked.

"Every night for weeks after Doc disappeared. That's why I had to try and find him."

"Mom put up a fuss about us going alone," Dub said. "She thought it was too dangerous, but we finally convinced her to let us go. More than once during the trip, we wished we'd listened to her and the premonition she had, didn't we, Tommy?"

"Yeah, every time we turned around, something else scary happened. After Dad let us off at a trail where we could hike through the woods, I went inside the old Thompson house to look for Doc, because that's where he was waiting for me in one of my dreams."

"What was about the Thompson house?" Jake asked.

"A guy people called Buzzard Thompson used a shotgun and killed his entire family in the house. Anyway that's what people thought at the time. So once I got inside the house, I thought I saw Buzzard point a shotgun at me and I got so scared I accidentally fired my .22 rifle at him."

"Oh, Wow," Jake said. "That's more scared than I've ever been."

"I was standing outside in the yard when I heard the loud crack of the .22 shell exploding. I thought Tommy had shot himself when I heard him scream. Afterwards he ran out the front door and fell down in front of me. It all happened because he got so scared his imagination ran wild," Dub said.

"How come you didn't go inside with Papa?" Jake asked.

"You couldn't have paid me enough money to set foot in that spooky house. I begged him not to go inside either. As usual he paid me no mind."

Nick looked at Jake and said, "That's being pretty darned scared to shoot at a ghost."

I figured Nick thought I might have made up some of the story, so I decided to really lay it on to gain credibility. "You know the haunted house you went to before Halloween? That was kindergarten compared to what I walked into that day. Think of it being just you and your little brother standing in front of a rundown shack in the deep woods. Not another living soul within miles. Wasp and yellow jackets flying around and copperhead snakes in the weeds, not to mention black widow spiders. You're barefoot of course."

"There had been a mass murder in the house your Papa was about to walk into and Buzzard, who everyone thought was the killer at the time, was still on the loose," Dub said. "In this case, anybody could have imagined they saw a ghost."

"It was a hundred degrees or better inside the house. Sweat burned my eyes and made everything blurry."

"Maybe that's why you thought you saw a ghost?" Jake said, giving his old Papa the benefit of the doubt as usual.

I looked at him and nodded my head. "Thank you, Jake. Maybe it was. Anyway, I had to open a creaky wooden door and climb a stairway covered with cobwebs to get up to the second floor. That was where the three Thompson kids used to sleep. The room was bare, except for a couple of mattresses and a broken down army cot. I'll remember until my dying day a little green dress hanging on a nail beside an open window where a torn lace curtain flapped in the wind. After I hurried back down the stairs was when I saw the ghost of Buzzard Thompson."

"Who did the dress belong to?" Jake asked.

"A little girl with blond hair about your age. Another thing I remember plain as day was a brownish-red hand print on the white kitchen wall."

"You're right, Papa," Nick said. "That would be a lot worse than a haunted house."

"What happened next?" Jake wanted to know.

"Next, we hurried down the trail toward the river to get away from the spooky Thompson place and Dub got attacked by a fox."

"No way," Nick said.

"I really did," Dub said. "I lucked out because the critter only got a mouthful of my pant leg. It had to be rabid or it would not have been out in the middle of the day trying to bite people."

"I was attacked by my friend's little dog once," Jake said. "It bit me on the foot, but I had my shoe on."

Everyone looked at Jake and smiled.

"After that we ran into the Conner brothers, a couple of old codgers that made moonshine whisky and lived back in the Ozark hills. They scared us because we thought they may have done something to Doc which was the reason he had gone missing," Dub said.

"Then it got dark on us before we reached the river and we had to walk down the steep trail from on top of the ridge." I pointed at a spot on top of the bluff where a winding path led down to the river.

"The next day we found a dead man in the Blue Hole and another one in Leatherwood Cave," Dub said.

"It almost seems unbelievable," Nick said. "But I know it's true if you told it."

"There's more," I said. "After all this spooky stuff happened, we decided to head down river to get back home. We didn't want to go back through the woods because for all we knew the Conner brothers may have been the killers of the dead men we found. Another reason not to hike back to where Dad let us out at the trail was we didn't want to go past the Thompson house again," I said.

"Anyway, as we walked down the gravel bar toward home, who should jump out of the brush almost on top of us but Buzzard Thompson? He had been living out in the woods like a wild animal for over a year ever since his family was killed. You may find this hard to believe," Dub said as he looked at Nick and raised his eyebrows. "Buzzard drowned in the river right before our eyes before we made it back to town."

"No way," Nick said.

"Here's the end of the story. With his last breath, Buzzard claimed he had nothing to do with killing of his family or anyone else and we had no reason not to believe him. When we told the folks in Lewiston what had happened, they believed him as well. The big mystery for all these years has been that the real killer was never found. Here and now, fifty years later, a human leg bone shows up. So Dub and I figured there's a chance it may belong to the evil person who committed the murders. The two dead men we found and probably Buzzard's family. It's crazy, but stranger things have happened."

When I finished the story I expected to see a mask of fear cover the boys' faces and Jake might want to pack up and go home.

"Holy smoke!" Nick jumped up off the log and threw his hands in the air. "This is like something in a movie, only it's real and lots better."

"Yeah, really," Jake said. "This trip's turned out to be ten times more fun than I thought it would be."

"So anyway, that's why I wasn't going to tell you I put the bone in the Jeep so we could turn it over to the Sheriff."

Nick asked if he could touch it before we gave it up and I said for all I cared he could hold it in his lap all the way back to town, and he smiled.

"Look, the turkey buzzards are back." Jake pointed at a couple Perched in a dead tree on top of the river bluff. "I wonder if they ate that man?" he said.

"You mean the one that used to belong to the leg bone?" Nick sounded brave talking about it.

"Remember the bunch of buzzards we saw eating on a dead deer?" I said to Dub. "It was the same day we ran across the Conner brothers?"

"What dead deer?" Nick wanted to know.

"I'm not sure you want to hear a story about buzzards," I said.

"I do," Jake said. I like buzzard stories. I don't care if the birds only eat dead things or not."

"Okay then, here goes. It all started when the radiator on Dad's pickup truck boiled over. He sent Dub and I off down a log road to fetch some water from a sinkhole. When we walked out of the woods into a clearing there were buzzards everywhere."

"Were they pecking off pieces of rotten meat?" Nick asked.

"Yeah, that's what they were doing. I wasn't going to go into the gory details, but if that's what you want I will," I said.

"The more gory, the better," Jake said. "I want the best story I can get to tell my friends."

"This one should take care of you," I said as I continued with more detail than I had planned. "The buzzards on top of the carcass were in a bloody, decayed flesh-ripping frenzy. They squawked and pecked at one another. Hundreds of blow flies swarmed the buck's bloated body like tiny airplanes circling a landing strip."

"I bet it smelled bad," Jake said.

"It was gut wrenching," Dub said. "I pinched off my nose and still I almost threw up."

"That's enough buzzard talk," I said. "The day's getting on. We've got a lot of stuff to do."

"What's next?" Nick asked. "I'd like to look for more arrowheads. I might be rich by the time we leave the river."

"The boys found a couple up river where you picked up the stone axe." I figured Dub might suspect me of planting them when he looked at me and grinned. "They wanted to know how much they're worth."

Before I could say anything else, the boys jumped up, pulled the arrowheads out of their backpacks and handed them to Dub. He studied the stones closely the way a skilled appraiser would before rendering a monetary guess. "I'd say they're worth one hundred dollars each, maybe more. You boys were lucky to find two arrowheads in such good shape. Some people look a long time and never find anything." Dub looked at me and grinned again.

"its worth going for another look don't you think, Uncle Dub?" Nick said.

"Sure, it is. No reason not to go. That's what we'll do."

"We've also got to try and catch that big bass again," Jake said.

Dub looked at me and grinned. "Did somebody hook a good one?"

Jake puffed out his chest and smiled. "I did," Jake said. "A big Smallmouth broke my line. I almost landed it. I saw it up real close."

"Yeah, Jake's monster bass put on some show," I said. "He jumped out of the water and tail-walked for us, you know how they do. We've got a few minnows in the bucket. We can seine more if need be."

"Let's look for arrowheads on the way back from Leatherwood Cave?" Dub said.

"I don't know about going into a cave," Jake said. "It's too dark."

"We'll have flashlights," I said.

"What if they quit shining? How would we find our way back outside?" Jake wanted to know. "I don't want to be around a bunch of bats either."

"We've got two flashlights. The odds are they won't both burn out," I said. "The bats won't bother you. Another thing is the floor of the cave will be slimy."

"You don't have to go inside," Dub said. "I don't care much for caves myself. You and I will fish the river while Nick and your Papa go exploring."

"Okay." Jake smiled. "Are there blind fish in Leatherwood Cave too?"

"I suppose there could be blind fish in any cave where there's water. So, are we set to go?" I asked.

"Yeah, I want to go to the cave first," Nick said. "I'm not afraid of anything in the dark."

Nick grabbed a couple of flashlights out of a backpack and waved them around above his head. "Okay, let's go. I want to see some bats."

The rocky path that followed the river for a quarter of a mile up to Leatherwood Cave was a narrow trail used mostly by animals. I hoped we did not run into any wild hogs, as they could be dangerous, especially if the sows had young pigs. After all the squealing I heard the night before, I was concerned that an injured hog might be hiding in the brush. If we walked close it might attack us. They have sharp tusks that could rip apart flesh like a can opener.

A thick green mat of moss covered the hillside along a towering limestone bluff. Broad-leaved ferns hung from the rock ledges. Water seeped through the cracks from underground springs and moistened the grey and white rock wall. The boys yelled with delight each time a cool droplet of water splattered on their face or ran down their bare back. Flowering plants with red and yellow blossoms grew along the path and large Sycamore trees shaded the riverbank and the edge of the water.

The further I walked down the trail toward the cave, the more vividly I remembered my childhood. The gurgle of running water and birds calling in the distance, even Dub's voice sounded like it did when he was twelve years old. "Remember the time Doodle fell into the deep pool in Leatherwood Cave?"

"It was even more scary because he lost his flashlight," Dub said.

"Yeah, I had another one but the batteries were weak. We barely made it back out before they ran down."

Jake looked over his shoulder. "Can't think of a much worse thing. Can you, Nick?"

"I can," Nick said. "You know what would be worse?"

"No, what?"

Nick reached out and gobbled up Jake's hair with the tips of his fingers. "You getting attacked by a bat. Its claws are stuck in your hair. There are hundreds of 'em flying around in caves."

"Stop it," Jake yelled as he pushed Nick away. "I mean it, too."

Nick ran ahead of us and jumped up on a log. He beat his chest with his fist like Tarzan and yelled "Ah Ahhhhhhhh." Everyone laughed.

It could not have been a more perfect morning. Golden rays of sunlight shown through the tops of the Sycamores and a warm breeze rustled the leaves. The rippling water sparkled like icicles on a Christmas tree. "Tutut-eee-ay-eee. Tutut-eee-ay-eee." A Wood Thrush called from across the river.

"Remember when we caught all those goggle-eyes out from under a root wad right here?" Dub said as we passed the spot where a Cottonwood tree was wedged up under the bank.

Jake laughed and looked down into the water. "What are goggle-eyes? Fish that wear goggles?"

"They're a game fish about the size of a Perch," Dub said. "They're named that because they have big eyes that are dark in the center and surrounded with red circles. They're also called rock bass. Look, there's some now."

Dub pointed at a couple of greenish-brown fish that had left the cover of the submerged tree limbs and were swimming upstream.

"The time we caught all those it had rained upstream the night before. With a lot of food washing into the river they went on a feeding frenzy," I said.

"We caught a bunch all right," Dub said as he stepped over a tree that had fallen across the path.

Jake hurried down the trail when he saw a snake drop into the water from a low hanging branch a few feet off to our right.

"It was a water snake," I said. "They're not poisonous and mean like a cottonmouth moccasin."

"Look at that," Nick yelled as he pointed at a beaver swimming along the bank across the river under the cover of an overhanging Willow tree. The furry brown animal slapped the water with his tail and disappeared under the water.

"How long do beavers live?" I asked Dub, thinking how the last time he and I walked the trail together we saw one in the same place.

"Not sure exactly, but they live a long time." Dub pointed up ahead when he saw the entrance to Leatherwood Cave and we picked up the pace.

I looked around when I heard the cry of a blue jay. I hoped the warning was not because of a wild hog nearby. I remembered when a sow attacked one of Uncle Ira's hounds, ripped its belly open and the dog had to be put down.

I could imagine the conversation the boys might have with their parents when we got home after the camping trip. The list would be endless, starting with the near death experience coming down the hill in the Jeep, killer ticks, snapping turtles big enough to bite off a finger, rabid bats, the bloody display when Dub cut the head off of the eel and the discovery of a human leg bone that may have belonged to a killer. More than enough worrisome items around without adding a wild hog attack. The scary thing being there was still time left to stay at the river.

Chapter Nine

We stared at the entrance in the side of the towering limestone bluff when we walked up in front of Leatherwood Cave. It was a magnificent sight. I rubbed my arms when I felt a rush of cool air pour from the opening. A picture of the dead man lying on the floor that Dub and I found when we were there last flashed into my mind. I groaned.

"What's wrong, Papa?" Jake asked.

"Nothing. I'm a little sore from sleeping on the gravel bar last night. Not so tough as I used to be, I guess."

"Wow, that hole's the size of a house," Nick said as he walked closer.

I thought about the waterfall and the deep pool at the base, which was about fifty feet away from where I found the dead man.

"The cool air feels good," Nick said as he rubbed his arms.

I looked at him and grinned. "Nice of Mother Nature to provide the air conditioning."

"Anybody ever get lost in the cave?" Jake asked as he picked up a rock and tossed it inside the mouth.

"Yeah, two boys got lost once," Dub said. "They went in to explore the cave and never came out."

"Did somebody see them go inside the cave?" Jake asked. "Maybe they ran away from home and went someplace else."

"There's an interesting theory," Dub said. "This young man might grow up to be something famous."

"Actually, I wondered the same thing," Nick said.

I laughed. "I'm sure they went inside, Jake. But you're right, I don't know of anyone who saw them. So anyway, remember I told you that Dub and I found a dead man in Leatherwood Cave." I spread my arms wide as a salute to the big dark cavern. "Well this is the place it happened."

"Weird you found so many dead people." Nick said.

"What happened to the man in the cave?" Jake asked.

""Somebody killed him and nobody ever knew who did it. When Dub and I searched for Doc Barnes, Leatherwood Cave was the last place we looked."

"How far back inside the cave was the dead guy?" Nick asked.

"Not far, maybe five hundred feet or a little more," I said as I stared at the mouth of the cave and remembered the events of the day. Someone had made a cross by tying a couple of sticks together and stuck it into the ground. In front of it was a blood stained rock. Even though Dub came up the river with me to the entrance, he was afraid to go inside. I had no choice but to go alone, I was on a mission to find Doc and nothing would stop me. We forgot and left the lantern at our campsite, so I set fire to a pine knot and used it to light my way. The resin scented smoke that burned my nose and made my eyes water, also stirred up the bats.

"What are you waiting on, Papa?" Nick said, breaking me out of my daydream. "We going inside the cave or not?"

"I'm ready," I said as I looked at Dub and Jake. "Are you two going with us?" I asked, knowing what the answer would be.

"We'll stay out here and fish," Dub said. "How does that sound, Jake?"

"Sounds good. You can't eat bats."

"That's funny," Nick said. "You can't eat fish either if you don't catch any."

RIVER'S EDGE

"You remember why I don't like to go in a cave, Tommy?" Dub said.

"Yep, because it's darker inside when your eyes are open than when they're closed. There is no doubt you are right."

"Turn the flashlight out when you get inside, Nick. You'll see what I mean," Dub said.

"We don't care if it's dark. Nick and me are natural born explorers." I grabbed one of the two flashlights Nick had in the pockets of his cargo pants and we walked into the darkness. I shined my light up at the ceiling when I felt a droplet of water splatter on the back of my neck. Already, the musty smell of the cave and the golden silence set the stage to return to the scene of the crime, after fifty years.

A bat hanging upside down above our head spread its wings and flapped off into the cavern. I shined the light down at floor when I felt something cool and damp squish up between my toes. I could hardly wait to see the expression on Nick's face when he realized it was a mixture of mud and bat guano. I took in a deep breath and could smell the scent of the earth. Feel the energy of ancient old souls all around me.

Nick tapped me on the shoulder. "You're not afraid are you, Papa?" He sounded more humble than I had ever known him to be, another nice moment.

"Nope. Like I've said before, there's nothing to fear but fear itself." I patted Nick on the shoulder as we walked further inside of the cave. "You doing okay?' I said when we stepped into a large room with jagged rock walls and stalactites hanging from the ceiling, some of them six feet long.

"Why was it you thought Doc may be in the cave?" Nick asked.

"Because in a dream I had he was sitting on the big rock at the entrance. When I didn't find him there I came inside the cave to look.

I had searched everyplace else and figured if I didn't find him here, I'd give him up for dead."

"Did Uncle Dub not come inside with you back then because he was afraid?" Nick said.

"He doesn't like being in a confined space. Claustrophobia's what he's got. You'll have to admit it's a little tight in here. If you get afraid, let me know and we'll head back outside."

"I'm okay for now. It'd be spooky in here with only a pine knot for light. How long will one burn?"

"An hour or so at best."

I shined the light up at the ceiling and a half-dozen bats took to the air and fluttered all around us.

"How many bats are in this cave, I wonder?" Nick said as he shined his flashlight all around.

"Five hundred at least, maybe more."

"Know what, Papa? We could be standing in the same spot where a caveman was thousands of years ago."

"You're right. This cave has looked like this for thousands of years."

"How far back inside are we going?" Nick said. "Not sure if I want to go a long ways."

"We'll stop at the waterfall up ahead then turn around. The waterfall's the main reason I wanted to bring you here. It's an awesome sight."

"Are we going to the spot where you found the dead man?" Nick asked, as he put the lens of the flashlight under his chin and opened his mouth so his face would look ghoulish.

"It'd be too spooky to go back there again," I said. "We'll turn around at the waterfall."

Nick shined his light on a stalagmite that rose up waist high from the floor of the cave. He turned around quickly when he though he heard a noise.

"Who's there?" Nick yelled. He shined his light at a crevice in the rock wall up ahead.

"Could be your mind playing tricks," I said. "The further back inside a cave you go, the more the walls seem to close in around you. Sometimes you hear things that aren't there and your sense of direction gets messed."

"That's really creepy."

"Another thing is that it really is darker when your eyes are open than when they're shut. Turn out your flashlight and see."

After we turned out our flashlights then opened them back up, Nick said, "Uncle Dub was right again. It's darker when my eyes are open. How much further to the waterfall?"

"We're almost there. Good thing we're not burning a pine knot for light, the smoke stirs the bats up like crazy. You know even though hundreds of them flew past me and around me, I wasn't touched by a single wing."

Nick turned his flashlight on and shined it around to make sure nothing had sneaked up on us.

"Being in a black cave with black bats all around and no light sounds scary as anything," Nick put the flashlight under his chin again. His shadowed eyes looked dark and hollow. "Except if you stumbled onto the Riley Brothers."

With all the other strange things that had happened at the Blue Hole, that would not surprise me at all, I thought. "You're right, that would be the most scary. Be careful right here." I turned sideways with my back to the rock wall and eased along a narrow pathway. Another fifty feet and we would reach the waterfall where a spring ran off a rock ledge and splashed into a cool pool of water.

"What's that smell?" Nick said.

"You mean kind of like ozone after a rain?"

"Yeah, I guess."

"It's a combination of unpolluted air from the cave deep in the earth, mixed with the smell of the earth, mud and bat guano."

"What's bat guano?" Nick asked.

"It's manure, like the stuff that's oozing up between your toes every time you take a step."

Nick shined the light down at his feet. "Oh brother. I wish I'd worn my shoes."

I smiled when I saw a streak of sunlight up ahead shining down through an opening in the top of the cave. "What a beautiful picture," I said as I shined my flashlight on the pool of water at the base of the falls where droplets of water splashed up in the air and sparkled like diamonds. When we walked up to the edge of the pool a brightly colored rainbow appeared.

"Wow, Papa. This place is past awesome. It'd make a great underground church," Nick said because the rainbow of colors showcased so well as we walked up to the edge of the pool and stared down at the water.

"Wow, Papa. This place is as good as it gets," Nick said.

"Figured you'd like it," I said with a smile. "I've been all over the world. This is the most unusual site I've seen."

"How much further to where you found the dead man?" Nick asked again as he shined the flashlight along a path that ran around the pool of water, past the waterfall and into a narrow passageway.

"Not too far. But there's nothing to be gained from visiting that sad and sorry site again. It would be like walking on somebody's grave."

"My friends would think it was cool. In their whole life they will probably never go to a place where a dead man was found in a cave. Someone that was found by their Papa."

I debated about what to do. Having the boys go home talking about their list of adventures that were born of natural events was one thing, visiting a place where I found a dead man might be stretching it some. We already had the discovery of the leg bone. I did not want their Mom and Dad thinking I fed the boys a steady diet of gore.

"How would your Mom feel about it?" I raised the light so I could get a look at Nick's face.

He was smiling when he told me she would probably think it was just swell because she liked for him to go places where he could learn new things.

"I don't know if this would qualify as a very good place to learn new things, but what the heck, let's go." I shined the flashlight up ahead at a hole in the ceiling of the cave that was about the size of a picture window in a house.

"There's a lot of water dripping down," Nick said as he tilted his head back, looked up at the ceiling and caught a droplet. "I hope the cave's not about to fall in on top of us."

"No kidding," I said. "That would be just one more thing people would never forgive me for."

After we passed the waterfall Nick walked up in front of the passage and shined his light inside. "The tunnel looks pretty small. What would I do if you got stuck and I was up in front of you?"

"Let's do this. I'll crawl through first, that way you can go back and get help if I do get stuck."

"Yeah, right. What if I took a wrong turn trying to find the entrance? I'd be lost in the cave like the Riley brothers."

"How about if I think I'm about to get stuck, I just won't go any further. The last time I was here, there were hundreds of bats hanging from the ceiling on the other side of the passageway. We're better off not to stir 'em up. They may flutter us to death. Whatever you do don't yell or scream."

"Why would I do that?" Nick asked, in a voice that had shifted to high alert.

"I don't know? Maybe if you got scared. Or because a rock fell on your foot or you fell into the pool of water, or something."

"How come people say they're blind as a bat? Are bats blind?" Nick asked.

"They're not, that's right. They see better than we do at night. Not only that, they can hear an insect walking on sand six feet away."

Nick flashed his light past my face and gave me a questioning look. "So they can hear us talking right now, even though they're on the other side of the tunnel. So much for not making noise."

"If we don't make loud noise we'll probably be okay. You sure you want to do this, all you're going to see on the other side is more rock and lots of bats."

"Are bats mean enough to bite you?"

"Bats are mammals, they're so kind they adopt orphans and even risk their lives to share food with less-fortunate bats. Only time they might bite is in self-defense. Are you asking all these bat questions because you really don't want to go through the passage? It's okay. Like I said, the only thing you'll see is more rock, probably. I'm not that keen on going any further myself."

Nick grabbed my arm and turned me around so he could see my face. "I want to see the place where Uncle Dub saved your life."

His words cut through me like a sharp blade. How could I have spent all those years not having a civil conversation with my brother, the man who saved my life?

"Okay," I said as I looked away from the glare of the flashlight. I climbed into the passageway and crawled toward the loud screeching sound made by the bats at the end of the tunnel. I had forgot how confined the space was and about the bite of the jagged rock when I brushed against the wall of the cave. Nick was so close behind me I could hear him breathing

"Can't imagine being in here with only a burning pine knot for light. You and Uncle Dub must have been two of the toughest kids ever."

"For sure it was a spooky deal. We'll crawl on through here; check the place out real quick and head back to the entrance. Dub and Jake will be worried if we stay too long."

When we reached the end of the tunnel I grabbed Nick's arm and he stood up beside me. I shined the light up at the ceiling and it was covered with bats nervously flapping their wings and screeching louder.

"Okay," Nick whispered. "Where was the dead man?"

I shined my flashlight out in front of me at the floor of the cave and moved it around in a circle. "He was right there and Dub's pine knot that he'd dropped was lying beside the dead man's head. Dub screamed when he accidentally touched the man's face as he reached down to pick up the knot. He scared me really and scared the bats even worse and they took to the air. Everything was a blur."

"What did the dead guy look like?"

"He was old and had shaggy grey hair. His face was sunken in and it looked like he'd been badly burned."

"What happened then, Papa?"

"Our light had gone out. My throat was so dry I could barely talk. My ankle was badly sprained or maybe broken. There was a dead man ten foot away for us. Whoever killed him could still be around to kill Dub and me. The most terrible thing being there was that no doubt what Dub had kicked in the Blue Hole the night before was probably the body of Doc Barnes. That horrible site was waiting for us if and when we got out of the cave and made it back to back to camp."

"It sounds awful. I would have had a heart attack. How did you get out of the cave?"

"At that point, both of our pine knots had flamed out. To save ourselves, we had to get one burning again and we only had one match. Since I promised our mother we would for sure not go inside Leatherwood Cave that would be the last place they would look for us.

"It would be like you were buried alive."

"Buried alive with a cave full of bats."

"What happened next?"

"We knew using a match by itself wouldn't catch a pine knot on fire. I checked my pockets and found a crumpled up piece of paper in my overalls, which turned out to be my camping gear list."

"So with that piece of paper you got the pine knot to burn again?"

"Yeah, there was still a lot of sticky resin that oozed out of the wood so it caught quickly."

"Then what happened?" Nick took a step forward and was so close he touched my shoulder.

"We lit the second pine knot and had light once again."

"That's wild, Papa. Really wild. Was Uncle Dub as scared as you? Doesn't seem like he'd get scared very easy."

"Yeah, he's pretty brave all right. But anyone in their right mind would have been scared."

"With your ankle hurt, how'd you get past here?" Nick asked as we started to crawl back though the passageway.

"Crawling through here wasn't too bad. But by the time we reached the waterfall and I stood up, my ankle hurt something terrible. I eased along the ledge and dug my toes into the gooey substance as I searched carefully for finger holds along the wall, just like we did today."

"Bat manure seems to be a lot slicker than mud."

"It is slicker, that's why it oozes up between your bare toes when you take a step. So anyway, once I made it past the pool of water, I put my arm around Dub's shoulders and hobbled to the entrance of the cave."

"Was this the worst experience ever in your whole life?" I had to think about what Nick had asked me. The experience in the cave was scary all right, but so were the two times I almost drowned. When I got snake bit; along with the day I shot Doc Barnes accidentally had to be at the top of the list. But all of that together did not compare to the very worst experience, which was the estranged relationship I had for so many years with my brother.

"Yeah, the cave was close to the most scary thing, I guess." I thought about what happened between Dub and me and I could not remember anything significant enough to cause so much damage. Oh, there was the silly disagreement over what to do with our parent's farm. The sale of some antiques I thought my Dad had wanted me to have. There was that and the argument over who would get Grandpa Tom's .30-30 rifle.

"So then you and Uncle Dub hightailed it for home, right, Papa?"

"Yep. Dub said if he had to stay at the Blue Hole one more night he might die from being scared to death. I said it would be slow going with my hurt foot, but I'd get us home no matter what. I would have endured any kind of pain to get away from the crazy things that had happened. Problem was, the bad stuff was not yet over. After finding the guy dead in the cave, we still had to go back to camp and see what Dub kicked. Even though we had talked about it being something like slimy weeds or a dead fish, we figured we knew better."

"When I get scared for a long time I feel numb. Is that the way you felt or something?"

"The only good thing I could think of was if we made it home alive, we'd have a great story to tell the kids at school on Monday. That and I would get to see your Grandma Lucy again who had been in St. Louis all summer."

"You and Nana have been together almost forever," Nick said as we walked out of the entrance to the cave.

"I'm sure it feels like it's been longer than that to her," I said as we walked out of the cave. I smiled at Dub and thought about the day I hobbled along beside him with my arm around his shoulder after he saved me from the underground tomb.

Chapter Ten

"How was the darkness?" Dub said. "Did your Papa show you where we found the dead man?"

"Oh yeah. It was creepy," Nick replied.

"I figured he would," Dub said. "See any bats?"

"Lots of 'em," Nick said. "The waterfall was awesome."

"We were as close as two brothers could be back then, weren't we, Tommy?"

I nodded my head and looked away when a lump filled my throat.

"You would have been scared I bet. Not only was it dark and spooky. Bat manure squished up between my bare toes." Jake stuck his tongue out and played like he was going to throw up when Nick held up his foot that was coated with brown bat guano.

Jake squinted his eyes. "No more than you was I bet. Was Nick scared, Papa? I thought I heard him scream."

I laughed. "I figure most everyone gets a little scared in a cave. You can't help but think about stuff, like what if your light went out. Or you took a wrong turn and went deeper into the cave. Which is what I figure happened to the Riley brothers."

"Look what Jake caught while you boys was crawling around with the bats. We get another one like this, we'll have a enough for dinner."

Jake smiled and held up a golden brown Smallmouth bass that weighed at least three pounds. Dub had cut off a Willow branch, ran it up through the gills and slid the fish down to the fork so Jake could carry it back to camp.

"You caught one that size when you were Jake's age," I said to Dub. "Got so excited you fell in the water while landing it."

Dub looked at me and grinned as we started down the trail.

"What did you catch the bass on?" Nick asked in a whiny envious sounding tone.

"A Crawdad. They're the best Smallmouth bait, aren't they Uncle Dub?"

"I bet you didn't put the craw on the hook," Nick said.

Jake got defensive. "It doesn't matter. I caught the fish and you didn't. You're jealous because you never caught one so big."

"Look, everything's gone back to life as usual," Dub said as he pointed at the water snake that had crawled back up on a low hanging branch. The snake dropped into the water and swam downstream when we stopped. The beaver that swam along the bank under the cover of a Willow tree slapped his tail and dived under the surface of the water. The turtles were all in a row sunning themselves on a log. Goggle-eyes that fanned their tails back and forth to maintain a position along the edge of the fast moving current had ventured out from the root wad once more.

When Dub asked the boys if they wanted to stop and search for arrowheads, they decided to go back to camp and do it later.

"Who's going to clean the fish?" Jake asked when we walked into camp and he held the Smallmouth up in front of him so Nick could get a close look.

"The one that catches 'em, cleans 'em. That's right ain't it, Dub?" I said.

"I can't clean a fish. I don't know how. I bet Nick's never cleaned one either."

"I helped clean a bunch of fish one time, didn't I, Papa?"

"You mean those Perch we caught? I don't remember you doing any actual cleaning. Best I recall all you did was get me some water in a pan."

"See I told you I'd helped." Nick picked up a spinning rod and walked over to the edge of the water. He cast a red and white Lazy Ike into the water and reeled in the lure, hoping against hope that he might luck into a bass bigger than the one Jake had caught.

"The biggest bass I caught out of the Oak River when I was a kid. I caught it on that same wooden Lazy Ike lure. It still looks good."

I looked up the river at the sunlight sparkling on the water and saw myself standing on the riverbank with a rod-n-reel in my hand.

Dub took Jake's fish off the Willow branch and put it on a rope stringer so it could breathe better and live until someone took on the fish-cleaning chore. The bass splashed around and tugged at the rope when Dub tied one end to a rock.

"There are other things we can eat besides fish. Loan me your .22 rifle, Dub. I'll go up on the ridge and shoot a couple of squirrels. You boys can come along if you want to."

Jake looked at me and frowned. "Are we really going to eat a squirrel? Are they the same kind that hops around in our yard? They seem more like pets."

"People in the country eat squirrels all the time. We pretty much lived on them and other wild game growing up. Didn't we, Dub?"

"We really did, Jake," Dub said. "We ate squirrel once a week at least."

"Tell ya what I'll do. While your Papa goes hunting, I'll catch us some Bullfrogs. We'll fix the potatoes and tomatoes I brought from the garden. Have us a dinner fit for a king. I'll go get the .22 rifle from the pickup truck and be right back."

Nick leaned his rod and reel up against a bush on the gravel bar. "I'm going with Papa. I want to shoot a squirrel. Can I carry the rifle? My friends won't believe we ate all this weird stuff."

"I'll stay with Uncle Dub," Jake said. "I want to see him catch a frog. Not sure I'll eat one though."

"Frog legs and quail are my two favorite kinds of meat," I said as I looked up and watched a red-tailed hawk being chased by a lowly blackbird.

"Even better than steak? You eat a lot of that," Nick said.

"Yep, I like frog legs and quail even better than steak."

"What are you doing?" Nick asked when he saw me putting on long pants.

"Long pants will help keep the ticks off. You best put on a pair yourself. It won't stop 'em completely, but it will help."

"Okay, that's what I'll do too," Nick said as he walked to the tent and crawled inside to slip on a pair of jeans.

I watched Dub as he came toward me carrying the rifle. Not only was he trim and fit, he had a bounce to his step like a man half his age. I looked down at my belly hanging over the top of my jeans and groaned. There was no doubt in my mind that when I got back home I would start a serious exercise program.

"Why the frown?" Dub asked as he stopped in front of me and pulled back the bolt on the rifle to show me it was not loaded. "What were you thinking about?" he asked as he handed me the firearm.

He caught me off guard. "I was thinking about the day we came back from Leatherwood Cave after we found the dead man. About how we were afraid to look down into the water once we had climbed up on the ledge."

"Yeah, we even talked about heading home without looking. That's how sure we were we would see Doc Barnes body."

"You must have been two of the bravest boys around," Nick said.

I shook my head and sighed. "Mainly we were trapped in a bad situation and had no choice but to keep going. We grew up a lot during those two days."

"The most scary time in my life for sure. Here are some extra shells." Dub handed me a box of .22 cartridges. "How long has it been since you shot a rifle?" Dub asked.

"Been awhile. But I can still shoot the eye out of a squirrel in a treetop. Always was better than you." If Dub had wanted to be cruel he could have brought up the fact that I accidentally shot Doc Barnes. I was glad he didn't, if the story had to be told, I would rather tell it in my own time. I patted Nick on the shoulder and smiled. "Let's go get some meat for the table?"

"I bet you'll be afraid to shoot a squirrel, Nick." Jake said.

"Why would I be?" Nick asked.

"You don't like to see blood. Remember the time you fainted when you cut your finger?" Jake gave some extra effort to his snicker.

"I was little like you then, Jake. Wait until you clean the fish. There'll be blood all over the place when you cut the head off."

"You don't know anything about it. You've never done it. Come on Uncle Dub, let's catch some frogs."

Dub and I laughed. Nick and Jake sounded so much like us when we were their age that it was like watching a re-run of our lives.

"Can I carry the rifle?" Nick said

"Sure, just be careful," I said as I handed it to him.

Nick grabbed the wooden stock and safely pointed the barrel toward the ground beside his leg.

"I'll show you I can shoot as good as anybody," Nick yelled back over his shoulder at Jake.

I looked up at the buzzards circling overhead as we waded across the river on our way to the ridge. I remembered they followed Dub and me all the way home the day we found the bodies. We talked about how if we keeled over dead the big black birds would peck us to pieces like they did the dead deer.

"What did Uncle Dub do after he saw the dead guy in the Blue Hole?" Nick asked as he took a couple of quick steps to catch up with me.

"He screamed and fell backwards against the bluff. Smashed his head into the rock wall so hard it made him dizzy. I was standing on the gravel bar watching him at the time. After I saw how Dub reacted to what he saw, I ran across the spring branch and climbed up on the ledge beside him. When I looked down into the water I thought the dead man I saw was Doc, too?"

"Must have been really bad."

"Dub was shaking' all over like you were when you jumped into the pool of spring water. He was scared that bad."

I looked around when I heard the chatter of a Kingfisher as it winged its way down the river.

"Those Kingfishers fly through a lot don't they, Papa?" Nick said as we stopped and watched the bird fly away.

"Do you believe in reincarnation?" I asked.

"What?" Nick gave me a startled look.

"You know, where people come back to life as some kind of a creature or another human being."

Nick cocked his head to one side and said, "I don't know. Why'd you ask me that question?"

"Because if I get to come back as a bird, I want to be a Kingfisher."

"That's pretty weird, Papa. Why would you want to be one of those?"

"They're beautiful and get to fly free every day. They live on the river where there's plenty of food and water. Look at the way they dip and dive up and down when they fly. Don't you think that would be fun?"

Before Nick could say anything there was a loud crash in the woods up in front of us. He grabbed my arm and we stopped. "What was that?" he asked.

"Sounded like a tree fell. Either that or the ghost of Buzzard Thompson."

"You mean the guy you and Uncle Dub captured that drowned in the river?"

"That would be the one. I'm sure it was just a tree. If you would rather not go into the woods, we can get along without the squirrels."

"No problem, Pop. I've got you to protect me." Nick looked at me and grinned. He had never called me that name before, Pop. "Is it okay if I call you that sometimes?" he asked.

"Okay with me," I said with a smile. Feeling really good that he did it.

"When can we load the rifle?" Nick asked.

"Not until we get to where we're going to shoot a squirrel. Fact is I had a bad accident with a rifle when I was about your age. I was always a little nervous around a firearm afterwards."

"What happened? Did you get shot or something?" Nick asked.

"Exactly the opposite. I'll tell you about it later, maybe?"

"Why not now?"

"Let's just get on up to the top of the ridge."

"I hope you tell me. I want to know."

"I wish I had never brought it up. Come on, let's go."

Gravel crunched under our feet as we walked across the riverbank toward the woods. When we reached the tree line where a spring ran into the river, I stopped and cupped my hands to scoop up a drink. I splashed some of my cool water in my face and rubbed the back of my neck. It looked to be about a three hundred foot climb up the steep slope before we reached the top of the ridge where we would stop and hunt for a couple of squirrels.

"We need to check for ticks after we come out of the woods," I said as I picked up a piece of sun-bleached driftwood to use as a walking stick.

"What about the long pants. That'll help won't it?" Nick said as he looked down and saw a brown seed tick crawling up his leg. He flipped it off and groaned.

"Sure they help. The tick would have crawled up into your crotch if you still had on a bathing suit." I parted the scrub brush with my hands and exposed a well-worn path. "Looks like a game trail going up the side of the hill. This will make it easier to reach the top." I looked over my shoulder at Nick and saw he had the barrel of the rifle pointed up the air. I was happy to see his safe practice.

When we reached the top of the rocky ridge, we stopped and stared at the greyish-white limestone bluff across the river that towered above our camp. Even though the bluff was taller than the ridge and still looked daunting, we could see up and down the river for a quarter of a mile where a layer of fog hovered above the surface of the water and followed the bank like a meandering ghost. I blinked when a soft summer breeze rustled the leaves of a big oak tree and let in a ray of sunlight.

"Is this a mystical site or what?" I said as I spread my arms out in front of me and looked up at the cloudless blue sky.

"Where are the squirrels, Papa?" Nick asked as he raised the rifle stock up to his cheek, pointed the barrel up at a tree and looked down the sights.

"They're around. We just need to sit down and be quiet. Are you going to skin the ones you kill?"

Nick wrinkled up his nose. I started to tell him that hunters cleaned what they killed. Then decided I would first wait and see if we shot any squirrels. We walked over to a hickory nut tree, sat down and leaned our back again the trunk. Nick sat the butt of the rifle on the ground between his legs and followed my lead as we scanned the tops of the trees but did not see any squirrels. It dawned on me when I looked across the river at our campsite that Nick and I were in the same spot on the ridge as the mysterious old man was standing. He had been standing in a circle of light with his arms above his head looking up toward the heavens.

"Humph," I grunted when I remembered how I told Dub to look at the old man that night and all he did was stare at me. By the time he finally turned around to look the old man was gone. He said he figured I was trying to trick him, again.

"Something wrong, Papa?" Nick asked.

"No, why do you ask?"

"You said humph. Were you talking to yourself?"

"Sometimes older people who have experienced lots of different things do that you know."

Nick looked at me frowned. *Maybe it's statements like that makes him question things I say sometimes.*

Down in the hollow, a blue jay screeched a warning danger cry. Nick picked up the rifle and cradled it across his chest. "Is it okay to load up now?" he asked.

I thought about the day I accidentally shot Doc Barnes and I blurted out, "I shot Doc with that same rifle you are holding, Nick."

Nick's mouth fell open. "You did what? You shot someone with this rifle? Was it on purpose?"

"No, it was an accident. I'd never shoot anyone on purpose. Unless I was being attacked."

"Wow. I've never known anybody that shot somebody."

"It's easy to make a mistake with a gun. That's why I'm telling you, okay? There's a lesson to be learned."

"Okay. What kind of lesson is it?"

"My friend Doc Barnes and I were hunting down river a few miles on a ridge like this one. I spotted a squirrel and shouldered the rifle. Got the eye of the critter in the bead of the front sight, curled my finger around the trigger and fired. Next thing I knew I was on the ground, I heard Doc groan and saw the side of his head was covered with blood.

"How did it happen?"

"It sounds crazy, but right before I pulled the trigger, a dead limb broke loose from a tree, hit me on top of the head, knocked me down and caused me to shoot Doc."

"Weird. Really weird."

"Yep, a lot of hunting accidents are caused by weird things."

"We've got frogs!" Jake yelled at us from across the river and waved his arms. "You got any squirrels?"

With the sound of Jake's voice echoing down the river, Nick shouted back, "We're catching slugs to eat instead."

That was the end of the conversation.

"I thought we were too far away from camp to hear anything. I guess not, I heard Jake just fine."

"Sound carries well over water. Plus, there is a two hundred foot bluff for it to bounce off of which helps."

"I bet you were really scared. What happened next after you shot Doc?" Nick wanted to know.

"Doc said he couldn't move his legs. I started to cry and say I was sorry. Even though it wasn't really my fault. I figured people would not believe me about what happened."

Nick looked at me and squinted his eyes. "Since Doc got shot in the head, how did that cause him not to feel anything in his legs?"

RIVER'S EDGE

"He did something to his back when he fell. It was temporary, but I thought I'd crippled him for life. By that time my old hound Trouser was licking my face and I started to think straight again."

"How come you never told me the story before?"

"Never had a reason, I guess. That's why I'm glad we're on this camping trip. I can tell you boys about some of the things I did when I was your age. For some silly reason, grandpas like to do that sort of thing."

"Are you glad Uncle Dub's on the trip, too?"

I looked across the river at the smoke curling up from our campfire and smiled. I turned my head and stared into brown eyes that looked at me shrewdly. "Yes, I'm glad Dub's along. More than you'll ever know. You want to hear the rest of the story about Doc?"

"Sure. Go ahead."

"I said over and over how sorry I was. Doc finally yelled at me to stop yakking and go get help. I jumped up off the ground and headed down the trail toward the pickup truck as fast as I could go."

"Did Trouser go with you?"

"He stayed with Doc to protect him. I stubbed my toe on a root wad, fell down and cut a gash in my knee. Almost fainted when I saw blood run out the rip in my jeans. Got up and hobbled along down the trail when I thought about Doc suffering a lot worse and how he depended on me."

"Then what did you do?"

"My next worry was about how to tell Mom and Dad what I had done. Imagine how terrible it would be to say you shot somebody, especially the town doctor. Over the course of fifty years he had delivered most of the residents in town. I kept thinking about how Dad reminded me over and over to keep the safety on until I was ready to pull the trigger."

Nick looked up at the limbs overhead and said, "I don't see any dead wood, do you, Papa? So what did you do next after you shot Doc?"

"I rehearsed my story in my mind as I made my way down the trail. Above all else, people had to know it was an accident that could not have been prevented. I figured it would be best to drag the story out and include many details. First I'd tell how Trouser chased the squirrel up a tree. Then say how Doc walked to the other side of the tree so the squirrel would move around closer to me so I'd have the best shot. I'd for sure tell how I did not take the safety off until I was ready to squeeze the trigger. It was at that Moment a dead limb broke loose, hit me on the head and knocked the gun barrel down so it was pointed at Doc when the rifle fired. I would even show the lump on the back of my head as more proof."

"It sounds like an accident that might happen," Nick said.

"Thanks for your kind thought, Nick. So anyway, I figured with that story I'd be cleared of not handling the rifle safely and people would know it was not my fault. That's what I told myself over and over until I reached Doc's red pickup truck that was parked alongside the road. When I climbed inside the cab, I reached under the seat and dragged out a canteen filled with water. I took a long swig and poured some on the back of my neck to cool me off and help calm me down. Then I felt guilty knowing poor Doc was hot and thirsty too, him lying on the ground with his head all bloody."

"How old were you, Papa?"

"Six months shy of my fifteenth birthday. Dad taught me how to drive that summer so I could steer the pickup truck around to haul hay. When I fired up the engine of Doc's truck and glanced in the rear view mirror, I didn't even look like the same person. My eyes were red, my face was scratched and from running into a thorn bush and I was pale as a ghost. I shifted into first gear and headed down the rough gravel road."

"I bet you were worried about a lot of things," Nick said.

"That's for sure. In a small town, not much excitement happens on a daily basis. So when some kid shoots the town doctor, it's a big deal. Of course, the more folks talked, the more the story grew."

"I'd have been sick and throwing up. Did you do that, too?"

"Maybe. I don't remember."

"Go on. What happened next?"

"When I drove over the low water bridge by the northeast corner of our farm and I saw Dad standing in the front yard, suddenly, I couldn't remember a thing I'd rehearsed in my mind that I was going to say. When I pulled up in front of our house and Dad walked toward me, Mom yelled at me from the garden. She wanted to know why I was driving Doc's pickup truck. I told them what had happened as best I could. Said how sorry I was a least a dozen times and repeated over and over that it was an accident."

"I hope nothing so bad ever happens to me. What did you do next?"

"Dad drove Doc's pickup truck back to the trail. When we walked to where I'd shot Doc, he was sitting up and seemed to be okay. Except for a bad headache and blood on the side of his head where the bullet grazed him. So anyway, the lesson to be learned is that it pays to be extra careful when you handle a firearm."

"Did you hear that noise?" Nick eased up off the ground when I nodded my head. "Can we load the rifle now?" He whispered.

I took a .22 cartridge out of my pocket and handed it to Nick. He raised the lever on the side of the rifle, slid the bolt back and opened the chamber. He slipped in the cartridge, shoved the bolt forward and locked it down. The barrel of the rifle was pointed straight up in the air.

The raspy, barking chatter down in the hollow was the unmistakable sound of a squirrel.

I got up and stood beside Nick to give him advice on how to make the kill. "Have you shot anything before?" I asked. "I've shot targets at the arcade. Good at it too."

I looked at him and grinned. Never thought of that being a good training ground, but there was no reason why not.

"When you're ready to shoot click off the safety. Lay your cheek down on the stock and hug it close. Look down the barrel and take a fine bead so the front sight blocks out the squirrel's eye. Take a deep breath, let it out slowly, curl your finger around the trigger and squeeze off a shot.

I talked back to the squirrel; my imitation chatter sounded a little rough since I had not used it in many years. It was good enough that I got a response. I saw the bushy red tail of a Fox Squirrel as he hopped from branch to branch, headed our way.

"I see him," Nick said quietly when the squirrel was a couple hundred feet away in the top of an oak tree. "Is it too soon to take off the safety?"

"Go ahead. Wait until you can see the eyes before you pull the trigger."

When the squirrel was close enough for a shot, Nick shouldered the rifle and clicked off the safety. Then the squirrel hopped to another limb, out of our view. Nick clicked off the safety and pointed the barrel of the rifle up toward the sky while he leaned back against the tree and waited.

"We've got another frog," Jake yelled extra loud and he laughed. "Hope you got something to eat or you'll get hungry."

Nick raised the rifle again and clicked off the safety when the squirrel climbed around to our side of the tree. "Crack," by the time the sound of the exploding .22-shell bounced off the bluff across the river, the furry red body of the squirrel had plopped onto the ground.

"Yes," Nick yelled. "I got 'em."

"Nice shot," I said.

"Told you I could shoot. It was just like in the arcade."

"You were right, nice shot," I said as we walked over and looked down at the squirrel twisting and turning in a bed of leaves. "You got him right in the eye."

Nick groaned and looked away. "I don't think I want to shoot any more. You can get the next one, Papa."

"Don't think we need any more squirrels. Let's take this one and head back to camp." I gave Nick a pat on the back, reached down and picked the squirrel up by the tail and we tromped off down the ridge toward camp.

"What will Mom say about me shooting a squirrel? She doesn't like guns."

"A gun used to hurt somebody is one thing. Using it to kill something to eat is different. You know?"

"Yeah, I know. Maybe I'll only tell my friends."

"Good idea. Some leaves are best left unturned," I said. Nick looked at me and grinned.

"This will be a strange meal. Fish, Frogs and a Squirrel. Who's going to clean all this stuff?"

"I'll probably clean it and Dub will cook. You can help if you want. I'll show you what to do."

Nick shook his head. "We'll see. I'm not sure about all that blood."

We walked down the hill from the ridge when we reached the bottom and started across the gravel bar toward camp, I held up the fat red squirrel by its bushy tail. "Look what we've got you guys. We'll be eating' high on the hog tonight."

I laughed when Jake yelled back and asked if we had killed a pig. I remembered that the famous feud between the Hatfield's and the McCoy's got started because of a lowly pig. Not much different than what Dub and I had rowed about over the years.

When we waded across the river and stepped out onto the bank, Dub was grinning from ear to ear.

"What's made you so happy?" I asked.

"When I climbed up on the rock ledge and looked down into the water. I saw a reflection of the way I looked when I was twelve years old. So you wouldn't think that I was losing it, I shot a picture of myself."

I tossed the squirrel down on the gravel bar and smiled. "Okay, Dub. Only time will tell."

Chapter Eleven

I looked out across the water and thought about the dead man and Doc's hound Lucky that Dub and I found tied to a rope. His arms floated up above his head and his hands flopped back and forth like he was waving good-bye. That was all it took for us to hightail it down river toward home. At that point I was so scared I was numb.

"I might sleep in Dub's pickup truck tonight," I said.

"Why is that?" Nick asked.

"Because you boys are past due to have a couple of nightmares. I don't want you screaming in my ear."

"Yeah right, Papa," Nick said. "If anyone does it'll be you."

Jake walked up and patted me on the shoulder. "If you did we wouldn't have to hear you snore."

"How many bull frogs did you get?" Nick asked.

"Three really big ones. Guess how we got them?" Jake asked. Nick threw his hands up in the air. "Uncle Dub used his fishing rod and caught them on a red fly. One even jumped through the air to get it."

"Where are they?" Nick asked.

When Jake pointed at a gunnysack in the spring branch with the top tied shut, one of the frogs kicked and the sack moved. "I caught one all by myself."

I had not seen Jake more excited about anything, even video games.

"I shot the squirrel," Nick said. "Hit him in the eye. All that practice in the arcade paid off."

Jake gave Nick a crooked smile. "What will you tell Mom? She doesn't like guns."

I looked at Jake and frowned. "What we do on the river is between us boys."

"We've got a mess of meat for dinner," Dub said. "You and the boys do the cleanin'. I'll be the cook."

I could tell by the way Jake wrinkled up his nose that part of the deal did not seem like much fun.

"Sounds good," I said. "We'll clean 'em now and put the meat in the cooler."

"What will we clean first, Papa?" Nick asked.

"Let's start with my fish," Jake said.

I picked up a knife and walked to the edge of the water. "Okay, let's clean the bass. A nice fish that will weigh two pounds or better. Go ahead, Jake. Take him off the stringer."

Being in the cool spring water had caused the bass to become lively and he was flopping around.

"What do I do next?" Jake asked.

"Hand 'em to me. I'll filet him. Then cut him in a half-dozen pieces so he'll fry up crispy brown."

"You boys seen anyone clean a fish or wild game before?" Dub asked.

"I haven't seen anybody clean anything," Jake said. "Not sure I want to either."

"I saw you clean a pheasant, Papa," Nick said.

"That was a long time ago. You were a little tyke."

"I was in first grade. I didn't eat any of it. But I do want to eat this stuff."

"There's enough to go around," I said as I watched Jake pick up the stringer and hold the bass out in front of him.

"What do I do now?" Jake asked.

"Slide the fish up the rope past the metal guide on the end then hand him to me."

"Can I help?" Nick asked.

I pointed at the red and white cooler by the log close to the campfire. "Get me the lid off the cooler. I'll use it to lay the fish on while I clean it."

I looked around when I heard a splash and saw the bass swimming toward the deep water. "Oh no," Jake yelled as he jumped up and down.

I splashed out and tried to grab the fish, but it disappeared in the deep water.

"Crap, Jake," Nick yelled. "What happened?"

Jake looked like he was about to cry. "I couldn't help it," he said. "The fish jumped right out of my hand."

"It's okay," Dub said. "It was a powerful fish and hard to handle."

"That's right it was. I'm glad it got away." Jake sniffled and held his head up high.

"Hey, you guys. It's okay. We have frogs, a squirrel and hot dogs. That's plenty to eat. Plus we've got deer jerky and a jar of peanut butter." Even though the combination seemed a little unusual, it conjured up a tasty image.

"People have survived on a lot less," Dub said.

"What do you want to clean next?" I asked.

"How about the frogs?" Nick said.

"I'll clean the first one, you can clean the other two," I said.

"Okay, I guess." Nick did not sound very committed to the job.

"Hand me the gunny sack, Jake. Nick, grab the pliers out of my tackle box. We'll do some frog cleaning."

I reached inside the sack, grabbed a frog and held on tight so he would not kick free and escape like the bass did. I laid the slimy green creature on the cooler lid and in one quick swipe of the blade I cut into the body above the back legs. A dark red gush of blood flowed across the white cooler lid and dripped off the sides onto the gravel bar. Jake whimpered and looked away.

"My Dad would have given me a fit for not cleaning the entire frog from the head down," I said when I threw the torso into the water. He was right that even though there wasn't much on the back and front legs, it was meat that could be eaten. I'm too lazy to clean the upper part of the body. I clamped the pliers down on the greenish-brown hide that covered the legs and stripped off the skin exposing the muscular white flesh. I cut off the feet and threw them and the hide into the water. I held up the pair of legs and said, "Here's frog number one for the frying pan."

"Is it okay to throw frog parts into the water?" Jake asked.

"Yeah, the Crawdads and Turtles will eat them before morning. Okay, Nick. It's your turn to clean the next one?"

Nick looked at the frog legs lying in a pool of blood and wrinkled up his nose. The blank stare on his face was a dead giveaway that he was having second thoughts.

"You don't have to do it. I'll clean the other two."

"I guess I'll do it," Nick said. "I said I would."

I rinsed the frog legs I cleaned off in the river and laid the meat on a piece of aluminum foil. I reached inside the gunnysack and pulled out the second frog, a strong kicker. When I squeezed down on the torso, a nylon leader popped out of its mouth. The frog had swallowed one of Dub's red flies.

"Open the belly and get my fly out," Dub said.

"Are you serious?" Nick said as he turned his head quickly and looked at Dub.

"I sure am. It's the last red fly I've got until I tie more."

The frog croaked loudly when I opened its mouth with my fingers and looked down its throat. "Okay, Nick. Here's your frog. Let me know if you need help."

Nick grabbed the frog as I let loose. He turned it so the white underbelly was facing him and stuck the knifepoint in the frog's belly. When he ripped it open, blood squirted in his face. He wiped away a clot on the side of his cheek and took a deep breath.

"You okay?" I asked.

He nodded his head up and down and proceeded to cut the red fly loose from the frog's intestine. Jake jumped back when Nick tried to hand it to him, so I took the fly and put it on a rock. Nick laid the frog down on the cooler lid and as if he were operating under a spell, he cut into the body above the back legs in one slice of the blade.

"You did that good," Dub said as he winked at me and I winked back.

"Real good indeed," I said.

Nick looked pale and sweat covered his forehead. "I'll finish this one. But I don't want to do anymore."

"That's okay. I'll clean the last one."

"How old were you when you cleaned your first frog, Papa?" Jake asked as he stared at the lifeless pair of legs.

I handed Nick the pliers. "About your age, I guess. Go ahead, peel the skin off down to the feet."

Nick clamped down with the pliers and pulled off the hide. He picked up the knife and cut off the feet. He laid the frog legs down on the lid of the cooler, waded out into the river and washed the blood off his hands.

Nick shook his head when Jake said cleaning frogs was a nasty job and he did not think he wanted to eat any of them.

"Frogs are as good as any meat," Dub said. "You eat chickens, don't you, Jake? They've got blood and entrails too. You've just never seen anybody clean anything before."

"Yeah, I like chicken. But I don't know about these frogs. They seem too slimy. I don't want to eat the squirrel either. They're like rats with bushy tails."

"What are you going to eat?" Dub asked.

"I'll eat Molly's deer jerky. I'd go hungry if I had to clean wild things to eat."

I cleaned the last frog and put the three sets of legs in the cooler. "It's squirrel cleaning time. Come on Nick, hold it up by the hind legs."

Nick hesitated for a Moment, and then grabbed hold of the squirrel and I cut a circle through the hide down to the meat around all four feet and at the base of the tail. I split the hide at each of those points and pulled the skin off the body until I reached the neck. I cut off the squirrel's head and feet, gutted the carcass and threw the inedible parts into the woods.

I wrapped the squirrel in aluminum foil and placed it in the cooler with the frogs. When Dub got ready to cook, the meat was ready.

"Thanks for cleaning the game," Dub said. "We'll have ourselves a nice dinner."

"What would you boys like to do next?" I asked as I washed the blood off my hands. When neither of them said anything, I pointed at the bluff. "You can climb up to the high ledge and jump off if you want to, Nick. It may be one of the biggest thrills you've ever had."

"What about me?" Jake asked.

"You'd probably get up there and freeze," I said. "It's a lot scarier when you look down at the water than it is looking up at the ledge from here. It's no fun at all if you have to climb back down."

RIVER'S EDGE

Nick scanned the bluff from top to bottom. "You go up with me, Papa?" He said.

"No, I don't think so. I'll hang out on the raft and watch as you jump. That way I rescue you if you don't come back up."

"Come on, Tommy. You don't want the boys to think you're gettin' old. Show 'em how it's done." Dub poured himself a cup of coffee and sat down on the log to watch the show.

"I won't climb up to the high ledge. But I will swing off on the rope. Back in the old days I could turn a flip in the air. Not sure if I'm up for it any more. I'll put on my bathing suit. Don't forget to check for ticks, Nick."

He tossed his arms in the air and looked down the front of his pants.

"All right for Papa." Jake said as I crawled out of the tent wearing a pair of red trunks, my belly sticking out over the top like a loaf of bread. Jake and Nick jumped into the water on top of the air mattress that was floating close to the bank and positioned themselves so they could watch me sail over the top of their heads.

I looked at the ledge sticking out from the side of the bluff ten feet above the water and froze when I thought about the dead man Dub and I found in the Blue Hole.

"Go on, Papa. What are you waiting for? Climb on up. I'll toss you the rope." Nick grabbed the end of the rope and began to whip it back and forth through the air so he could flip it to me.

I looked at Dub and smirked. "Do you want to go first since you're an old river rat?"

Dub laughed. "Age before beauty, big brother."

"Come on, Pap?" Nick said.

Jake laughed. "Yeah, Pap. Go on ahead."

I waded across the cold water in the spring branch and climbed up onto the ledge. I stood with my back against the rock wall and a knot in my stomach. I felt the way I did the Halloween night that I walked through the graveyard under the light of a full moon when I was a kid. I looked over at Dub sitting on a log by the campfire drinking coffee and he tipped his hat. The surface of the water was a mirror image of the wide-open sky. A couple of buzzards circled overhead effortlessly. Below the image of the big black birds was a deep pool of refreshing cool water waiting for me to take the plunge.

"Toss me the rope," I said as I felt a burst of courage and at the same time, knew something spooky was waiting for me in the water. Nick whipped the rope up toward me when I held out my hand and I caught it on the first try. I gripped it tightly above the knot with both hands and I was all set to go.

"You look like a pro," Dub said. When he gave me thumbs up, I jumped off the ledge and swung out over the water, feeling the same exhilaration that I had when I was a kid. It was like I was as free as a bird.

"Yeah, Papa!" Jake yelled as I flipped around in midair and splashed head first into the deep blue water. Instead of shooting back up to the top, I swam toward the bottom. Kicking my legs up and down, I moved my arms in a wide sweeping motion. I felt the water get colder as I descended into the depths and the light began to fade. As the pressure built up inside my head my ears began to ring. Determined to touch the bottom like I could when I was a kid, I swam deeper into the darkness. When I reached out and picked up a rock, as proof that I had gone the distance, inches away from my eyes I saw the chalk white face of the dead man. There was no doubt in my quest to prove to myself I had gone too far.

Chapter Twelve

I panicked! I took wide sweeping strokes and kicked my legs as hard as I could to escape from the watery grave. My lungs hungered for air like they might explode and everything was blurry. I exhaled forcefully when I shot through the surface and snorted like a goat as I blew water out of my nose.

Nick and Jake clapped their hands. "We was worried, Papa," Nick said as I rolled over on my back and sucked in a couple deep breaths of air.

"You may have set an underwater record," Dub said.

"Yeah, I know," I said, still gasping for air. I held up the rock that I picked up from the bottom and threw it onto the bank. I pulled myself onto the air mattress up to my waist and laid my head down. I was dizzy and my ears were clogged up, but I felt like a champion. Never again would I swim to the bottom of the Blue Hole. It was as if my life had made a full circle and where I started out was where it came to an end.

"Just like the old days," Dub said. "Except it took you longer to get down and come back up."

"You did good, Papa," Jake said. "Nobody could have done better."

I laid on the air mattress until I got my breath back. "Your turn," I said to Dub as I swam toward the bank. I crawled out onto the gravel bar, rolled over onto my back and stared at the sky. I started to tell Dub about seeing the face of a dead man again, then decided we had already talked about the ghost from the past enough.

"The boys can represent me on the rope swing," Dub said. "I tore a tendon in my shoulder not long ago. I'm not healed yet. Go on, Nick. Get up there and swing off, it's a great feeling."

Nick shook his head. "I'm afraid I'll go down too deep."

Jake laughed. "I don't care what you think. You do it first. I'll throw the rope,"

"Okay, I will," Nick, said. "I'm not afraid of nothing."

Jake swam over and grabbed the end of the rope while Nick waded across the spring branch and climbed up onto the ledge. After a couple of failed attempts, Jake tossed the rope hard enough that Nick caught it and he was ready to sail through the air.

"It's easy if you want to turn a flip. Play like you're on the trampoline, lower your head and turn yourself around," I said.

"What are you waiting on?" Jake said after Nick had stared down at the water for some time. "Don't be a chicken."

That was all the encouragement Nick needed. He pushed off the ledge and yelled like Tarzan as he sailed through the air. He dropped into the water and was back up on top in a couple of seconds.

"That was great," Nick said. "Go on, Jake. You'll really like it."

To my surprise, Jake swam to the bank, waded across the spring branch, and was up on the ledge, waiting to swing off, all in one continuous motion.

"Wow, what made you so brave all of a sudden?" Nick asked as he flipped the rope up to Jake and swam off to the right to get out of his flight path.

"What's the matter, Nick? Afraid I'll fall on you?" Jake let out a yell and sailed off the ledge. When he reached the top of the swing, he did not let go of the rope and headed back toward the bluff.

"Let go of the rope!" I yelled, figuring he would end up with a broken arm or worse if he smashed into the bluff.

Like a graceful bird, Jake raised his legs and landed on the ledge. He let go of the rope and climbed down, waded across the spring branch and dived into the water.

"You little rat," I said when he came to the surface. "You might have hurt yourself."

Jake grinned at Nick. "Told you I didn't want to drop into the water. But I wasn't afraid to swing on the rope."

"No doubt who that kid takes after," Dub said.

"What's next?" Nick asked. "I don't think nothing can be more fun."

Dub pointed at the high ledge sticking out from the face of the bluff about sixty feet above the water. "Don't know if that's more fun. But it's more daring."

"You mean jump from way up there?" Nick said.

"That's right," I said. "It's the highest point you can get to on the bluff. Many a boy has gone up there and got afraid to jump, then had to climb back down. Which is actually more scary than the climb up."

"How come?" Jake asked.

"The fear of scraping your body along the face of the bluff on the way down if you fall. That's how I got this scar on my chin," Dub said.

Jake frowned. "I'm not going for sure. Are you Nick?"

Nick studied the situation. "What about after you get up there. Do you just close your eyes and jump?"

"Probably as good as a way as any," I said. "Whatever you do, don't look down. It's too scary."

"The reason I jumped the first time was because Tommy said he was going to leave me on the ledge and go down river to fish," Dub said.

I laughed. "You had climbed up and down a half-dozen times. Fact is you may have set a record for being the biggest chicken."

"Your mind plays tricks on you up there. You know that, Tommy. What worried me most was that I might turn over in midair, hit flat on my back, knock myself out and drown."

"It sounds really dangerous," Jake said.

"I just wanted to let you know what it's like if you decide to make the climb," Dub said.

"Anybody ever gets killed?" Nick sounded as serious as I had heard him be about anything.

"Red Lewis did. He slipped on the ledge, hit the back of his head and knocked himself out," Dub said.

"But did he get killed?" Nick asked.

Dub laughed. "No, he lived and wasn't much sillier than before the accident."

I stared at the ledge and remembered the last time I jumped off. How simple life was in those days.

"What would you do if you were me, Papa?" Nick asked.

"Can't say, Nick. You've heard talk from a couple of old-time jumpers. The decision is up to you."

"I'm going to jump. If you and Uncle Dub did it, I want to do it too," Nick said as he walked over and put his fingers in a crevice in the face of the bluff. Before he started his climb, Dub and I gave him a few words of advice.

"Hug the wall," I said. "Take slow, deep breaths and stay relaxed. Make sure you have a firm grip with one hand before you reach for the next hand hold."

"Whatever you do, don't look down," Dub added.

It took Nick about twenty minutes to climb to the high ledge.

"Good job." Jake clapped his hands when Nick stood up and hugged the bluff with the flat of his back.

"The kid reached the ledge in record time and looked like a professional climber," Dub said. "He must have some experience."

"Him and his buddies climb the rock wall at a shopping mall. This was a lot further and there's no protective harness."

"You can see a long way from up here," Nick shouted as he pointed down river. "That's where Jake hooked the big fighting bass." He looked up the river. "There's where we found the arrowheads. I wish you hadn't told me about the guy that hit his head. If I get knocked out, will I sink to the bottom?"

I grabbed the air mattress, jumped into the water, paddled out into the middle and looked up at Nick. "If anything happens, I'll pull you out. Try this and see if it helps. I used to take a deep breath and close my eyes, then play like I was about to leap into the back of the pickup truck with the tailgate down. That way I'd jump away from the face of the bluff."

The words were barely out of my mouth when Nick yelled, "Look out below." He flapped his arms up and down like a bird as he fell toward the water. He had jumped further away from the bluff than I anticipated and was headed toward me like a cannon ball. I flailed the water with my arms as I hurried to paddle out of his way. He hit the water only a couple of feet from me and quickly popped back up to the surface. He was laughing and yelling that he wished his friends could have seen him make the jump.

"You're a real pro, Nick," Dub said. "Are you going to do it again?"

"Not today. Maybe tomorrow. It was fun though."

"Anybody hungry?" Dub asked.

"I'm a little hungry," Jake said.

"What about you guys?" Nick and I agreed by the time Dub got dinner cooked we would be ready to chow down. In the meantime the boys and I would do some swimming to work up an appetite.

We put on our diving mask to explore the deep water close to the bluff. We swam a few feet back inside of an underwater cave, where we chased out a couple of Smallmouth bass. Nick found the shell of a snapping turtle about the size of a hubcap and Jake picked up a red and white Lazy Ike fishing lure with most of the hooks rusted away.

The boys and I grabbed the air mattress and hung onto the sides while we kicked our feet and splashed water up in the air. We tilted our heads back and opened our mouths to catch droplets of cold spring water that dripped from a crack in the bluff. I rolled over on my back and swam along under a cover of green ferns and purple flowers that grew along a rock ledge. The air smelled fresh and clean, like after a rain. A Bullfrog jumped off a broad leaf lily pad when we worked our way toward the slough. I turned over on my back and watched a hawk circle overhead in the cloudless blue sky. It could not have been a more beautiful day. I could not have felt more in touch with the earth.

"Bet the Indians liked it here," Jake said.

"Did you see the fish jump?" I pointed at a ripple up ahead.

"What kind was it, a bass?" Jake asked.

"I believe it was a gar. They get good sized in the river. Dad caught one once that weighed seven or eight pounds."

Jake crawled up on one end of the air mattress. "Gar have sharp teeth. Do they ever bite?"

"No reason to be afraid. They don't bite people. They do eat a lot of game fish, however."

"Do people eat gar?" Nick asked.

"No. They're scavenger fish and not very tasty. Got lots of bones. I'd rather eat a turtle or a snake than a gar," I said.

"Is there anything you haven't eaten, Papa?" Jake said.

"I haven't eaten a buzzard. Even if I were starving, I'd never eat a slug."

RIVER'S EDGE

Jake wrinkled up his nose and shook his head.

"I'd throw up if I had to eat a slimy slug," Nick said.

I put my feet up on the side of the bluff and pushed away. Gliding out into the middle, turned over and floated on my back with my eyes closed.

Jake swam up beside me and pecked me on the shoulder "How deep did you go before you touched bottom, Papa?"

"Maybe thirty feet."

"I couldn't make it that far. My ears clog up when I go to the bottom of the swimming pool."

"You want to swim down and touch the bottom?" I asked Nick as he floated up beside us on the air mattress.

"Might later. If I jump off the ledge again I can go on down to the bottom."

"You boys hungry yet?" Dub asked as he held up a long-handled black metal skillet.

"I'd eat as soon as it's ready," I said. "What about you boys?" I got a nod from Nick as Jake splashed water in his face and swam toward the lily pads where yellow dragonflies darted back and forth in an aerial display. Nick was in hot pursuit and gaining with each stroke.

"Be careful," I said as I swam toward the bank to give Dub a hand with supper. "That back water slough is snake country." I no more than got the words out of my mouth when I looked over my shoulder and saw that Jake had stopped and began to back paddle.

"Snake! Snake!" Nick yelled, as he thrashed the water wildly with his arms and started to swim toward the bank. Slithering toward the boys with its head held high was a dark brown cottonmouth moccasin the size of my forearm. Jake struggled to swim faster than the poisonous creature but he was losing the race.

"Hurry!" I yelled. Jake kicked frantically and a spray of water shot up in the air.

"Help me, Papa!" Jake screamed when he headed back toward shore with the snake only a few feet behind him. "Please," he begged.

I froze. I could not bring myself to jump into the water. My stomach churned, the taste of bile filled my mouth.

When I heard the sharp crack of a .22 shell I did not know if the explosion was for real or something I imagined. The snake shot up in the air and lunged forward, coming to rest only a couple of feet behind Jake's bare foot. The snake began to twist and turn, churning the water, finally sinking out of sight.

When I looked at Dub, he still held the rifle to his shoulder and the smell of gunpowder filled the air. He had made a perfect shot over the top of Jake's head to hit the snake, a gamble I was sure he did not want to take, but obviously felt he must.

Jake was crying when he reached the bank and Nick was pale white. "You saved us from being bit, Uncle Dub," Nick said. He was out of breath and his eyes were big as quarters.

Dub sat down on the gravel bar and looked at his bandaged foot. "I couldn't let you get bit like me."

I walked over and patted Dub on the shoulder. "That shot was a miracle. A complete and total miracle."

"Even better than on TV," Nick said as he took a deep breath and pushed his hair back away from his face with his hand.

"I hope the snake's dead. Not just wounded," Dub said, putting the situation into a different light.

"He looked dead," I said, hoping that it was true.

"Did he look dead for sure, Papa?" Jake said.

"He did for sure," I said, even though I knew that one shot from a .22 rifle would not usually kill a big cottonmouth moccasin. In many cases it would just make them mad.

"Most scary thing ever happened to me, that was," Nick said.

"What about a video of the snake chasing me and Uncle Dub shooting over my head. Maybe they would show it on Animal Planet," Jake said.

Amazing how quickly young people rebound, I thought when Nick asked Jake if he wanted to go for a swim and laughed.

"I'm not swimming anymore today. Maybe not again in the river," Jake said as he walked to the tent and grabbed a towel to dry himself off. Nick agreed as he walked over and sat down on the log by the campfire.

I looked at the lilies to see if the snake may have survived the rifle shot and crawled on top of a broad leaf pad. I saw nothing but a couple of dragonflies hovering above the top of the water.

"If everyone's not too upset, let's eat?" Dub said as he laid the rifle down beside a log.

Nick picked up a rock and threw it in the water. He looked at Jake, laughed nervously and said, "All the excitements made me hungry."

Jake walked up beside Dub and grabbed his hand. "You're the best shot in the world, Uncle Dub."

Dub patted Jake on the head. "I'm good all right. In this case, it may have been a power greater than my aim that caused the bullet to hit the snake."

I smiled and nodded my head up and down. Who was I to argue with a preacher that had pulled off a miracle?

"You should have seen your face," Nick said to his brother. "Like you was trying to out swim a ghost."

"Yeah, well. I've not seen you move so fast either." Jake tried to sound brave, but his fingers still trembled.

"What time is it?" Nick asked.

Dub looked at his watch. "Almost seven. We've got a couple of hours before dark. If you want to do anything else, you best get going.

"What would we do?" Jake asked. "I won't go back in the water. I'm afraid the snake might still be alive."

"You could go down river and fish. Or, you could go up river and look for arrowheads," Dub said.

Jake and Nick agreed the best plan was to stay in camp. Obviously the encounter with the snake had put a damper on any activities for the remainder of the day.

"Okay. I'll put you to work." Dub picked up a sack from the grocery box and handed it to Jake. He gave Nick a knife. "Be careful when you peel the potatoes. That knife is sharp."

Jake looked at the bag and frowned. "I don't know how to peel potatoes."

"Me either," Nick said. "I don't think I want to learn."

"I'll show you how it's done." I walked over to the edge of the water and motioned for the boys to come join me. After I looked all around to make sure the snake was nowhere in sight, I hunkered down.

Jake squatted down beside me and pulled a potato out of the sack and Nick handed me the knife. I kept the peeling together and made one long curly strip. I rinsed the cleaned white potato in the river and dropped it in a pan that Dub brought over and sat down on the gravel bar. I grabbed another one from the sack and handed it to Nick, along with the knife.

"Here you go," I said. "You peel a couple, then Jake can peel a couple. That's all we'll need for supper."

Nick dug the knife blade in deeply and left a quarter inch of potato meat attached to the peel. When he finished the process the potato was only about half its original size. He tossed it into the pan. He adjusted the cutting pressure on the second potato and did a much better job. As usual, Jake learned quickly by watching Nick and when it was his turn, he peeled off a perfect curl. I took over and cut the potatoes into thin slices so they would fry up crispy brown.

"I need this red beauty peeled too," Dub said as he tossed me an onion.

"Ok, I'll take care of this chore. I don't want to see these boys crying from onion juice." I cleaned the onion and chopped it up into small pieces.

I carried the potatoes and chopped onion mix over to Dub and set the pan down beside the campfire. Dub had the game cut up into small pieces and laid out on a sheet of tin foil. He rolled the frog legs and five pieces of squirrel in cornmeal so they would not stick to the frying pan. The hot dogs he would fry in the grease that was left over from the wild game.

Dub set the black cast iron skillet down on a wire grill, which was supported on both sides of the lapping yellow flames by two flat rocks. He poured in Crisco from a bottle until the liquid was a half-inch deep. When smoke began to rise off the surface of the cooking oil, he dumped in the potatoes and the hot grease sizzled.

"Those will be great," I said. "I love fried potatoes and red onion." We looked around when there was a splash close to the bluff.

"You think it was the snake, Uncle Dub?" Jake asked. He sounded anxious to hear the right answer.

"If not dead, he's holed up sick as hell," Dub said. "Nothin' to worry about."

It was hard to tell if Dub really believed what he had said or was just putting on for the sake of the boys. I would not dare say a word under the circumstances, but I thought about the time I shot a cottonmouth moccasin with my .22 rifle. I barely clipped it in the neck and it actually chased me down the riverbank. I finally killed it with a rock.

"Bet none of your friends in the city are having a dinner like ours," Dub said as he stirred the potatoes with a spatula and the sweet smell of the onions filled the air.

"Most of them would be afraid to eat this stuff," Jake said. "Especially girls."

Dub and I laughed.

"What about you?" Nick asked. "Will you eat some of everything?"

Jake squinted his eyes and said, "I'll eat anything you do."

I looked down the river when I heard the cry of a Kingfisher and saw a swarm of cicadas flying around in the treetops. Their constant high-pitched chirping had caused me to wake up more than once the night before. I could not believe I forgot the sleeping pills that I laid on the dresser. No way Dub would have any, no doubt when his good old country soul lay down at night he slept like a man without a care in the world.

Dub laid a strip of tin foil on top of the cooler lid to put the fried food on. He set a pot filled with water and ground coffee on the edge of the grill to boil.

"Looks like dinner will be ready before long. Hope you boys are hungry?" I said.

"I'm all of a sudden hungry as a bear," Jake said as he and Nick walked to the edge of the water and looked at the slough.

"See any sign of the snake?" I asked.

Both boys shook their head, but did not say a word.

Dub scooped the potatoes out of the skillet onto the tin foil and was ready to fry the game.

"I'll fry the frogs and the squirrel first, save the hot dogs for last." Dub dropped the game meat in one piece at a time and the hot grease steamed up and danced. "We've got tomatoes if you want to slice up a couple, Tommy. Might as well get the bread and honey out of the camp box. We need the plates and some tools to eat with, too."

Jake walked up close to the fire and pointed at the frying pan. "What's going on with those frog legs?" he asked. "They're kicking in the pan."

"Frogs have tendons in their legs. When they start to fry up, the tendons shrink. That makes the legs move," Dub said. "I have actually seen them jerk so hard they jumped out of the pan."

"Have you really, Uncle Dub?" Jake said.

"I have, I'm serious."

"Pretty spooky," Jake said and there was no doubt by the sound of his voice that he really meant it.

"What if we cooked a couple of Crawdad tails too?" Nick said. "I can catch some real quick."

"Sure. Bring 'em on over. We'll fry 'em up. Crawdad tails are tasty."

By the time Dub scooped up the frog legs and got the squirrel pieces out of the frying pan, Nick and Jake had caught four Crawdads and peeled the hull off their tails. Dub rolled them in flour and dropped them into the frying pan. Within minutes, our odd game combination was ready for consumption.

Jake and Nick each ate a hot dog, a pair of frog legs, one squirrel leg and a couple of Crawdad tails, along with a side of fried potatoes and a slice of honey-covered homemade bread. Dub and I split what was left of the frog and the squirrel, then finished off the rest of the homemade bread and fried potatoes. We washed it down with a cup of black coffee.

The sun was setting behind the ridge across the river as the boys and I were washing dishes. Long dark shadows covered the gravel bar. I hated it that the snake had put a damper on our trip. Going back into the water would not be the same, so maybe it was good that we were headed back to Lewiston the next morning, then on to Kansas City the next day.

A breeze came up that helped cool down the hot humid air. The sound of the cicadas and tree frogs had started with their chorus. I was bone tired. Surely I would sleep until morning.

Chapter Thirteen

We had finished an exciting and exhausting day eating a mixed bag of wild game, scrambled eggs and honey-covered homemade bread. We spent our final hours before going to bed sitting around the campfire telling stories, poking at the coals with marshmallow sticks and watching the sparks fly. We were a contented group of campers. Except in the back of everyone's mind was the snake.

"Look, a bat," I said as one of the dark brown creatures dipped and darted past. "There goes another one."

"They're gobbling up mosquitoes," Dub said. "Bring on more bats."

"Now that you're done cooking, is it okay to put more wood on the fire?" Jake asked. With a nod from Dub, the boys tossed a half dozen limbs and a pine knot on the coals and flames shot up within minutes.

"Are there really blind fish in the Blue Hole Cave, Uncle Dub?" Nick asked.

"People say so, I've never seen any. Uncle Ira claimed he caught one once. We can walk up there and throw some breadcrumbs in the water. Maybe one will come up to eat. We should do it now because it will be dark soon."

Jake jumped up and got a slice of bread. "Okay, let's go."

"I'm not going," Nick said. "The snake might have crawled up the spring branch and be waiting for us."

"If the snake's not already dead, he'll be back in the slough. You're safe to walk up the spring branch if you want to go with us," Dub said.

"Are you going, Papa?" Nick asked.

"I think I'll stay here. I've done all the exploring I want to do for one day. Go on ahead. You might see a blind fish."

"I'm going to stay with Papa. Yell if you see one."

"Goes double for me. If you see a blindfish I'll give you fifty dollars. If you catch one, I'll give you five hundred dollars," I said as Dub and Jake headed for the pool of spring water at the mouth of the cave.

"I want to ask you some questions, Papa," Nick said when we sat down on the log by the campfire. "I didn't want Jake to hear because I thought he might get scared. He's already scared enough."

I had never heard Nick sound so serious about anything. "Okay, go ahead. I hope I don't get scared."

"Do you really think the leg bone might belong to the killer of those two guys you and Uncle Dub found?"

"It would be far out if after fifty years it showed up now. Stranger things have happened. We'll give it to the Sheriff and see what he can find out. What's your next question?"

Nick reached down and flipped a spot of brown mud off his knee. In the fading light it looked like another tick. "Once on TV I saw a wounded snake chase somebody. If the snake were still alive, would he crawl up into our camp tonight?"

"Why worry about it? You'll be in the tent."

"I may have to go outside to pee. I'm afraid to step out onto the gravel bar barefooted."

"Take a can inside to pee in. Throw the tent flap back and dump it when you're done."

"I don't want anybody to see me pee in a can."

"Good Lord, Nick. We'll be asleep, unless you wake us up and make an announcement. I'm sure the snake's dead. Don't worry about it."

"Another thing is I pulled a tick off me today that was down between my legs. Do you think I might get tick fever?"

"Not if the head of the tick didn't stay buried when you pulled it off. Don't worry you'll be fine."

Jake stood up on top of the boulder in front of the cave and waved his arms. "We saw something. It might be a blind fish."

I looked at Nick and grinned. "Go check it out if you want. You won't run into the snake."

"I'm coming," Nick yelled as he jumped up and headed up the spring branch, hoping to get a glimpse of the elusive blindfish.

I looked to the west at the reddish-purple glow in the sky as the sun set behind the ridge. It would be pitch dark for an hour or so until the moon rose above the top of the bluff and flooded us with white light. I set a bag of marshmallows on top of the cooler and laid out a couple of sticks so the boys could roast some when they returned from their blind fish-sighting trip. I stood up and looked at the water when I heard something thrashing around. Even though I would never admit it, Nick's concern about the gunshot snake crawling up on the gravel bar had me a little concerned as well. I sat down on the log by the fire and moved the coals around with my stick.

"We might have seen one, Papa," Jake yelled.

I waved and told Jake to let me know when he was sure. I stared at the fire and thought about what a nice time all of us had camping. Even though the snake caused a little ruckus, the creature spiced things up and left us with a trip to remember. At first it bothered me that the boys admired Dub's outdoor skills more than mine. Why wouldn't he be a better fisherman and hunter? He had fifty more years to practice than I did. It was a good thing or he would never have been able to pull off the shot that stopped one or both of the boys from getting snake bit.

I wondered if my wife Lucy and the boys' Mom and Dad were worried the whole time we were gone. They were uneasy about my taking the boys to a wilderness area in the middle of nowhere. I had told too many stories about the strange and spooky things that happened when Dub and I were kids. Things like describing my snakebite in great detail, and the dead men we found, not to mention our eyewitness account of Buzzard Thompson drowning in the river. They knew the rugged country could pose a certain amount of danger, even if a person was extra careful.

"The blind fish turned out to be a Perch with its eyes open," Jake said as he and Nick splashed along down the spring branch toward me with Dub close behind.

"Sorry," I said. "I hoped we could have fried blind fish for breakfast."

"Looks like the fire will last until bedtime," Dub said as he walked into camp. "Lots of coals and the pine knot will burn for hours."

I pointed at the cooler. "I laid out a bag of marshmallows if you boys want to do some roasting."

"Okay." Jake walked over and opened up the bag. Nick followed Jake's lead and they slid a couple of marshmallows on the sticks.

I started to remind Jake about the right way to roast a marshmallow, by that time they had already caught fire. Nick laughed as Jake huffed and puffed to blow out the flame.

Nick held his marshmallows a few inches above the flames, rotated the stick slowly and they turned a toasty brown.

Dub pulled a pipe and a can of Prince Albert tobacco from the pocket of his bib overalls and sat down on the log.

The boys watched as he filled the bowl with tobacco and lit it with a flaming stick he pulled out of the campfire. He exhaled a big white smoke ring that drifted up toward the sky, another thing that I could never do.

"When we were boys, most people who smoked either rolled their own cigarettes or puffed on a corn cob pipe. The first time I tried to smoke, I got sick. So did you, Dub. Do you remember?"

"Oh yeah I did," Dub said. "We were in the barn and I threw up on my shoes. It was a hot summer day. When I got back to the house, Mom kept saying she smelled something like hog slop."

"I'll never smoke," Jake said. "It makes peoples' lungs black. That old Mrs. Netter that lives down the street smokes and she can't hardly breathe."

"You're a smart boy," Dub said as he blew out another smoke ring. "What about you, Nick?"

Nick shook his head and changed the subject. "Do you know for your whole life there's a spider within three feet of you? That's on the average. I saw it on the Discovery Channel."

"What's that got to do with smoking?" I asked

"Nothing, I just wondered if anybody knew it or not. It's spooky."

"I hope you don't snore so loud tonight, Papa," Jake said. "For a while the tent was shaking."

"Bull! Nobody could snore that loud," I said.

Nick laughed and said I also made a yipping sound like a hurt dog and whistled through my nose.

"You boys could sleep outside the tent tonight," I said. "You wouldn't hear me so loud."

"Yeah, right. Real funny, Papa." Nick poked the fire and looked all around. "It got dark all of a sudden. How long until the moon comes up?"

I looked up when I heard the screech of a common Nighthawk, a cousin to the Whippoorwill and I watched the bird circle overhead. "There should be moonlight in an hour or so."

A breeze rustled the leaves on the Sycamore tree. I watched the yellow flash of a lightning bug's tail as it slowly winged its way toward the woods. The hoot of an owl echoed off the bluff and from down river came the yodel sounding bark of a coyote.

Jake stood up, looked at Dub and me with a frown as if something was bothering him and said, "I'd like to ask a question."

Dub looked at me and raised his eyebrows. I figured without a doubt we were thinking the same thing. It was only a matter of time before one of the boys would want to know what happened between us and why we were estranged for so many years. To my surprise said, "What's a premonition?"

Dub nervously laughed. It was obvious that he was taken by surprise as much as me.

"Good Lord, Jake. Why have you been thinking about a premonition?" I asked.

"Because when you told us about why you and Uncle Dub came here to look for Doc Barnes. You said your mother had a premonition that you shouldn't go. Is it like a promise or something?"

"No, it's where you get a feeling something's going to happen, before it actually does. In the case of our mother, she had lots of premonitions about things before they happened and she was usually right."

Nick threw a piece of driftwood on the fire and we watched the sparks.

"Doc Barnes said our mother was the best at predicting the future of anyone he ever saw. She'd get a 'gut-level' feeling before something happened, like an accident or a death was about to occur.

We all knew to leave her alone when she got a certain look in her eye until she was ready to talk," Dub said.

"She'd drum the tips of her finger on the table and get a distant look in her eyes," I said.

Jake sat down beside me on the log, locked his arm inside of mine and laid his head on my shoulder.

"So is a premonition like magic?" Nick asked.

"Some people think so. Some think it has to do with religion. Some think it's Witchcraft."

There was a long silence and everyone stared at the dancing red and yellow flames.

"Jug o' rum, jug o' rum."

"You boys didn't get all the Bullfrogs," I said when I heard one bellowing back in the slough.

"Need to leave some for seed," Dub said with a smile.

There was a loud crash in the woods toward the mouth of the cave and something squealed. Dub grabbed the rifle and jumped up off the log. Whatever it was ran away through the bushes.

"What was that?" Jake asked wide-eyed. When nobody answered he said, "What do you think it was, Uncle Dub? It sounded like something got hurt."

"Probably a wild hog," Dub said. "Nothing to worry about, they squeal a lot."

"When you were boys what did you and Uncle Dub do for fun?" Nick asked.

"We hunted and fished a lot. Pretty much lived on wild game and fish we caught out of the river. We worked as well, helping out with the chores. Milked cows, slopped hogs and put up hay. What else did we do, Dub?"

"One of us gathered eggs every day and fed the chickens," Dub said. "Since Uncle Ira owned the pool hall, he let us play free. So we shot pool about every day and got really good at it. We also explored a lot of caves."

"Each year in the fall, I helped Grandpa Tom butcher a hog," I said. "He passed away before Dub was old enough to help with that chore. I'm going to visit his old river cabin before we leave town."

The image of my grandfather sitting in front of the fireplace had been on my mind ever since we arrived in Lewiston and drove across the bridge he helped build. I could feel the presence of his spirit all around me. It would be spooky walking into a room where hides and stuffed animal heads had covered the cabin walls.

"How did you see after dark with no electricity?" Jake asked.

"We used candles and kerosene lamps," Dub said.

"What else did you do?" Nick asked.

Dub scratched his head for a few seconds. "Played cards and told stories. Sang songs and made music. On Saturday night we usually had a dance at the schoolhouse or in somebody's barn."

Jake giggled. "In somebody's barn with the animals? What about the poop?"

"We moved the animals out before the dance started. It was our job to clean up after them before the dance."

"What about when you had to go to the bathroom at night?" Nick asked. "Was it scary and cold in the winter?"

"It was scary sometimes, but we were used to it. Winter was bad all right, but summer was worse, ask your Papa." Dub looked at me and grinned.

"What's Uncle Dub talking about?" Jake asked.

I looked at Dub and went on to tell about how much courage it took to tromp off after dark to use the outhouse. How you walked as fast as possible to get there and do your business, then hurried back to the house.

"How big is an outhouse?" Jake asked. "I've never seen one."

"There're about the size of a small car turned up on end. You'll get to go inside one when we visit the old farm place."

"How come Uncle Dub said it was more scary in the summer, Papa?" Jake wanted to know.

"It had to do with spiders. Once you got inside the little white building with the rusted tin roof and the heavy wooden door slammed shut, spiders would scamper across their webs and hide in the corners. So you were in a hot little building with spiders all around and there were no light."

"Will there be spiders in the outhouse at the farm?" Jake asked. "If there are I don't want to go."

"Yep, they'll be divided up in two different bunches. The up-top spiders—the ones you can see. Those are not so scary as the down-in-the-odorous-hole spiders. Many an outhouse was accidentally set on fire because of those."

"That's weird," Nick said. "How come it happened?"

"Because back then sometimes people used catalogs for toilet paper. They'd rip out some pages and set them on fire. Then stick the flaming paper down inside the hole to scare the spiders away. It was a trick I used myself when I was a kid."

Nick frowned. "You ever set an outhouse on fire?"

"I did once. But there was not much damage."

Dub busted out with a belly laugh. "The damage was more to the butt-naked boy that ran from the outhouse. Everyone in the family was standing in the front yard when the door flew open. Smoke boiled out behind as Tommy ran outside with his pants down around his ankles. He smashed a ripe red tomato with his hand when he tripped and fell in the garden. He screamed when he looked down because he thought it was blood.

After Jake and Nick stopped laughing, I went on to tell how, even though I had been warned not to, I set fire to a page from the catalog and stuck it down in the hole. I claimed I had to do it in self-defense.

Dub looked at me with a smirk on his face. "Was you gonna tell the boys about the rifle shell?"

"What rifle shell?" Jake asked.

"I guess I got no choice but to tell now that you've brought it up. One day when I was about Jake's age. In my constant battle with the outhouse spiders, I came up with a plan to blow them up. I took a .22 rifle shell out of Dad's hunting coat and picked up a match from the kitchen. I went to the outhouse, laid the shell on the edge of the seat close to the hole and struck the match. When I held the flame under the brass casing, the shell exploded.

"You could have put your eyes out," Nick said.

"That's what Tommy thought had happened to him, he'd been blinded by the explosion. Go on, tell 'em what happened next," Dub said.

"When the shell blew up, a piece of brass casing went half way through my thumb. When I looked down and saw the blood oozing out around it, I fainted. My final thought was that part of the casing hit my eyes and I was blind."

Dub chuckled, but the boys seemed too concerned with the outcome to think it was funny.

"Did you kill any spiders when the shell blew up?" Jake asked.

I groaned. "Not enough that I'd try it again."

"How did you get the shell casing out of your thumb?" Nick asked.

"Dad pulled it out with hog-nosed pliers," I said, remembering that Dub got a little pale watching the operation that day as well.

Dub walked over and gave a pat on the back. "I was afraid to go back inside the outhouse for a long time," he said.

"How come?" Jake asked.

"All your Papa did was make the spiders mad."

"Interesting how something that was so scary at the time is funny when you look back on it," I said.

Nick stood up and stared at the slough. "I wonder if the snake attack will ever be funny," he said.

Chapter Fourteen

I looked over my shoulder and saw Jake watching the neon flash as a lightning bug slowly worked its way across the gravel bar toward the woods.

"If I knew the snake was dead, I'd swing off on the rope again tomorrow," Nick said.

"Don't worry, Nick. I'll stand by with the rifle," Dub said.

"Yeah, but what if you missed this time?" Jake said.

Dub looked at me and grinned. "I hardly ever miss."

"Now that's funny, Uncle Dub," Nick said.

"Whatever we do, I'd like to head for town by mid-morning. I have many places to visit before we start back to Kansas City. For sure I need time to play Dub a few games of pool. I used to beat him on a regular basis."

Dub looked at me and smiled. "We'll see about that big brother."

Everyone looked up when I pointed at the moon rising over the top of the bluff. I thought about the mysterious old man Dub and I saw last time we camped here. It would be even weirder than finding the leg bone if he came back again.

"You boys have been on the move all day. I bet you're plumb tuckered out," Dub said. "I'm going to turn in early myself."

"What time is it?" Jake asked. "I don't feel a bit sleepy."

Dub pulled a watch attached to a gold chain from the pocket of his bib overalls. "Nine o'clock on the nose."

The watch was another thing Dub and I got into an argument about during the years we were feuding. Like Grandpa Tom's .30-.30

rifle, Dub had put it to good use. I would have stuck it away in a drawer.

"Ever had to fix the watch?" I asked.

Dub snapped the face cover shut and slipped it back in his pocket. "Only once in fifty years."

"Those old railroad watches are tough." I remembered when I was a little kid watching Grandpa turn the stem on the top back and forth to wind the timing mechanism.

"Grandpa Tom got it when he worked on the railroad," Dub said.

"That must have been a long time ago?" Nick said.

I thought for a few seconds to remember the date and said, "It was sometime back in the mid-1800s."

"People have used watches from the time railroad travel began. As soon as there were two trains moving in opposite directions on a single-track line, there arose the need for a watch. Train movements were described in terms of scheduled times and by how far off of scheduled time a train was."

"Wow, Uncle Dub. You know a lot about railroad watches," Nick said. "I've got a model train, but I never heard any of that stuff."

"Tell you what, boys. I have a dozen old timepieces at the house. I'll give you each one when we get back. This one I got here is the only one I ever carry."

"Oh, neat," Nick said. "I promise I'll take good care of it." He looked at me and I nodded my head.

"Yeah, me too," Jake said. "I won't let my sisters touch it."

Once again Dub had endeared himself to the boys, giving them something else to look forward to when we got back to town. I changed the subject from railroad watches to music. Maybe it would be good for everyone if Dub played a few songs.

"You still play a fiddle and the banjo?" I asked.

"Play every Saturday night. Get together with some of the boys at church, or the VFW hall. Got a good group. We even made a recording. Sold enough to replace the old songbooks and buy a couple of things the church needed. I'll give you a CD when we get back to the house."

"I'll be glad to buy one to help the church. You played good even as a kid. Don't guess you brought an instrument along to the river?"

"You're in luck tonight, fellas. Just happen to have my banjo and fiddle in the pickup truck."

"What kind of music do you play, Uncle Dub?" Nick asked.

"Don't know it's anything you listened too much. We mostly play gospel at the church and bluegrass at the VFW hall. Lots of folks like to square dance, too."

"What kind of music is bluegrass?" Nick asked. "Probably nothing like rap, I guess?"

"Well, like rap, lots of our songs do tell a story. Bluegrass is old time music that folks in the country like to hear. Songs that conjure up an image of a simpler time. Back when a tune and a good tale was all it took for people to be entertained and happy."

Dub stood up and headed for the pickup truck to get his fiddle and banjo.

"You boys are in for a treat getting to hear your Uncle Dub play," I said as I picked up a log and tossed it on the campfire.

"I thought preachers only liked church music," Jake said.

I watched Dub as he walked down the gravel bar toward his pickup truck and disappear into the shadows. "Where did you hear such a thing, Jake?" I asked.

"My friend, Bobby told me. His Mom said that all other music comes from the devil."

"That's bull," Nick said.

Jake tossed his hands in the air. "That's what he said. That's all I know."

I started to tell Jake not to say anything about it to Dub. Then I figured him being a preacher he was confronted with all kinds of questions and dysfunctional problems. It would be interesting to see how he handled such an inquiry from a kid. I might get an idea of what he was going to talk about on Sunday when I was trapped inside the church.

"Tell you what, Jake. When Dub comes back you can ask him."

Nick looked at me through the lapping yellow flames of the campfire and scratched his head. "You think that's a good idea, Papa?"

"Dub's a man of the cloth. He deals with all kinds of questions and sorry sinner stuff. I'm sure he's real good at it by now."

The way the boys looked at me, I figured I might have come on a little strong. The talk about the devil prompted me to stand up and look across the river at the ridge where I saw the old man in a circle of light. I looked around quickly when I heard a big splash. When Jake snickered I realized that Nick had thrown a rock in the water.

"Don't be trying to scare me, boys. I know some tricks to scare people that can leave 'em shaking." I walked over to the edge of the water and watched the silver ripples that were created by the rock as they shimmered along working their way to the bank.

"Ready to get your feet tapping?" Dub asked as he walked back into camp with his fiddle in one hand and a banjo slung over his shoulder. He reminded me of a picture I saw of a hobo standing beside the boxcar of a train with his travelling instruments.

When Dub sat down on the log beside me, I said, "Don't mean to put you on the spot, but Jake has a question you can answer."

"Okay, Jake. I'll do the best."

"My friend Bobby said his mother told him music was from the Devil, unless it was church music."

Dub lowered his head and looked up at me through bushy white eyebrows. "Don't know about all music! I do know a good country tune goes a long ways to pickin' up folk's spirits. One time on Saturday Night Live, somebody asked Father Guido Sarducci, the actor, if Rock and Roll was the work of the devil. He said he didn't think so because there was no music in hell. Personally, I can't give the devil any of the credit for the talent of gospel, blues or bluegrass music. I do figure he probably hangs around to listen. Without any tunes in hell, he's got to be a lonesome fella."

I looked at Jake and he smiled. I gave Dub a pat on the shoulder and said, "That sounds good enough for me." I would never have thought about Dub being a Saturday Night Live fan.

Without another word, Dub put the base of the fiddle up under his chin, ripped the bow across the strings and began to play a hot fiddle tune called "The Devil Went Down To Georgia." He sang the words in the first verse.

"Fire on the mountain, run boys run
Devil's in the house of the rising sun.
Chickens in the bread pan, pickin' out dough.
Granny does your dog bite? No, child, no."

The boys clapped their hands and tapped their feet. They made up their own words as they sang along. A spray of gravel flew in the air when they danced and swung one another around and around until they fell down. We laughed and hollered so loud a body could have heard us a mile away up and down the river.

Dub switched off between the fiddle and the banjo, he played one tune after another. Many of the songs I remembered from when I was a kid. "The Wabash Cannonball," "Arkansas Traveller," "Cripple Creek," "Old Time Religion" and Lordy, he even picked out the song from the movie *Deliverance*, "Duelling Banjos." Of all things, he somehow played both parts all by himself. To finish off the musical display, he pulled a harmonica out of his pocket and the sweet sound of "Amazing Grace" floated through the air so softly it seemed like the notes were riding on the wings of an angel. I stood up and walked away from the campfire so the boys would not see my face. Nostalgia had slipped in and taken my breath away.

Dub was plumb tuckered out after playing so many songs. When he stood up in the firelight I saw the front of his shirt was wet with sweat.

The boys and I clapped loudly after his wonderful performance. He laughed and took a long deep bow. There seemed to be a letdown after all the upbeat excitement, which was probably more due to exhaustion than anything.

"We should all sleep good tonight," Dub said. "Don't you think, boys?"

Jake and Nick nodded their heads. "You know what, Uncle Dub?" Nick said. "I never danced that much to rap music."

"Glad you enjoyed it. All that playin' has tuckered me out. I'm ready to turn in for the night."

"Would you tell us one story before we go to bed, Uncle Dub." Jake said. "It doesn't have to be a long one."

Dub looked up at the moon while he thought over Jake's request.

"Or, you could tell one, Papa," Nick said. "You're a good story teller."

"Thanks, Nick. Let's see what Dub comes up with first," I said.

"Okay, here's a true story that took place in the Ozark Mountain wilderness. Say something if it gets too scary."

Nick looked at Dub and said, "It might bother Jake. But it won't be too scary for me."

"Yeah right, Nick. You're more afraid than I am. You won't even walk into a dark room by yourself."

Dub cleared his throat. "Okay, here goes. Back in the mid-1800s there was a Catholic priest named Father John Hogan. He led a group of Irish immigrants from St. Louis into the wilderness to escape oppression."

"What does oppression mean?" Jake asked.

"Mainly it's not letting people do what they want to do," I said.

"Sometimes I don't get to do what I want to do," Nick said. "Am I being oppressed?"

Dub and I laughed. "Maybe, but it's for your own good. Go on with the story, Dub."

"So anyway, these poor souls tromped through bug-infested, snaky overgrown woods, up steep rocky hillsides and down into deep hollers, across rivers and spring branches until they were in the middle of the most rugged country in the Ozarks. It was there they stopped and established a settlement which today is part of the National Wilderness Preservation System called the Irish Wilderness."

"How come they went so far into the woods?" Jake asked.

"They wanted to escape from people who had treated them mean. Figured the place was so remote that nobody could find them," Dub said.

"How did they know where they were at without a GPS?" Nick asked.

Dub smiled. "They were guided by the sun and the stars."

"So nobody found them in the wilderness, right Uncle Dub?" Jake said.

"That's what should have happened, but it didn't. The problem was that they arrived shortly before the Civil War broke out. When the war ended, Hogan and the Irish had mysteriously disappeared into thin air. Not even so much as the trace of a little kid's shoe was ever found."

"That's an interesting story," I said. "Seems like in the past hundred and fifty years somebody would have figured out what happened."

"Oh, there's a bunch of theories. I've a couple myself, which some people think are strange. So I don't bring them up very often."

"What would those be?" I asked, thinking it was one of the few times I had seen Dub seem vulnerable about anything.

"One theory is they could have been grabbed up by aliens. The mysterious old man that appeared behind our tent last time that night wasn't a mortal being you know, Tommy." I nodded my head in agreement. "My other theory, which is probably closer to right, is they were killed and eaten."

"Bull, no way they got eaten," Nick, said. "That only happens in the jungle."

"Tell you what, Nick. Many people who roamed the wilderness during the Civil War were mean and vicious as junkyard dogs. They were common criminals and not very bright. You figure they were cold and hungry much of the time and only thought about their own survival."

"I'd have no trouble believing' your theory about the aliens," I said. "Not sure about the cannibalism."

"I don't know that the whole bunch got cooked. Some may have run into the woods. But I don't think they all escaped. Like I said it was hard times back in those days and the bad boys wouldn't stop at doing anything."

Nick gave Dub a sober look and Jake stared at him wide-eyed. "That's a scary story. Somebody could walk into our camp tonight and we'd be cooked by morning."

"You're not scaring me, Nick. They would cook me last because I'm little. I would probably escape," Jake said.

"What mysterious old man are you all talking about?" Nick asked.

"I think there has been enough scary stuff for tonight. I don't want you boys to have bad dreams. We'll talk about the mysterious old man tomorrow."

"Come on, Papa. It can't be any worse story than people being eaten," Nick said.

"That I'm not so sure about. What do you think, Dub?"

"Don't know, I guess it's all right. If you boys promise to stop me before you start shakin' in your boots."

"Go on, Papa," Jake said. "I've never been shaking in my boots before."

"Okay, here goes the last story of the day. What I'm about to tell happened to Dub and me the night before we found the two dead men. Dub got up in the middle of the night to go pee. When he didn't come back, I crawled outside to see what was wrong. There he stood staring at a pulsing bed of coals that were only a few feet behind our tent.

"How did a fire start all on its own?" Jake asked.

"I asked Dub the same question but he didn't know. At the sound of my voice, the Sycamore tree by the spring began to sway back and forth. In the pale white light of the moon, the branches looked like a gathering of ghosts. From the corner of my eye I saw an owl sail across the river. The wind stopped and the sound of the night creatures got dead still. During the eerie silence, a flowering Dogwood tree grew up out of the pulsing coals. Rising up through its branches was a white-headed old man with a long beard. It was the same man that I saw standing on the ridge in a circle of light earlier in that evening."

Jake shivered. "I would have been scared enough to pass out," he said.

"That was another strange thing," Dub said. "We were not scared at all. I just felt numb. Next a cloud moved slowly across the sky and blacked out the light of the moon and it seemed like time stood still. When the moon reappeared, the fire was out and the old man had disappeared."

Nick rubbed the goose bumps on his forearms. "I can believe ghosts probably live in a place as wild as the Ozarks," he said. "I'd never want to camp here alone."

"Me either," Jake said. "Even if old Trouser was along to protect me."

"Wasn't that the name of your dog, Tommy?" Dub said.

"Yep, probably not fifty people in the whole country got a dog named Trouser."

"Both Trousers are in dog heaven now," Jake said. "Mine got backed over by a car."

"I'm sorry," Dub said. "It's a terrible thing to lose your dog."

"What happened after the old man disappeared?" Nick asked.

"When I touched the gravel where the fire had burned so hot we could feel it fifteen feet away, it was cold, like in the dead of winter."

"I'm not going outside the tent tonight," Jake said. "Will you sleep with us, Uncle Dub?"

"You don't want me inside the tent. I snore."

"Papa snores so bad nothing else matters," Nick said.

"I'm ready to turn in," I said. "You can sleep with us if you like, Dub. It's a four-man tent. We've got plenty of room."

"Okay, I might as well. I'll go to the pickup truck and get my sleeping bag."

Jake and Nick jumped up to tag along and the three of them headed up the river. I watched until they disappeared into the darkness. I wondered if Dub might not be afraid to stay in the pickup truck by himself after telling the scary stories.

I walked to the tent and threw back the front flap. I shined the light all around and shook the sleeping bags. The possibility of a wounded cottonmouth moccasin crawling inside bothered me more than I would ever admit.

I slapped the back of my neck and smashed a blood-sucking mosquito as I walked toward to the campfire. I laid a pine branch on top of the coals and the needles crackled and popped as they burst into flame. I thought about Jake saying his dog Trouser was in heaven. My old Trouser was in my bed the cold winter night that Dub was born. So long ago, I thought. So long ago

"I've got the leg bone," Nick yelled as he walked into camp behind Dub and Jake, he was swaying from side to side and hunched over. He grunted loudly like a caveman and smashed the bone into the ground, spraying gravel in the air.

"Good Lord. What are you doing?" I said. "Dub did you give Nick the bone?"

Jake got started laughing so hard that he got off balance and fell down. "Did Nick fool you, Papa?" Jake said when Nick tossed his fake leg, a piece of sun-bleached driftwood into the fire.

I forced a grin and composed myself. "No, not at all. I knew it was a stick all along."

"Anybody care where my spot is in the tent? I'm headed to bed," Dub said as he held up a sack of jerky. "Here's our breakfast. Can't beat deer meat and boiled coffee in the mornin'."

"You can sleep beside me, Uncle Dub. The red bag's mine."

RIVER'S EDGE

"Okay, Jake. I will." Dub opened the cooler lid and tossed in the package of jerky. He walked over to the tent, threw back the flaps and crawled inside.

I nudged Nick on the shoulder. "That was a funny trick with the wooden bone. Did you try to get Dub to give you the real one?"

"How'd you know?"

"That's probably what I would have done."

"I might have asked if I could pick the bone up, that's all. I wasn't going to carry it around."

"What did he say?"

"He asked me if I'd want my leg bone treated like a toy."

"I'm all set. My bag's laid out beside yours, Jake," Dub said as he crawled outside the tent.

"Remember that old canvas tent Dad got from Buzzard Thompson?"

Dub laughed as he walked up close to the fire. "Do I ever. It weighed about forty pounds and smelled like the hair of a wet dog."

"Did it keep out the water?" Nick asked.

"No. It leaked like a sieve," I said. "But it was better than nothing."

"Who would call somebody Buzzard?" Jake asked. "That's the worst name I've ever heard."

"It was the nickname for a guy that looked like a turkey vulture. He was tall and skinny and had a thin red nose." I stopped short of telling the story about how we watched Buzzard drown in the river. The boys had been exposed to enough gore for one day.

"Do you remember Buzzard's brother? Folks called him Razzle Dazzle because he talked so much. His wife's name was Milly. A real nice lady who put up with a world of grief from Razzle D."

"What I remember most is he was drunk a lot. One time when I was little he came to our front door and I hid under the bed. Why'd you bring him up?"

"Because he disappeared one day. People thought Milly might of had something to do with it but nobody cared that he was gone so nothing much was done to find out if she did our not."

"So you think his wife did it?" I asked.

"All I know for sure is after Razzle D. was gone, I saw Milly smile for the first time," Dub said.

"Somebody should write a book about all the stuff that's gone on around here," Nick said.

"That's what you should do, Dub," I said. "You've got all the spooky details."

"I've thought about it and I just might. But for now, I'm going to hit the sack," Dub said. "We'll leave for town mid-morning tomorrow. You boys can swim and use the rope swing before we go if you want too. I'll watch over you with the rifle."

"What about going down river to fish again. Maybe try to catch the big bass," Jake said.

"That would be okay. If we get up early, we'll have plenty of time," I said as I started toward the tent.

We crawled into our sleeping bags, the boys in the middle, Dub and I on the outside by the walls of the tent.

"Did you tie the flaps tight?" Jake asked Dub, since he was the last one inside. "I don't want something to slip in and get us."

"Don't be a scaredy cat," Nick said.

Nick yelled when Jake gave him a kick. "Didn't ask you. I asked Uncle Dub."

I crawled to the front of the tent and pulled on the cords that secured the flaps. "You're safe, Jake. Let's settle down and get some sleep. Nothing can get us with your Uncle Dub and me on guard."

RIVER'S EDGE

Within minutes after everyone had said good night, Jake and Nick were sound asleep. I stared into the darkness as I listened to their slow, deep breathing and thought about the places I would visit in Lewiston. After we dropped of the leg bone, I wanted to go to the schoolhouse, from there to the pool hall and then to the old farmstead. I figured I would visit the cemetery and Grandpa Tom's river cabin by myself on Sunday morning before going to hear Dub preach at the church. I would probably not run into anyone from the old days since most people I knew had either moved away, or were dead. It would be interesting to see what the Sheriff had to say when Nick handed him the leg bone. It could be one of the biggest mysteries to try and solve that any law official in Lewiston had run across in the past fifty years.

My last thought before I fell asleep was about the climb back up the steep hill and that I should to do it alone.

I woke up when a streak of moonlight flashed across my face. I saw the tent flap close when someone crawled outside. Jake groaned when I laid my hand on his shoulder and I heard Nick roll over. I figured Dub must have gone out to pee. When he did not come back after a couple of minutes I crawled outside and stood up beside him. A few feet behind our tent was a pulsing bed of coals.

"How could this happen to us again?" I said. "Maybe it really is a dream this time?"

Dub laid his hand on my shoulder. "No, it's more powerful than a dream."

It was all happening again just like the last time. Out the corner of my eye I saw an owl sail across the river. The wind stopped and the sounds of night creatures were dead still. A flowering Dogwood tree grew up from the bed of coals and the face of the mysterious old man appeared.

At the same time a dark cloud moved across the sky and swallowed up the light of the moon, the fire went out and the old man disappeared. I walked over where the blaze had burned like an inferno. Like the time before, when I reached down and touched the gravel, it was as cold as ice.

Dub walked up beside me. "I take it as a sign from God that our family bonds are back together. Sunday's sermon may be one of my best. It's hard to beat a story about the power of love. I'm going to bed and sleep on it."

After we crawled inside the tent, I reached across my sleeping grandson and shook my brother's hand. With tears in my eyes, I drifted off to sleep, knowing the new day would bring freshly born hope that had eluded me for so many years.

Chapter Fifteen

When I awoke the next morning and crawled outside the tent, Dub was sitting on the big log by the campfire smoking his pipe. We gave each other a nod and a half broken smile.

Still clinging to the remote possibility that the mysterious old man might have been a dream, I asked Dub if he went outside the tent during the night.

He gave me a solemn look and puffed on his pipe. "I did. How about you?"

"Stood right beside you," I said. "Do you have anything to say?"

"Don't right now." Dub picked up the blue and white speckled pot and poured himself some coffee. He set the steaming tin cup down on the log beside him to cool. "I hope to have some kind of an answer before you leave town Sunday."

"That's a bold move on your part. I can hardly wait to see what you have to say. I figured if anybody can solve the mystery, it surely would be you."

"I wonder what the boys will want to do before we head back to town?" Dub said.

"Not sure. The snake's got 'em spooked about swimming. Jake wants to go fish for the big bass again. We'll see what they say when they get up."

I shivered when I thought about how to solve the snake dead or alive dilemma. Somebody would have to swim to the bottom of the hole and recover the slimy body.

"Sounds good." Dub looked up when a cloud blocked out the sun, and shade covered the gravel bar. "Looks like it might rain. Been dry for a long spell."

"Let me ask this about last night. Before when we saw the old man there was a full moon. This time he came the night after a full moon. I wonder why."

"You're mixed up by one day, Tommy. Last night was a full moon. Not the night before."

"There's the easy answer," I said as I wondered what Dub could possibly say on Sunday that would clear up the mystery. "On another subject, I wonder what's in the package I've got in the car?"

"Don't know. It had your name on it. I'm not one to open other people's mail. Yep, come Sunday there may be all sorts of answers."

"I didn't have even one bad dream last night," Jake announced as he crawled out of the tent. "What time is it, Uncle Dub?" he asked.

"Time to eat if you're hungry. We have milk, bread, jelly and deer jerky. Molly will fix a nice lunch when we get to the house." Dub gnawed off a bite of jerky, chewed on it for a while and washed it down with gulp of black coffee.

Nick crawled out of the tent, raised his arms up over his head and let out a yell that echoed off the bluff and faded away down the river.

"You ready to eat?" Dub asked.

Nick yawned again and nodded his head. "Hungry as I can be."

"Okay, all we've got is milk, bread, jelly and deer jerky. That's what was stashed away in the cooler. Everything in the food box was gobbled up by the raccoons. The smart little devils figured out how to open the latch," Dub said.

"I'm having all that stuff," Jake said as he strolled over to the sack and picked up a piece of dried brown meat. "Nick will probably just want bread and jelly."

Dub and I laughed as Jake gnawed off a bite and began to chew the tough meat, making a growling noise like a bear.

Nick walked up to the fire and looked at the coffee pot. Not to be out done by Jake, he said, "I'll have jerky and a cup of black coffee."

Dub poured Nick a cup and handed it to him. "Be careful, it's hot. Don't want to burn your tongue. Here's a piece of jerky."

Nick spilled a little coffee when he set the blue tin cup down on the gravel bar. He gnawed off a piece of the stringy, home-cured deer meat and began to chew and chew.

"Didn't know you drank coffee." I said.

Nick looked at me and continued to chew. "Don't usually, but I am today."

I grinned. "That coffee's strong enough to turn a person's hair white. Look what it did to your Uncle Dub."

"Not mine," Nick said. "I'm tougher than most people."

When Dub handed me a cup of coffee, I slid the lid off the cooler and picked up some ice. I dropped a cube in my cup, one in Jake's and the other in Nick's cup. "No need to get a tongue burn and not be able to savor the flavor." I blew away the rising steam and watched the ice melt. I slurped in a sip and swallowed the thick black liquid. I looked at Dub with a coffee ground or two stuck to my teeth and smiled.

"Nothing like coffee boiled in river water," Dub said. "It's got a kick of its own, like moonshine whiskey."

I looked at Nick and raised my cup. When I slurped in another sup, Nick followed my lead.

"What do you think of it?" I asked after he swallowed and wrinkled up his nose.

Nick sucked in a deep breath of air and exhaled with his cheeks puffed out. "Not sure I'm ready for boiled coffee. You can have the rest of mine, Papa. I'll eat jerky and drink milk."

"Wise decision," I said. "It takes awhile to acquire a taste for river water coffee. Fact is some people never do like it all that much."

"You think I might?" Jake asked.

Nick looked at him and frowned. "Only if you like to drink pond water and chewing on an old shoe."

"What do you want to do before we head back to town?" I asked.

"Catch the big bass." There was no doubt by the excitement in Jake's voice that he was hooked on fishing for smallmouth.

"Fine with me," Nick said. "I'll only swim in the Blue Hole if I see a dead snake body. A snakebite might be as bad as Uncle Dub's coffee."

"Whoa, comparing my coffee to a snakebite is over the line." Everyone laughed as Dub picked up the pot and poured the last of the coffee into his cup. I was still thinking about Nick's quick-witted response.

"The snake's either dead, or holed up sick. He has no energy to chase you boys," I said. "I wouldn't be afraid to swing off on the rope myself."

"Okay, Papa. You do it, I will too," Nick said.

Why not, I thought. I may never be back here again. I walked across the spring branch, climbed up on the ledge and looked down at the water along the base of the bluff. I had hoped to see the cottonmouth turned belly-up laying on top a boulder. I saw nothing but a couple of Sunfish about five feet below the surface, slowly fanning their tails back and forth. I scanned the lilies in the slough, thinking a wounded snake might lay on top of a broad leaf pad to soak up some sun. I saw no living creature but a couple of dragonflies darting back and forth.

RIVER'S EDGE

"Go on, Papa. I want to see you swing off before I head down river to fish," Jake said.

Something caught my eye when I waved at Jake. It was the end of the sign I had torn down which announced hundreds of snakes. There may not have been that many, but there was at least one who did not like us being around.

After Nick used the swing the day before, he stuck the knot into a crack in the bluff so it would be there for the next person to use. I grabbed the rope, took one last look down at the water and jumped off the ledge. I sailed through the air, let loose of the rope, dropped into the water and popped right back up to the top. Never gave a second thought to swimming down to touch the bottom.

When I broke the surface, Jake yelled, "All right, Papa."

I looked at Dub and he smiled. "You did good, Tommy. You've not lost your nerve."

"I'm ready to catch a big fish." Jake picked up his rod and reel and walked to the river's edge, ready to wade across the riffle and head down river.

I turned over and floated on my back. I watched a yellow butterfly flutter by as it headed up the river. It had been a long time since I felt so relaxed and happy to be alive. The tranquility of the moment made it seem like I was moving in slow motion.

"Are you ready to go, Papa?" Jake asked, obviously anxious to start down river.

"Okay. Grab the bucket, Nick. See if the minnows are still alive. If not, we can seine a few real quick."

Nick walked over and grabbed the rope that was tied to the minnow bucket. He flipped open the lid and looked inside. "Only a couple of dead ones. Most are still alive."

"Are you going, Uncle Dub?" Jake asked. "I'd like to see you catch a big bass too."

"Sure, I'll go. Like you, I've hooked some nice sized Smallmouth in that chute. I landed one that would weigh five pounds."

"Maybe this will be the day," Jake said. "Come on guys, let's go."

"I'd rather stay here," Nick said. "Will you stay with me, Papa? We'll swing off the ledge. Maybe go look for a blind fish again."

"That okay with you, Jake? Your Uncle Dub is a better fisherman than me anyway."

Jake frowned, not sure if he liked the idea. I figured he wanted everyone gathered around if he hooked into another big bass. "Okay, I guess so," he said. "If I catch a really big one, you'll be sorry you didn't come along."

"Take the camera, Dub. Hold the fish out in front of you arm's length, it will look even bigger."

Dub grabbed the camera out of my backpack and snapped a picture of Nick and me with the Blue Hole in the background. He and Jake waded across the riffle and headed down river to stalk a record Smallmouth bass.

"What do you want to do first?" I asked as I swam to the bank and walked out onto the gravel bar.

Nick looked at the rock ledge sixty feet above the water, then over at the rope swing. Next his eyes followed the spring branch toward the cave. "I might want to jump into the water later. Right now I'd rather look for blind fish."

What a strange choice, I thought. He knew the odds of seeing a blindfish were about the same as Jake catching a record-breaking Smallmouth bass. It had to be a fear of the snake still being alive that kept him from going into the water.

"That's okay by me," I said and we walked up the spring branch. "Whoa," I yelled when I slipped on a moss-covered rock and almost fell down. I was preoccupied and not paying attention. From the time we started the trip, I wondered if I should talk to Nick about sensitive subjects. Things like, girls and safe sex might be a place to start. Even though he probably already knew as much as me from health class in school, but maybe not. The thing was, I might never have a better chance to get his undivided attention. Drugs were always worth discussion. I could ask him if any of his friends smoked cigarettes to get things started, that way it would not seem like I was asking him about it personally.

"Be careful, Papa. You're too big for me to drag back to camp."

"Have you had much to do with girls?" I blurted out.

Nick looked at me funny as if he suddenly had a crick in his neck. Then we climbed on up to the top of the boulder that overlooked the pool of water at the mouth of the cave. From that vantage point we could see a blind fish if there was any around. Nick looked at me and grinned. "Don't worry, I know about girls and sex. Unless you can tell me why they act so weird sometimes. Like saying they want to do one thing, then do something else. They get mad easy too. It's hard to know what they want a lot of the time."

"Sorry, I don't have the answer to why girls act the way they do. If you ever find out, please let me know," I said.

Nick must have read my mind about what the next question might be. "None of the dudes I run with think it's cool to do drugs either."

"Glad to hear it, Nick. Really glad."

We stared as the surface of the water as droplets of water fell from the roof of the cave. "Plot, plot, plot" was the sound.

I pointed at the mat of green ferns hanging down from the side of the bluff. "Ferns are one of the oldest plants on earth," I said. "They've been around over two hundred million years."

"Yeah, I saw something about it on the Internet. They called ferns the ancient plants," Nick said as he stared at the pool of water. "This river is the nicest place I've ever been. The trees are all different colors of green and there's no loud noise."

I was surprised to hear such a comment from a kid who listened to loud rap music and played video games. Nick had hit on a subject that upset me a lot, loud noise.

"There's no reason for loud noise," I said. "I hate the shriek of leaf blowers. Car alarms set off by accident caused dogs to howl and bark. Cell phones ringing everywhere and people talking all day about what absolutely nothing of hardly any value."

"I saw on TV where more people go deaf all the time," Nick said. "It would be awful not to hear."

I looked behind me when I heard something rustle the leaves and saw a Fox Squirrel leap from one branch to another in a hickory nut tree.

"How'd you like the deer jerky and coffee breakfast?" I asked.

"The jerky was fine. But it will be awhile before I drink any more river water coffee," Nick said.

I smiled. "You're probably better off. I've gulped down enough coffee to float a house. Some people think it's bad for you. I can't tell it's hurt me none. Do I seem jittery?"

"You seem okay, except you wiggle your nose sometimes." Nick laughed.

"Yeah, right," I said.

"It'd be wild if Jake caught a bass that broke a record. He'd never stop telling the story. Would he, Papa?"

"Probably not. Jake's a good fisherman, he's got a knack for catching 'em."

Nick looked up at the top of the bluff and pointed at the buzzards sitting in a dead tree. "You think they're hanging around because of the leg bone?"

"I doubt it, they eat meat, not bones."

"Do you really think the leg bone belongs to the killer?"

"I don't know. We'll see what the Sheriff finds out. It would be double spooky if it was."

Once again Nick talked about a DNA test. I said I had no idea if it would work on something fifty years old. He told me someone on TV said age did not matter. To avoid getting into a conversation with a twelve-year-old who knew considerably more about DNA than me, I changed the subject.

"Did I ever tell you about the time I got lost in the woods?"

Nick hesitated for a few seconds. "No. What happened?" he said.

"We were squirrel hunting and I wandered off, you've got to stay with the pack is what I learned from this experience. I got turned around and went in the wrong direction."

"How long were you lost? How did you find your way out?"

"I was lost most of one day and all that night. The next morning, Dad, Uncle Ira, and Trouser, my hound, found me asleep under a tree."

I had not thought about the frightening experience for years, but it came back to me as clear as day. Especially the part about when the darkness closed in and the night creatures roamed the woods.

"What did you think about when you were lost?" Nick asked.

I grunted. "You mean after I stopped crying and feeling sorry for myself? What helped me most was thinking about other bad situations that I had survived in the past. Like snakebite, almost drowning in the river, twice. Being bucked off a horse and having my head stepped on by a cow."

"How did that help?" Nick asked.

"It helped me stay calm so I could think better. When you have bad trouble, no matter what it is, don't let your imagination run away with you. If you can do that, you can survive better. Remember that nothing is over until it's over and don't worry about things that may never come to pass."

Nick nodded his head up and down slowly and actually seemed to be considering my advice.

I picked a tick off the calf of my leg and flipped it into the river to give it a ride downstream. "Check yourself good for ticks before you go to bed tonight," I said. "Just found one on my leg."

Nick pointed at the water close to the edge of the bluff. "What's that swimming back in the shadows, right there where the fern's hanging down almost into the water?"

"It might be a blind fish," I said. "The eyes look funny. Nobody will believe us if it really is one."

When Nick moved his foot, a pebble fell into the water and the fish darted back into the darkness.

"That's the way the blindfish looked I saw on a TV," Nick said. "Skin covered the eyes to protect them from sharp rocks."

I looked at him and grinned. "Thought you didn't think there were any blind fish?"

"The blind fish I saw on TV were in another country. I didn't think there would be any here. Since blind fish live in the darkness, I wonder why that one was out swimming around?"

"Good question," I said. "I don't know why. The fish's eyes were covered with something. I know that for a fact." We stared at the water and waited for another ten minutes, hoping the fish would reappear. "I doubt if it will come back out again, I scared it off when I moved my arm," Nick said.

RIVER'S EDGE

I gave Nick a pat on the back. "You're probably right. I'm going back to camp and pack some things. We can take another look before we head to Lewiston."

"Okay. I'll break the tent down. I might swing on the rope once more, if you think it's safe."

"I think the snake's dead. He was twisting and turning after Dub shot him. That means a serious hit to the body. If you get bit, I've got a sharp knife to cut you open with so I can suck out the poison." Even though I knew the technique did not actually work, it was a common technique used by many old timers.

"Maybe we just thought the fish was blind," Nick said.

"Maybe, but I'm sticking' with my story."

We climbed down off the boulder and walked along the spring branch where towering cottonwood trees formed a dark canopy of shade. We splashed along the edge of the clear rushing water where small brown snails clung to moss-covered rocks and sliver minnows darted in front of us. "Okay, I'm going off on the rope swing again," Nick said when we reached camp and without hesitation he walked across the spring branch and climbed up on the ledge.

"I'll toss you the rope," I said as I dived in and shot back up to the surface. I grabbed the end of the rope and flipped it through the air into Nick's out- stretched hand. "Nice catch. Let me get out of your way."

Nick stood on his toes to get a better look as he stared down into the water. "What's that down under you, Papa?" he asked.

When I kicked my foot, I felt something slimy wrap its self around my ankle. If it was the snake and it still had an ounce of life left in its body, it would bite me for sure. I screamed and swam for shore as fast as I could churn the water. Panting, I dragged myself onto the bank and looked down. Hanging on my foot was the green, slimy skin of a Bullfrog I had cleaned the day before.

The sound of Nick's laughter cracked the still morning air. "I guess the turtles didn't eat that one like you said they would right, Papa."

I rolled over on my back and took a deep breath. Glad Dub was not there to hear me scream and see my reaction when I thought I was about to get snake bit, again.

Nick pushed off the ledge and sailed out over the water. He turned a flip in the air and dropped down in headfirst. He shot back up to the top quickly, swam over to the bank and sat down beside me. "I've had a real good time, Papa. Let's do this every year."

I laid my hand on his forearm and smiled. Nobody had ever said anything to me that I appreciated more. "Don't see any reason why not. I'm sure Dub would like to camp with us again."

"Think you might move back here someday?" Nick asked.

"I wouldn't mind. Don't know if Lucy would do it though. I'll see what she has to say. Would you and Jake stay with us some of the time if we did?"

"Heck, yes. I'd come here for the whole summer."

"Hey, you guys. I caught the big one," Jake yelled from down river as he and Dub walked toward us. "Maybe the biggest bass in the river."

"Bull," Nick yelled.

Dub verified Jake's story as they splashed across the ripple. "Jake caught the biggest bass I've seen in years. Maybe forever. I swear, Tommy. The fish would have weighed at least five pounds."

"Where is it?" Nick asked.

"Jake wanted to let it go, but we got a picture. It measured twenty-three inches, a fat golden brown beauty."

"Congratulations, Jake," I said. "You've caught the two biggest Smallmouth bass on the trip."

"For sure he has," Dub said as he patted Jake on the back. "The fish jumped four or five times. Jake handled him like a pro."

"We saw a blind fish in the pool at the cave." Nick sounded glad that he had something to combat Jake's fish story.

"Bull," Jake said. "Did you catch it? Where is it?"

"Did you see a blind fish, Tommy?" Dud asked.

"Looked like one to me. It was swimming along the edge of bluff, back in the shadows. Its eyes seemed grown over with skin."

"You want to try and catch it, Jake?" Nick said.

"Sure, I've already caught the biggest bass in the river. Might as well catch a blind fish, too."

"What should we use for bait, Uncle Dub?" Nick asked. "It's not very big."

"A Crawdad tail should work good as anything. Peel the shell and use the white meat."

Nick and Jake waded out into the water and Nick scooped up a Crawdad that backed out from under the first rock he turned over. "I've got one," he yelled. "Blind fish, here we come."

Nick peeled the hard orange shell off the tail and threaded the white meat onto a small silver hook. "I'd sneak up real careful and flip the bait as close to the bluff as you can. Let it drift down into the shadows. It will be something special if you catch one."

"We'll have it mounted," I said. "Plus you'll get your picture in the newspaper."

Dub and I watched as Nick and Jake walked up the spring branch on a mission that only a few boys would ever experience. The odds were against them catching a blindfish, but stranger things had happened.

Chapter Sixteen

Dub lowered his head and looked up at me through bushy white eyebrows. "Good boys, those two," he said. "You should of seen Jake fight the bass. He was calm as a cucumber."

"They say twenty percent of the fishermen catch ninety percent of the fish. It's the power of positive thinking more than casting technique that counts. How many pictures did you take?"

"Half dozen, I guess. Got one shot when the fish jumped and then tail-walked across the water. It was a beautiful sight." Dub held his hands apart and showed the size of the bass to be a couple feet long. "A nice memory for Jake," Dub said. "Nice one indeed."

Dub and I looked around when we heard a splash in the slough. We stared at the lily pads as they waved up and down on the surface of the water.

"Amazing what one snake can do," I said. "Look what happened to Adam and Eve."

"You got that right," Dub said. "I thought we'd pack up and head to town after the boys come back. Got lots of places to visit. First we'll drop the leg bone off at the Sheriff's office. Nick will probably fill him in on all he knows about DNA."

"Sounds good. I'm anxious to see how you fixed up the schoolhouse. I'm also curious about the package you sent me that's in the car." I started to say something about the ashes in the trunk, but decided it was not a good idea since that was the cause of our most bitter disagreement.

RIVER'S EDGE

Dub laid his hand on my shoulder. "We've got plenty of time to see and do everything. It's been real nice camping with you and the boys." I my head in agreement.

We walked to the mouth of the spring branch and watched the boys climb up on top of the big boulder to try their luck at catching a blindfish. Nick cast his bait and held the rod and reel out in front of him as he looked down into the water. Within seconds after Jake squatted down beside him, he let out a scream and grabbed Nick by the leg. After much flailing the air with their arms as they tried to regain their balance, both boys fell into the cold spring water. By the time Dub and I ran up the branch and climbed up the boulder, Nick and Dub had dragged themselves out onto the bank.

"Are you okay?" I asked. "What happened?"

"A spider crawled over my foot," Jake said.

"He grabbed my leg, I got off balance and we fell in," Nick said.

"We saw you," Dub said. "You probably scared the blind fish back to the center of the earth." The boys agreed and we all headed down the spring branch toward camp.

"Sorry I lost your rod and reel, Uncle Dub," Nick said, "I'll get you another one."

"No problem, I've got lots of rod and reels. That was an old one anyway."

"You boys want to go off on the rope swing one last time?" I asked.

"I don't," Jake said without hesitation. "I'm too cold to get back in the water."

"I don't either," Nick said as he looked at me and snickered. "I'm afraid I might get a frog hide wrapped around my foot."

"That's real funny, Nick," I said as he walked over to the tent and started to break it down.

"A frog hide. What's that all about?" Dub asked.

"Oh, he's making fun of me. When I was swimming before you and Jake got back to camp. A hide from one of the frogs we cleaned yesterday got wrapped around my foot. I thought it was the snake."

"Thought I heard someone scream," Dub said and everyone but me laughed. "Wish I could have seen it."

The boys attacked the campsite like a couple of machines. After Nick broke down the tent, he grabbed a trash bag and picked up every little thing, including the .22 cartridge that Dub ejected from the rifle after he shot the snake. Nick started to put it in the black plastic bag, then stuck it his pocket instead. Jake rolled up the sleeping bags. Dub packed the cooking gear while I dumped the minnow bucket and set the shiners free in the river. I scooped up some water and poured it on the fire. Dub cut the lures off of the fishing rods and put them in the tackle box. As the final outdoor activity before we headed back to civilization, Dub let each of the boys shoot the .22 rifle a half-dozen times each at a piece of driftwood floating down the river.

I looked around the campsite, up toward the mouth of the cave and across the Blue Hole at the slough where a yellow dragonfly darted from one green lily pad to another. The screech of a red tailed hawk caught my attention and I watched the graceful brown and white bird circle high above me in the cloudless blue sky. Sitting in a big dead tree on top of the towering bluff was a flock of buzzards, watching, waiting and wondering about their next meal. I stared at the high ledge where Nick had jumped off and remembered the many times I had climbed up there when I was a boy. I looked at the rope swing expecting it to move back and forth, but it remained motionless. I thought maybe the appearance of the old man during the night had broken the spell and there would be no more spirits, but deep inside I doubted if they would ever leave us alone.

"How many times did we camp here with Dad and Uncle Ira when we were kids?" I asked Dub as we started toward the Jeep with our gear.

He reached up and brushed away a spider web hanging from the limb of a Pawpaw tree as it drifted across his path. "I'd say fifty or more. We always camped here when we floated the river. That was six or eight times every summer."

"Old Trouser sure loved it here," I said. "Remember how he'd get up on the low ledge and bark when we'd swing out and drop into the water? Sometimes he'd jump in behind us. He was a tough old dog."

"Had a great nose, he could track like nobody's business," Dub said.

"Sounds like a really smart dog too," Jake said.

"He was almost smart enough to talk," Dub said as we reached the Jeep and laid our gear down on the ground. "I was convinced if he could just get out one word, he'd be able to carry on an entire conversation."

"Funny you said that, I used to think the same thing."

Dub laughed.

"Is it okay if we ride up the hill with Uncle Dub?" Jake asked and Nick agreed that sounded like a good idea.

"Sure," I said, as I looked at the boys and smiled. I did not blame them after the experience we had coming down and I was actually relieved not to have the responsibility. We loaded the vehicles; I took the lead and drove down the river road until we reached the bottom of the steep incline.

"Man you're loud with no muffler," Dub yelled as he pulled up beside me and motioned for me to head up first. I nodded, shifted into low gear and started the climb up the steep incline. The foul smell of exhaust fumes made me cough and burned my eyes. I gripped the steering wheel tight when the knobby tires kicked up a spray of gravel. I looked in the rear view mirror but did not see Dub behind me. I figured he was too smart to start up until I had reached the top, or until I rolled back to the bottom. I breathed a sigh of relief when I turned the corner and saw the crest of the hill fifty feet away. I was wet with sweat when I pulled to a stop on level ground.

"Shut it off for a minute," Dub yelled as he pulled up beside the boys and waved. I turned off the ignition. "Are you about suffocated from exhaust fumes?"

"It's bad, but I can make it back to town," I said. "Sorry I knocked off your muffler."

"No problem. I'm always knocking' something off on these rough roads. Molly will have lunch ready for us when we get to the house. Afterwards we can make the rounds. We'll take the bone to the Sheriff first, that will make his day."

"I'll follow you. No reason you guys should eat anymore of my fumes."

As Dub and the boys headed for home, I drove behind them in a cloud of dust for about five miles. I stopped for a few seconds when we reached the road that led to Grandpa Tom's river cabin. That would be my last place to visit on Sunday morning before I heard Dub deliver his sermon and we drove back to Kansas City. It would be good to dump the ashes. I should have done it years ago.

Molly waved at us from the porch when we pulled up in front of the house. She came down the steps and walked briskly across the yard, her curly brown hair blowing in the wind.

"I've got lunch ready for you campers," she said. "Did you have a good time?"

"Couldn't have been better," I said as I got out of the Jeep. "Could it boys?"

"I could live on the river," Nick said. "If I could get rid of the snakes."

Jake threw his hands up in the air. "It's the coolest place I've ever been. I caught a big bass and a really big bass."

"What about you guys?" Molly said as she looked at Dub and me.

"Just like the good old days," I said as we walked toward the house. "Only now, Dub's a better cook."

"Wow, after what we've eaten, this looks really good," Jake said when everyone sat down at the kitchen table for lunch. There were sliced tomatoes and corn on the cob from the garden. Smoke house ham, potato salad, and wheat bread fresh out of the oven and for desert, homemade ice cream and strawberries.

"You shouldn't have done that," I said as I looked at the ice cream freezer sitting by the kitchen cabinet.

"No bother at all since it's electric. Not like the old hand cranked freezer that wore out your arm. I'm glad everyone had a good time. So, what did you boys do on the river?" Molly asked. "Did you see any snakes?"

The boys told about Dub shooting the cottonmouth moccasin and how he may have saved their lives. Next came the story of the leg bone. Jake talked about the big Smallmouth bass he caught and the eel we ate for breakfast. Nick told about the blind fish and how we fell into the pool of cold water. He spent considerable time telling how he and I went inside Leatherwood Cave to the place where Dub and I found the dead man. Jumping off the high ledge and the rope swing got a share of attention. Of course, Nick telling about me screaming when the frog skin got tangled around my foot got the biggest laugh.

"Did you catch any frogs to eat?" Molly asked. "I know Dub usually likes to fry up a mess when he's camped out."

"Oh yeah, I forgot," Jake said. "Uncle Dub and I got three frogs and Nick shot a squirrel."

"Interesting mixture of wild game y'all ate on the trip," Molly said. "Bet your friends will find it hard to believe."

"Yeah, probably," Nick said. "The wildest food any of my friends will probably ever eat is shrimp at Red Lobster. "Jake finished up the story of our adventure saying how it bothered him that the buzzards watched us the entire time we were on the river.

The only significant thing not mentioned was the runaway Jeep ride down the steep hill. I could only hope the frightening experience would never raise its ugly head again, certainly not in the presence of the boys' mother.

"I figure the boys are up for about anything after their river experience," Dub said as he looked at me and grinned. "If everyone's ready, we'll drop off the leg bone and get started on our rounds. We'll check out the old homestead first, we'll go from there to the schoolhouse and swing back by the pool hall. The last stop will be the cemetery."

"Have they still got those little bottles of Grapette soda?" I asked, remembering the first time I reached inside the pop cooler and pulled one out when I was a kid. When I swallowed the sweet, cold grape flavored liquid I thought I had gone to soda drinker's heaven.

"Still got 'em," Dub said. "Remember how your tongue turned purple and when you stuck it out, everyone laughed?"

"I want a purple tongue too," Jake said.

Nick laughed. "You've already got a purple brain."

"If you're trying to be funny, Nick. You're not," Jake said.

"What about Grandpa Tom's river cabin?" Dub asked.

"Thought I'd visit the cabin by myself Sunday morning before church." Dub looked at me and nodded his head.

RIVER'S EDGE

"Okay, we're set for a tour of Lewiston, biggest little town on the Oak River. In the process, I'll beat your Papa at a couple games of pool. He shot a good stick in the old days. Figure he's out of practice now."

I looked at Dub and smiled. "All I know is the last time I played pool I ran the table. It wasn't that long ago."

"Thank you for the good food, Aunt Molly." Jake said. "Especially the ice cream." Everyone joined him in agreement that nothing could be finer. Molly handed Jake a sack of chocolate chip cookies for the road.

"What about our railroad watches, Uncle Dub?" Nick asked.

"Oh gosh yes, hold on I'll and get 'em." Dub walked over to a cabinet by the fireplace and opened a drawer. He picked up two gold pocket watches with shiny metal chains dangling from the stems. Both had old time locomotives engraved in the case covers and they looked to be in perfect condition.

"Oh wow!" Jake said. "Which one's mine?"

"They're both the same." Dub handed a watch to each of the boys and they grinned from ear to ear. "These watches each have seventeen jewels and are over one hundred years old."

"What's that mean, seventeen jewels?" Jake asked.

Dub patted Jake on the top of his head. "The jewels keep them from wearing out, even after decades of constant use. They're a treasure you can pass along to your children."

The boys stared at the watches in the palm of their hands like they had been given a sack full of gold. Finally Nick asked the question I knew he or Jack would get around to eventually. "How much are these watches worth?"

Dub grinned. "They're worth more than your Nintendo by quite a bit." Nick looked at Dub and squinted his eyes. There was no doubt

Dub's answer was not what Nick had in mind, but he accepted it and stuck the watch in his pocket.

We walked out of the house, across the yard and through the gate. I got the leg bone out of the Jeep and laid it on the floorboard as we climbed into Dub's pickup truck to tour Lewiston. A beautiful little river town where 510 country souls were deeply rooted into the Ozark hills and spring-fed rivers. The boys and Dub's hound Sunny, a black and tan coon dog that turned out to be the best tracker ever, even though he was the runt of the litter all huddled together inside a big tractor tire that covered most of the pickup truck bed. As he headed down the road, Jake's mop of silky black hair blew back in the wind exposing his sparking blue eyes and smiling face. Nick hugged Sunny with one arm and waved at a farmer walking across the barn lot with the other one.

"Couldn't be a nicer day," I said as I held my head out the side window and took a deep breath. The sweet smell of honeysuckle hung heavy in the air. Barn Swallows on a bug-gobbling mission dipped and darted over the newly mowed hay that lay in the field ready to be raked up and baled for livestock feed during the winter.

"I saved that hat for you," Dub said.

I picked up the baseball cap lying on the dashboard and pulled it down tight on my head. I flipped down the truck's visor and looked at myself in the mirror. My sunburned face blended in well with the red cap. The Mack Truck bulldog emblem reminded me of how tough I was once as I looked at the crowfoot wrinkled lines that ran from the corner of my eyes. I thanked Dub for the cap and tried to prepare myself for reliving a bunch of fifty-year-old memories that were closing in on me up ahead.

"Look at that," Jake yelled, he pecked on the back window and pointed at the edge of the woods.

Dub stopped the pickup truck and we watched a half-dozen Wild Turkeys take flight and fly across the road in front of us. Dub leaned out the window and looked back at Jake. "Come back during turkey season, we'll shoot a big gobbler."

I could tell by the way Jake squinted his eyes and threw his head back when he looked at Dub that killing a turkey or pretty much any creature would be one thing he'd never do. He was kind-hearted and would never blast away a turkey. We headed on down the road.

When we pulled up in front of the Sheriff's office and stopped, sitting on what looked like the same wooden bench from the old days was the grandson of Sheriff Johnson who had been the Sheriff when I was a kid. Lying on the sidewalk beside him was a black and white English setter that looked identical to his Grandad's quail hunting dog.

"Howdy, boys," Sheriff Johnson said, when we got out of the pickup truck. "What you got there young fella? Looks like a bone?"

Nick held the leg bone out in front of him with both hands as he walked up and handed it to the Sheriff.

"Is this the first leg bone you've seen all week," Dub asked and we laughed.

"Where did you run across this specimen?" Sheriff Johnson asked as he scraped on the bone with his fingernail during his examination.

"My brother Tommy dug it up from the gravel bar," Dub said.

"We've not met." When I reached out to shake the Sheriff's hand he laid the bone down on the bench beside him. The English setter stood up and sniffed it from one end to the other.

"I knew your Grandpa well," I said. "He was a kind man and a good peacekeeper. My grandson Nick actually found the bone and I dug it up. You probably know the story of Dub and me at the Blue Hole?"

"I know it well. It still comes up even after all these years. The fact the murders were never solved bothered folks more than anybody wanted to let on. Yeah, I've heard lots of stories told, but you and Dub have got the best one yet."

"We wondered if this could be the leg bone of whoever committed the murders fifty years ago? I know it sounds crazy, but I even think we saw a blind fish in the cave spring, so I figure anything might be possible," Dub said.

Sheriff Johnson cocked his head to one side and squinted his eyes. "You saw a blind fish? Are you sure? I've heard about 'em for years. Never met anyone who actually saw one."

"Do you think DNA will help see if the bone belongs to the murderer?" Nick asked, taking the Sheriff's train of thought from blindfish in a cave to modern technology.

Sheriff Johnson picked up the bone and studied it some. "Looks like the owner was about as tall as me," he said as he held the bone down to his side for a measurement. He surprised me when he began to talk extensively about forensics. He ended up by saying he doubted if it would work because there was nothing to compare the DNA in the leg bone to. He would do the best he could to solve the puzzle.

Nick looked disappointed. I knew he wanted the method of discovery to be high tech and him be a part of the process.

Leaving Sheriff Johnson with what seemed to be an almost impossible task of solving a crime from so long ago; we piled back into the pickup truck and headed east of town toward the homestead where Dub and I grew up.

For the next few miles we drove on a gravel road shaded by tall pines and oak trees. The road ran along the top of a ridge that overlooked deep hollows with boulders and rock ledges on either side. Gradually we descended into a river valley for the last quarter mile where three hundred acres of fertile bottomland lay that used to be our old farm place. Looming up in front of us when we rounded the last bend was the white two-story house where Dub and I were born. It was hard to believe someone else owned it. It was even harder to believe that sixty-five years had passed.

"I told the Conner's we'd be out to visit the old place today. They go to town on Saturday, so they won't be home," Dub said, as we got out of the pickup truck. Jake and Nick jumped from the back of the bed with Sunny the hound close behind. The boys ran up ahead as we walked toward the house and plopped down in a porch swing that was suspended from the ceiling by a couple of chains.

"The big elm trees are gone," I said, remembering there used to be one on each side of the front gate that Grandpa Tom planted when he built the house in the early 1900s."

Dub shook his head. "Dutch Elm disease killed 'em some time ago. Doesn't look the same without those big tall beauties."

"It looks naked." I remembered how I used to climb up close to the top, wrap my leg over a limb and ride along as the tree swayed back and forth. The stronger the wind was the better. I could see over the top of the farmhouse, up and down the Oak River for a quarter of a mile. "On the day Grandpa Tom died, I climbed one of the Elm trees and wouldn't come down."

"I was real young at the time, but I remember it like it was yesterday," Dub said. "Dad tried to talk you into coming down, then Mom and Aunt Millie took a turn and you wouldn't budge. I think it was Uncle Ira that finally got you down," Dub said.

"I'm surprised you remembered. You were only about four years old."

"Believe me, that's something not easy to forget," Dub said.

I walked to the edge of the garden and looked across the barn lot. "Where's the pond Dad and Grandpa dug with the horses and the metal scoop?"

"The Conner's filled it in with dirt. It was shallow and overgrown with moss. About all it was good for was growing' snappy' turtles and mosquitoes."

"That's the place I caught my first fish." I'd sit on the bank for hours and watch my bobber that was tied to a line and a long cane pole. "It was a Bullhead catfish. Dad helped me clean it, Mom cooked it and I ate it for dinner with scrambled eggs." The winds of change had begun to blow. If the elm trees and my fishing hole were gone, Lord only knows what else I would find changed before I headed out of town.

Jake had been standing behind us taking in everything. "What happened to the fish in the pond when they filled it in?" he asked.

"Probably got buried if nobody seined them out," Dub said.

We walked out into the barn lot and opened the door to the machine shed. There sat Grandpa's red tractor with the metal lug wheels. It still looked to be in good shape. "What's that doing here?" I asked.

"When the Coner's bought the place it was there. They never got rid of it," Dub said.

Seeing the old tractor put a couple of good feeling points back up on the board. I remember Grandpa saying a fancy tractor would never take the place of big brown eyes. He was talking about the pair of big black Belgian horses he worked the fields with for years before gas power came along.

I closed the door to the machine shed and we walked toward the red two-story barn with a silver tin roof. It was built almost one hundred years ago to hold loose hay, years before the invention of the hay bailer.

"What else did you and Uncle Dub do, Papa?" Nick asked as he swatted at a wasp that buzzed around his head.

"We used to catch a little bit of everything when we seined the ponds. We'd have a big fish fry and invite the entire town. Sometimes a hundred people or more would show up."

"Your Papa, was in charge of rounding up people to turn the handle on the ice cream freezers." Dub chuckled. "He got that job because he ate more ice cream than anyone else."

"What kind of fish did you catch in a seine?" Jake asked.

"Mainly catfish, carp, perch and a snapping turtle once in awhile," I said. "Sometimes we'd drag out a squirming black leech and a few snails hooked onto a rock. Also some Crawdads and a water snake or two. They were not poisonous like a Cottonmouth Moccasin, but they will bite you just the same."

"You should have seen Tommy dance the day a snake crawled out of the seine and slithered over the top of his bare foot," Dub said.

I laughed. "The snake scared me so bad I ran out into the garden yelling at the top of my lungs."

"You jumped up and down like a bucking horse," Dub said. "We seined lots of different ponds. The one that was close to Uncle Ira's house only had goldfish. Some of them weighed three or four pounds."

"Did you eat goldfish?" Jake asked.

"Yeah, we did. Fact is we ate about everything, except Snapping Turtles. Goldfish aren't bad, I never liked it much because the meat tastes sweet, but some people do," I said.

"We did all of those fun things and worked hard too," Dub said. "Come summer we'd cut hay. Let it dry in the field, rake it up and haul it to the barn. Lord it was hot. Sweat stung your eyes and the hayseeds caused you to itch something' awful. We were always in a battle to stop sprouts from growing in the field. Once we chopped our way to the end of the field, it wouldn't be long until a new bunch sprouted up. Sometimes I'd be so tired I'd go to bed before dark."

"I know it doesn't seem like much. But I take out the trash," Jake said.

"Was there anything good about all that work?" Nick asked.

"Of course. What kept people going' was when noontime rolled around," I said. "Grandma Jessica would ring the big iron bell and we'd break for lunch. Grandpa Tom said grace to bless the heap of fried chicken spread out on a big white platter, along with a bowl full of potato salad. There would be a pitcher of lemonade and apple pie for dessert. After lunch it was off to one of the shade trees in the yard for a thirty-minute snooze. We would head back to the field knowing that when the rest of the workday was finished, we'd jump in the pond to cool down."

"We hoed weeds in the garden, too," Dub added.

"Do you still work that hard, Uncle Dub," Jake asked, obviously overwhelmed by all the things that Dub and I used to do that did not sound like much fun.

"I still put up a little hay, but I don't buck bales. I mostly drive the pickup truck."

"We used to be as tough as a boot," I said. "We had other chores, too. We slopped the hogs, fed the chickens and gathered eggs. Milked the cow and helped butcher a hog every fall. You know what else, boys?" Jake and Nick looked at me wide-eyed waiting to hear about some other chore. "We never worked on Sunday, and there was still time to camp, swim in the river, fish and shoot pool."

Chapter Seventeen

When we walked up to the barn, Dub pushed open the heavy wooden door mounted on rollers that ran along a steel track. A half dozen Pigeons fluttered out of an opening above our head, a black cat with yellow eyes ran in front of us and disappeared behind a bale of hay. I started to say something about black cats bringing bad luck if they crossed your path but decided to let it go.

"It's hot in here," Jake said as he stepped inside.

"Talk about hot; imagine filling this barn with loose hay. That's what your Uncle Dub and I did every summer." I walked inside the big wooden structure and looked at the gable sixty feet above our heads. Bales of hay by the hundreds were stacked up on both sides of a ten-foot wide aisle that ran from one end of the barn to the other. Streaks of sunlight beamed through knotholes and cracks in the weathered grey oak siding. The smell of sweet clover brought back boyhood memories.

"What's loose hay, Papa?" Jake asked as he walked up beside me and looked up at the top of the barn. "How did you get it all the way up there?"

"Do you want to hear the long or the short version?" I asked as I looked at Nick and grinned.

Before he could answer, Jake said, "I don't care what he says. I want to hear everything about it."

Nick glared at Jake. "That's what I was going to say too."

"Okay, here goes. Before we had a tractor and a hay bailer, Grandpa Tom and Dad used horses to pull a mower with a sickle blade that cut the grass. The new mown hay would lie in the field for a couple of days to dry and then be raked up into haystacks. After that, Dub and me used pitchforks to load the hay onto a flat bottom wagon. Then we'd haul it to the barn and unload it with a hayfork."

"That must have been a big fork," Nick said. "Was there a knife to go with it?"

Jake looked at Nick and moaned. "It must have been hard work," Jake said.

"Real hard work. Hot as blazes. So dusty sometimes you could hardly breathe. Hayseeds stuck to you and sweat burned your eyes. Felt sorry for the horses. Their black coats would be soaked. Frothy white slobbers dripped from their mouths.

"How long did it take to put up hay?" Nick asked as he swatted at another Red Wasp that buzzed past his ear.

"We could put up a hundred acres in a couple of weeks. Sometimes there would be three cuttings each summer, depending on the amount of rain," Dub said.

"How did you get loose hay way up to the top of the barn?" Jake asked again.

"We used a metal hayfork that was shaped like giant ice tongs. It was attached to a pulley and secured to that rail." I pointed at a steel rail in the gable that looked like a train track. "With the hayfork dangling outside one end of the barn, it would be lowered into the loose hay on a wagon with the tongs open. Another rope was tied to a bar called a single tree, which was connected to the harness of the team of horses. When the horses were driven forward, the metal tongs would close and raise a shock of hay the size of a small car up off the wagon to the opening at the end of the barn. We'd pull the hayfork with the big hay shock inside, down the track to where we wanted it, yanked on the trip rope and dump it. Then we used a pitchfork to distribute it around evenly, building up the hay in layers until we stacked it almost to the top of the barn."

"Makes me tired to hear about all that work," Nick said as he wiped the sweat from under his chin with the back of his hand. "If it's this hot just standing here, I'd probably get sick and puke if I had to pitch hay."

"It was hotter than you can believe," Dub said.

I looked around and realized the hayfork was not hanging from the metal rail. "The hayforks gone," I said. "What happened to it?"

"Some antique dealer probably bought it," Dub said. "There are only so many hayforks around."

"Too bad. Thought I'd get to watch you ride across the barn one more time," I said and Dub laughed.

"What does riding across the barn mean?" Jake asked.

"See the scar over Dub's eye?" Nick and Jake looked at Dub's face. "Here in the barn is where he got hurt. He was lucky it wasn't any worse."

"What happened?" Nick asked. "Did you two get in a fight?"

"No, not at all," I blurted out; wishing Nick had used another example. "Even though the primary purpose of a hayfork was to load hay into the barn, we also used to grab hold of it and ride from one end to the other. To get to where the ride started, we'd climb that ladder up to the platform." I pointed at a ladder nailed to the wall and then at a wooden platform the size of a dinner table that was mounted close to the roof.

"Did you really climb all the way up there, Papa?" Jake asked.

"It was crazy, but yes we did. From the top of the ladder, we'd crawl out onto the platform and grab hold of the hayfork tongs, one in each hand. Then push off toward the other end of the barn."

Dub laughed. "Sometimes we would flush Pigeons from their roost on the rail. They would fly in front of us and escape out the other end."

"I remember spitting Pigeon feathers out of my mouth sometimes," I said and the boys giggled. "So anyway, about twenty feet before you reached the other end of the barn. You kicked your feet out parallel, let go of the hook and fell into a cushion of hay, flat on your back. It was not a game for the faint of heart."

"That sounds dangerous," Jake said. "What did your Mom and Dad think about the game?"

I looked at Dub and he frowned. "Don't think they knew anything about it until the day Dub smashed into the wall. See that scar over his eye. He didn't let go of the hay hook in time. He hit the barn wall so hard he was knocked out."

"I'm glad the hay hook's gone," Jake said. "I would be afraid Uncle Dub might hurt himself again."

"Thanks for your concern, Jake. I'm too old to do something that foolish now."

"I wonder what Sheriff Johnson's done with the bone?" Nick said.

"Oh, he's probably solved the crime by now," Dub said and everyone except Nick laughed.

When we stepped outside, I walked to the corner of the barn lot and looked at the Oak River. The Willow trees growing along the river's edge waved in the breeze and sunlight glistened on the rippling water. A Kingfisher sitting on the low hanging branch of a Sycamore tree took flight and headed downstream, its shrill cry echoed off the towering limestone bluff. How could anything be more beautiful, I started to say, but the words never made it past my lips. Tears welled up in my eyes when I thought about standing in the barn lot as a kid listening to my Dad and grandpa talk about things like the crops and the weather.

Jake walked up and stopped in front of me. "I want to use the outhouse."

"No you don't, Jake," Nick said. "You're afraid of spiders."

"I want to not be afraid of spiders anymore," Jake said. "Maybe if I go inside I won't be, maybe."

"Okay, if that's what you really want to do, follow me." I remembered how facing my fears after I got snake bit helped stop the awful nightmares. Jake followed me as I headed toward the small white wooden outhouse with a silver tin roof. I figured I would go in first and scare away some of the bad looking ones first. God forbid I let Jake go inside and him get spider bit. Half dozen brown and black spiders scurried across a network of silken webs on the ceiling and a couple more disappeared down the holes in the toilet seat when I opened the creaky door. When I looked around, Jake was standing a few feet behind me trying to get a glimpse of the action.

"Does it look scary?" he asked.

"It looks like there are lots of spiders and it's hot. At least one hundred degrees, maybe more. Are you sure you want to go inside?"

"How many spiders did you see?" he asked, moving his head from side to side for a better view.

"A half dozen scurried off to hide." I picked up a stick and propped the door open a couple of inches so there would be some light when Jake walked inside.

"I hope he doesn't get bit," Dub said. "You will be in big trouble."

I looked at him and frowned.

As I started to say something else to discourage Jake, he kicked the stick away from the door and walked inside the small wooden structure.

After a minute or so had passed and Jake did not reappear, I walked up and opened the door a crack to look inside. "There stood Jake taking a pee down in the hole where some of the spiders had gone. We're ready to go when you are," I said, letting the door slam shut, proud that Jake had shown so much courage.

"Alright," Jake yelled when he shoved the door open and jumped outside. Smiling, he followed us out the front gate and climbed in the bed of the pickup truck with Nick and Sunny. He threw his head back and grinned when I gave him thumbs up.

When we drove into the northeast corner of Lewiston and headed down Main Street past McDonnell's drug store, I commented on how good the town looked, no litter in the street or on the sidewalks, not a rundown building or a speck of peeling paint.

"Old man McDonnell was a smart guy. He knew a little bit about everything," I said, remembering not only his medical expertise, but also the ice cream floats he made that only cost ten cents. Every Saturday I would hop up on one of the swivel seats and twirl around and around while he made a special treat.

"He not only mixed medicine for people, he treated animals that got sick too," Dub said. "Fact is, he knew almost as much about what it took to cure a person as Doc Barnes. Of course Doc's specialty was delivering babies."

I stared at the hardware store, which was the only building that stood empty. "What happened to Virgil More's place?"

"When Virgil died the store went with him," Dub said. "Now people make a trip to Ashbury when they need hardware items. The town's too small for a person to make a living' dealing in nuts and bolts. No way for a little business to survive against those big chain stores anymore."

"Virgil was a nice old man," I said. "He'd fix about anything that got broke."

Dub pointed at the bank building. "A new bank with a drive through window is located south of town at the Ay junction. The old bank got turned into a restaurant."

RIVER'S EDGE

"Does the restaurant do a good business?" I asked.

"A group of ladies from the church took over the restaurant last year. Some people drive fifty miles to eat the homemade ice cream and cherry pie. The fried chicken they serve is so crispy good it ought to be a sin. We'll probably eat there tonight. Can you still eat five bowls of ice cream at one setting?"

I looked at him and grinned. "I never ate more than three or four bowls at any one time and you know it."

Jake slid the back window in the cab open and scooted up close to where he could hear what Dub and I were talking about.

Dub slowed down as we passed the pool hall. The two benches out in front on the sidewalk looked like the ones from when we were kids. There was one on each side of the door in front of the plate glass windows that had "Pool Hall" written across the top in dark green letters.

"We must have shot thousands of games of pool?" I said.

"Why did you play so much?" Jake asked

"One reason was that Uncle Ira owned the pool hall. So it didn't cost anything to play. Those the same wooden benches from the old days?" I asked.

"Yep, Black Oak is about as tough as petrified wood. I hope you can still make a ball or two when we come back to play," Dub said. I laughed and patted him on the shoulder.

I looked back at the boys and said, "We'll come back to shoot some pool. Who do you think will win?"

Jake hunched his shoulders up and shook his head. Nick said, "We'll know when the games over, I guess."

We drove past the white two story feed mill with a red tin roof where Dad and Grandpa Tom bought salt blocks for the cows and had corn ground into meal. I thought about all the fish I caught in the pond behind the big building using a cane pole, a bobber and a worm that I threaded onto a hook for bait.

Konk-la-ree. Konk-la-ree. I looked at the water when I heard the high-pitched sound of a Redwing Blackbird and saw one of the male beauties swaying back and forth on the stem of a cattail. I remembered lying in the soft cool grass on the pond bank and looking up at the sky as I listened to the melodious sound of the beautiful birds and the *jug-o-rum* of Bullfrogs sitting on green lily pads croaking the day away. A serenade I enjoyed while waiting for the next fish to bite.

"I bet I caught five hundred Perch out of that millpond during my day," I said as I pointed at a moss-covered pool of water the size of a softball field.

"I don't remember you catching anything close to that many," Dub said.

I squinted my eyes and raised my eyebrows. "That was before you started to tag along and scared them away."

When Dub pulled up and stopped in front of the one-room schoolhouse where he and I spent much of our youth, my mind flashed back fifty years. There we stood as plain as day in the schoolyard under the oak tree with a dozen kids gathered around.

"Is something the matter?" Dub asked when he opened the door and started to walk around to the front of the pickup truck?

"What are you looking at, Papa?" Jake said. "Are you getting out?"

"Sure, I'm getting out. I was thinking about something." I opened my door, stepped outside onto the gravel driveway and walked to the edge of the playground. Dub ambled up beside the boys and me headed for the swings.

"It looks brand new," I said. "Even the eagle over the front door is shiny."

I looked at the American flag hanging on a wooden pole by the front door. In my mind's eye, I saw the kids standing around it saying the Pledge Of Allegiance, something we did every day before school.

"Wait 'til you see inside the place," Dub said. "We restored it from the ground up. It looks really good."

I walked to the big oak tree and looked up at the cover of thick green leaves. I remembered swinging back and forth on one of the low handing branches, falling off and knocking the wind out of myself. When I came around Lucy had knelt down beside me and asked if I was okay. Through a squint-eyed haze I looked up into her blue eyes and felt as if I had gone to heaven and I was talking to an angel.

Dub startled me out of my daydream. "Remember Lonnie Chambers?"

"Sure, he was same age as me."

"He drowned a few years back."

"To bad, he was a nice guy. What happened?"

"River was running full after a spring rain. His canoe got crossways in the current and flipped him out. He was sucked under a root wad. I'm the one that found him. He looked like the guy that drowned in the movie Deliverance. His arm was twisted back behind his head. Eyes open, he was white like a ghost. Not a pretty sight."

"How many people have drowned in the Oak River since we saw Buzzard Thompson go down?" I asked.

"Half dozen or so, I guess. About the same that's been killed by lightning strikes and hunting accidents. There were two people died from eating poison mushrooms. Which raised some suspicion—everyone around these parts knows the difference between an edible morel and a poisonous mushroom much as they recognize their own dog," Dub said and he wandered off toward the schoolhouse. The boys waved as they ran from the silver metal swing set and headed for a wooden merry go round. I smiled and waved back.

I leaned my back against the oak tree and closed my eyes. I imagined I was a fifteen-year-old again, full of grand ideas and the center of attention.

The year was 1950. First day back after summer vacation. Every kid in school was hanging around waiting for Dub and me to tell our story about the dead men we found on our camping trip, who were probably murdered. If that was not enough, Buzzard Thompson had drowned right before our eyes. I see my friend Doodle standing in front of me as plain as day. He's asking me if the Crawdads had eaten the eyes out of the dead man we found in the Blue Hole. Not knowing for sure if they did or not, my best answer was that craw's were known to eat about any kind of meat.

The most baffling question came from a girl named Molly. She wanted to know why the Lord picked some people to drown in the river and let others live? After deep thought, during which time I looked up toward the heavens and hoped for a sign, which I never got. I told her as best I could figure it was because the Lord worked in strange and mysterious ways. I could tell by the frown that she had hoped for something a little more definitive. She gave me a half-baked smile and walked away.

"Come on, Tommy. See what we've done inside the schoolhouse. Come on boys, take a look," Dub yelled and snapped me out of my daydream. Nick ran past us with Jake hot on his heels as I started for the front door.

"I was thinking about the first day of school. All those kids huddled up under the big oak tree to hear our story. I could see them and heard the voice of every one as plain as day," I said, wondering if I my imagination could have gotten the best of me.

"I've done the same thing," Dub said. "When I painted the schoolhouse this spring, I was surrounded by the kids that were here that day we told the story. Like I said before, no doubt many of the strange things that have happened to you and me had to do with the mysterious man on the river. I don't know why we were picked by him, but for some reason we were."

"Without a doubt. I'm sure he caused the rope swing to move. I'm also sure his influence inspired you to become a preacher, while I was picked to be a lost soul." I said.

"It's never too late to make a change, Tommy. Many times things happen for a reason that we don't understand."

"Well, for whatever reason things happened the way they did, we're the only two people I know who have rubbed elbows with the spirits." I walked through the front door of the schoolhouse and looked around the room. Miss Simpson's desk was in the same place. The Willow branch she used to point at things on the black board and switch the butts of boys like Dub who acted up in class lying on top.

I smiled at Dub when I picked up the Willow switch.

"What was that used for," Jake asked.

"Probably to beat kids with," Nick said. "Teachers used to spank a lot in the old days too."

"How do you know?" I asked and of course Nick said he saw something about it on TV.

"Mostly it was used by our teacher Miss Simpson, to point at pictures and stuff that she had written on the blackboard," Dub said, without saying anything about how often he felt the sting of the switch. "I refinished all twenty of the desks in this room. Took care not to erase any of the initials that were carved into the wood over the years."

When I walked to the back and stepped into the cloakroom, there were the kids again. They were talking and laughing, putting their lunch sacks on shelves with their names written across the top and getting ready to take their seats for a day at school. When I looked at Dub he raised his eyebrows and nodded his head. There was no doubt that he was aware of them as well. I walked to my old desk in the corner of the room and stared at Lucy's initials, which I had carved inside of a heart along with mine.

"How could so many kids in one room keep things straight?" Nick asked. "What about when somebody read out loud while other kids were trying to study?"

"What most people don't understand about a one-room school is things being taught to older kids were learned by young ones as well. That's why I did so well in math. I listened and by the time I got to seventh grade, I already knew how to work advanced problems," I said.

I looked at Dub and started to tell about the day he let the black snake loose in the classroom that scared the girls and Miss Simpson, then decided there was no reason to stir up trouble and have him turn around and tell something on me that might even be worse.

"What do you think about the place?" Dub asked.

"Good job. Looks better than it did in the old days. I'm sure the new school across the road from the bank is nicer."

"It's nicer and got more room. Don't know if it's better."

Along with Dub's hound Sunny, Jake and Nick ran out the front door and jumped in the back of the pickup truck. I grabbed Dub by the arm and looked into his eyes. "Did you see all the kids in the cloak room, talking and laughing?"

So matter of fact that it caused a chill to run through me like I had stepped on somebody's grave, Dub said, "Did you notice some of them looked different? Your old friend Doodle for one."

RIVER'S EDGE

I stepped backwards, almost falling down. "He looked paler, so did Molly Brown and a couple of the others. Their eyes were like the black of night with a yellow glow in the center."

"Those are the ones who are dead. The eyes are supposed to be the windows to the soul. In the case of the people who have passed on, what you saw in their eyes was spirit energy."

"Did Doodle know I was in the room?" I asked.

"Not sure," Dub said. "Just not sure if he did or not."

"I noticed Lonnie Chambers' hair was matted down on his head, like it was wet."

"As I said, he drowned in the river.

We walked to the pickup truck and climbed inside. I looked in the rear-view mirror when Dub started the engine and there stood Doodle dressed in military fatigues, a combat rifle in his hand and the American flag waving in the breeze. I remembered when he called to say that he was going to war. He had turned eighteen the day before. It was the last time I heard his voice.

Chapter Eighteen

Dub pulled out his pocket watch when we stopped in front of the pool hall and flipped open the cover. "It's four o'clock," he said as he slipped the timepiece back in the front pocket of his bib overalls. "We can shoot at least three games. Maybe more if I run the table every time you rack."

I laughed as I piled out of the pickup truck and walked up the steps. I stopped and looked at the huge oak tree beside the grey wooden building. "Hard to believe the old oak is still alive. It's older than you and me put together."

"Tree's a tough one. Been struck by lightnin' two or three times."

Before I stepped inside the front door, I rubbed the tips of my fingers across the initials I had carved on top of the wooden bench to the right of the front door. My nose twitched when I smelled the scent of linseed oil that was used to treat the hardwood floor. I looked up at a ceiling fan with long black blades that turned around slowly and could not believe it was still in operation. The same metal talcum powder dispensers were mounted on the wall beside three cue stick racks, one for each of the pool tables. The cast iron, wood-burning stove which was used to heat the pool hall during the winter was still in place. Nothing seemed to have changed since I was there last.

"Wow, this place looks old," Jake said as he walked up behind me. "It smells funny too."

"Been here close to one hundred years," Dub said as he patted Jake on the top of his head.

RIVER'S EDGE

"Who are your friends, Dub?" Ron Simpson, the guy who had owned the pool hall for the past twenty five years asked as he stepped out from behind a glass front candy case filled with licorice snaps, candy cigarettes, red Atomic Fireballs and Baby Ruth candy bars.

"This is my brother, Tommy," Dub said. "He and I were in your great-Grandma Simpson's class at school. She probably told you some of the things he tried to pull." Ron looked at me and grinned. "Tommy used to shoot a good game of pool. I brought him here today to see if he's still got the touch."

"I want one of those Grapette sodas Papa talked about," Jake said.

"Me too," Nick said. "I want to see if anything can be that good."

Ron walked over to the candy counter and tossed us a bag of peanuts. "Got to have nuts with a Grapette soda, you know." He threw back the lid on a pop cooler beside the candy case and pulled out four little bottles of blue soda the color of the ocean. He used the shiny brass opener mounted on the front of the pop box to snap off the lids and gave each of us a Grapette.

"I've heard about you from my great Grandma, Tommy. But as best I can tell, you was a tame one compared to Dub." Ron looked at Dub and they grinned at one another. "I know all about the camping trip where you and Dub found the dead guys and saw Buzzard drown."

"A good story never dies," I said as I walked over to look at the pool cues lined up in the rack on the wall. To my surprise, the first cue on the end had my initials carved in the handle and was the one I used to shoot with from the time I was ten years old. I looked at Dub and he grinned, no doubt he had something to do with it being right up front after all that time.

"What you got there, Tommy?" Dub asked, as if he did not know.

"You're in trouble now, little brother. I've found my favorite stick." I picked up a cube of chalk and rubbed in on the felt tip, hit the button on the bottom of the dispenser to collect some white powder in the palm of my hand and rubbed the fine grained talcum up and down the cue until it felt as smooth as glass. A stick has to slide free and easy before this shooter can play his best game.

"You got no excuse now," Dub said. The boys sat down on a bench by the wall to watch the contest. "Go ahead and break the rack. It may be your last shot."

When I walked to the head of the pool table, I thought about the outcome of the game. Since the mission to patch up our long-standing feud was going so well, the ideal thing would be that neither one of us would win. I laid the white cue ball down on the green felt, placed the small end of the stick over the top of my thumb, wrapped my index finger around it and leaned over the table. I drew the butt end of the stick back slowly and with a powerful forward motion, I drove the cue ball into the rack. Fifteen multiple colored balls rolled around from one end of the table to the other. A blue and white-striped twelve ball fell into one of the side pockets and a solid orange three ball dropped into the corner, so I had a choice of shooting solids or stripes.

"You should quit while you're ahead, Papa," Nick said. I frowned when both he and Jake laughed louder than I thought was necessary.

I walked around the table and sized up the position of each pool ball so I could figure out my next best shot. The cue stick felt light and balanced in my hands, just like I remembered. I wondered if I could still suck the cue ball back toward me by hitting it down close to the bottom, which would create a backspin commonly referred too, as English and that would put me in a good position for the next shot.

"You have to shoot to make 'em," Dub said, after he thought I had taken too long to figure out my next shot. "You can't wish 'em in the hole."

I remembered Dub's tactic from the old days when he would say things to try to break my concentration. I played like I had not heard a word he said and continued to study the table. More stripes, the numbers 9 through 15, then solids the numbers 1 through 7, were out in the open on the table, so I decided it would be my advantage to shoot the high numbers. I leaned over to shoot the ten, hoping to draw the cue ball back for a good shot on the nine ball. As planned, I shot the ten into the side picket and backspin brought the cue ball back to perfect position. With the fluid motion of an old pro shooter pulsing in my veins, I drilled the nine ball into a corner pocket and I felt like I could do no wrong.

"I thought you'd not shot pool for a long while," Dub said. "He's been practicin' ain't he boys? Go on, tell me the truth."

"I don't think so," Jake said. "I didn't even know Papa could shoot pool."

I went on to run the rest of the stripes on the table down to the eight ball and missed a bank shot because I got nervous and shot too hard. Now Dub had an open shot at every solid ball, but during his run, he missed the last shot in a side pocket by a hair. I ran the eight ball down the rail and to my delight, I had won the first game. It was nothing so grand as having shot a killer snake and saved the boys lives, but a feather in my hat just the same.

"Playin' over your head wasn't you, Tommy? You can't be that good." Dub said.

"Once you've shot pool as good as I used too. You don't forget because it's been awhile."

The contest was a great idea, it ended with each of us wining two games and we got to relive the good old days when we were as close as any two brothers could be. The boys chugged down another Grapette soda; we headed out the door and climbed in the pickup truck.

"Sure you don't want to go by the cemetery on the way home? If you're going to Grandpa Tom's cabin in the morning, you won't have much time before church."

"Okay, you're right. Let's go there now. I don't want to miss any of your sermon."

Still reeling from the effect of seeing the kids in the cloakroom at school. It felt eerie going to the place where we would be surrounded by many of our departed friends and relatives. Even worse would be if the two murdered men that Dub and I found on our camping trip came up for a visit.

When we arrived I discovered that Lewiston Cemetery had been filled up with country souls and about twenty gravesites were in a new section across the road. Dub told the boys that Henry Hines, the groundskeeper, had found a few arrowheads while digging some of the graves. Jake and Nick jumped out of the back and were off on a hunt with Dub's hound Sunny sniffing the ground and trailing along behind.

"How many people are buried in the old section?" I asked as we stepped out of the pickup truck and I gazed out across the sea of tombstones.

Dub looked at me through the shimmering heat waves rippling up off the hood of the pickup truck and said, "Five hundred or so, I guess. Maybe a few more."

I followed Dub through the gate under a curved metal archway with black letters that read, "Lewiston Cemetery Est. 1888." I felt guilty as we walked toward Grandpa Tom's and Grandma Jessica's grave because I had not paid them a visit in such a long time. When I read the inscription on their tombstones, I noticed they were born in the same year, 1878, which was something I had forgotten. After Grandma passed away, Grandpa went downhill fast and they died within a couple months of one another.

"Do you see anyone?" I asked. "You know, Grandpa or Grandma or anyone buried in the cemetery?"

"I don't see anyone today," Dub said as calmly as if we were talking about the weather.

I took a deep breath as we walked toward our parents' graves. One of the most horrific disagreements Dub and I ever had was over the cremation of our father. It was something Dad had requested be done and for some reason, Dub was bitterly opposed to the idea.

The outcome was so terrible that neither of us had talked about it since. I gave Dub half of Dad's ashes to put in the coffin so there could be a regular burial service, closed casket of course. To my knowledge, Dub and I and Ned Thomas, the funeral director, were the only ones who knew there was no body. I was certain Dub figured I scattered my half of the ashes in some special place, when actually they had been in my closet all those years. Now they were in the trunk of my car, which was one of the reasons I wanted to visit Grandpa's cabin alone, so I could finally dispose of Dad's remains in the Oak River.

"What do you think of the roses I planted?" Dub said when we walked up to our parent's grave. "I planted them about ten years ago because of what Dad used to say to Mom a lot."

I looked down at the grave sites, which were covered in a carpet of beautiful red rose peddles, then looked at the inscription on my mother's tombstone, which read, "Summer, Winter, Spring and Fall, you are the rose in my life, Dreaded Benson." My father's tombstone simply had his name, dates of birth and departure and a picture of the American flag.

"You have been a better son, Dub," I said. "Staying here and taking care of things."

Dub gave me a solemn look. "I don't know about that, Tommy. But like I said earlier, it's never too late to change."

I thought about how doves mate for life when I heard one cooing in the distance and how Dub and I couldn't have had two kinder and more loving parents. I looked away when my eyes filled with tears.

"Hey, Papa, Jake might have found half an arrowhead," Nick yelled from the other side of the cemetery. I wiped my eyes and waved, wondering what half of an arrowhead would look like.

We moved along to my friend Doodle's tombstone. All that was written besides his name dates of birth, and departure, was "He died a long ways from the Ozarks."

"Have you ever seen him here in the cemetery?" I asked. "The only place I've seen Doodle is at the schoolhouse. I don't know why. I guess the only way I'll ever understand the ways of the spirits is when I become one."

Dub pointed at Buzzard Thompson's headstone up in front of us, but I told him I did not want to go there because everything about Buzzard's life made me feel too sad. The shocker of the cemetery tour was when Dub said that grave robbers had dug up the bodies of the two men we found dead at the Blue Hole soon after they were buried. A note was left inside each one of the caskets saying that the devil had a special place for them in hell.

"So I guess you haven't seen them around either?" I said and Dub shook his head.

The last grave we walked past was the resting place of Sheriff Johnson, Sr. Born 1889-Died 1954. Above his name were a bronze star and the words "Peace Keeper."

I don't know what came over me. I looked at Dub and in a weepy voice I said, "I never got over old Trouser dying. What is it about a dog that makes a person think about them forever?"

"I don't know," Dub said. "I never got over him dying either and he wasn't even my dog."

"What's wrong, Papa?" Jake asked as he and Nick walked up while I was drying my eyes.

"Nothing. Got sweat in my eyes," I said. "You boys ready to go? What about the half of an arrowhead you found?" I asked.

"We threw it away," Nick said. "It was just a rock."

On our way to Dub's house we stopped at a spring branch where the boys jumped out of the pickup truck and waded in up to their knees. They cried out with each step that the water was too cold, but stayed in it like a couple of troopers. Sunny splashed back and forth in front of them until Nick grabbed the stick out of his mouth and tossed it up on the bank for the hound to fetch.

"I've caught lots of Crawdads in this creek," Dub said as we drove away after the boys finally froze out. "Same goes for red fin minnows."

When we pulled up in front of the house, the picnic table under the shade of a hickory tree was draped with a red and white checked cloth.

"Decided to make dinner rather than go into town," Molly said. "I'm the one bakes the apple pies, so we've got the most important part."

Molly had fixed fried chicken and potato salad, along with an apple pie that was hot out of the oven. The spread looked like what Grandma Jessica used to fix when we came in for lunch during haying season and I wondered if she did it on purpose.

Dub got the boys interested in looking at old pictures of us when we were kids and of our parents, grandparents, friends and relatives.

Included was one of Uncle Ira sitting up in a tree with his pet Raccoon, Rowdy, which was a perfect name for the animal because it got into everything imaginable. One day the critter unscrewed the lid on a mason fruit jar where Ira kept a stash of money and carried it off to no telling where. Rowdy disappeared shortly after that happened. Uncle Ira was pretty tight when it came to his funds and $200.00 was a great deal of money back in those days.

There was even a photo of the Conner brothers on the day Sheriff Johnson and the Feds raided their whisky still, along with a great shot of Buzzard Thompson sitting bareback on a horse at the town square, smoking a corncob pipe and wearing a straw hat. The boys were about beat after all the activity during the past few days and Dub sent them off to bed with a book. What got their attention was him telling them it was one of the scariest stories he had ever read.

"I've got something in the woodshed out back might be of interest," Dub said with a smile that lit up his eyes. "It's only for special occasions. My parishioners might look down on me for it, so it's just between you and me."

I followed Dub to the woodshed. He opened the door and pulled a chain that turned on a bare bulb hanging from the ceiling. He rummaged around in a wooden box and brought out something wrapped in a gunnysack. There was no doubt about what it was when he pulled out a jug filled with a clear liquid. It was white lightening whisky—180 proof moonshine from somebody's Ozark Mountain still. It looked innocent enough, but from past experience, I knew it had the kick of a mule.

"I thought we'd have a drink to celebrate us burying the hatchet," Dub said as he passed the jug.

It had been many years since I saw a jug of the devil's brew. I put my index finger through the small round glass handle at the top, eased the cork out of the clear glass jug and lifted it up for a swig. The liquid went down as smooth as silk, but when it hit my stomach it literally caused me to gasp. I handed the jug back to Dub and wiped my mouth with the back of my hand. I inhaled deeply and when I exhaled, it felt like my breath was so powerful it might set the building on fire.

"Henry Hines, the feller that takes care of the cemetery and digs the graves. He runs off a batch of corn whisky once in awhile. He gave me this jug in case of an emergency." Dub laughed. "You're the first person I've shared it with and I've had it for a good long spell."

Dub sighed deeply after he took a swig, wrapped the jug back up in the gunnysack, stashed in the wooden box and we went back into the house.

"So, tomorrow you're going' to Grandpa Tom's river cabin, then comin' to church," Dub said as he looked at me across the kitchen table with clear untroubled eyes. "Hope you get to church in time to get a good seat."

"That's my plan," I said. "But for now, I'm going to bed. Two nights on the river and a town tour has worn me down to a nub."

"It's been a good day for brothers," Dub said as we stood up, walked around the table and gave one another a hug.

When I got to the head of the stairs, I turned around and looked at Dub standing under the deer head by the fireplace. "Thanks again for everything," I said and he gave me a nod.

I looked in the bedroom and the boys were sound asleep. The book Dub gave them to read was open and laying on Nick's chest. Sunny raised his head up off the red and green braided rug at the foot of the bed and looked at me with sleepy brown eyes. I took the book with me and fell asleep after the first couple of pages.

The next thing I knew, I heard Molly yell at me from the foot of the stairs that it was time to get up and eat breakfast.

"Okay. I'll take a shower and be right down," I said as I bounced out of bed onto a hardwood floor.

"Don't dilly dally. It's a beautiful Sunday morning." The cheerful sound of her voice put an extra bounce in my step.

I showered, shaved and combed my hair. Put on my jeans, a clean white T-shirt slipped on my sandals and headed down the stairs.

"Wow," I said when I walked into the kitchen and saw how nicely Dub had cleaned himself up. He had on a pair of khaki pants, a white shirt, a red necktie and shiny black loafers. I had not seen him in anything but bib overalls and a bathing suit most of his life, so he made quite a fashion statement. "Sorry I'm not dressed up better for church," I said feeling really tacky. "I've got a closet full of suits and I'd have brought something better if I had known about going to church."

"You'll fit right in just fine. Half the men there will have on bibs and work shirts. Since they know you're in town, they'll probably even wear shoes. Clothes don't make the man in the county. That's citified stuff. You know that, Tommy."

I smiled at Dub as I sat down at the table and as usual, Molly had prepared a nice spread of food for us to eat. I looked around the room to see if my mother's spirit might be present. She used to fix the same breakfast every Sunday morning before we went to church.

"Are you looking for something?" Molly asked.

"No," I said, feeling a little silly.

"Looks a lot like the breakfast Mom used to make don't it?" Dub said as he forked a patty of sausage onto his plate.

"Yeah, it does. Looks good. Where are the boys?" I asked.

Dub scooped a couple of eggs onto his plate and picked up a slice of bread. "They came down thirty minutes ago. Molly gave them some biscuits and bacon and they headed for the river. They're down at the rock dam by the spring branch, within yellin' distance."

"They're usually late sleepers," I said.

"Not today." Molly launched right in to thanking the Lord for the food and for Dub and I being together and for our families, then finished by saying that it was time to eat.

After I downed a last bite of biscuit with homemade grape jam piled high, I scooted my chair away from the table to get some breathing room.

"You and Lucy should spend a weekend with us soon," Molly said. "Maybe even stay a whole week. Bring your girls and their husbands and your grandsons if everyone wants to come visit. We'll try to gather up our kids and their grandkids. We need to have a family get together, it's been a long time, Tommy."

"I agree," I said. "I'll round up as many folks as I can and we'll make up a little for a lot of lost time."

"The boys enjoyed the camping trip," Molly said. "They talked about it non-stop at breakfast. They loved the rope swing, catching fish, both blind and sighted." Molly laughed. "Leatherwood Cave and the eel Dub caught. Of course Jake can't wait to get the pictures of his big bass loaded onto his computer. He also showed me the arrowhead he found. He said he was going to keep it, where Nick thought he might sell his and buy a motorbike. They were lucky, I hardly ever hear of people finding arrowheads at the river anymore."

I started to ask if they said anything about Dub shooting the snake, but decided to let it go. I hoped I would be so lucky when we got back home that neither of them brought up the subject. "Yeah, they were lucky to find the arrowheads. Especially two of them," I said as I looked at Dub and he grinned. "Did Dub tell you I'm going to pay a visit to Grandpa Tom's river cabin before church?"

"He mentioned it. The place has been run down over the years, but it will be a nice memory for you. You might as well leave the boys with us and we'll bring them to church."

"Sounds fine with me. It'll give them a more time to spend at the river."

"I forgot to mention, when Jake came downstairs this morning. He said he could still hear the sound of crickets in his ears," Molly said and we laughed.

"They were loud and chirped nonstop all night," I said

Dub looked at his watch. "It's eight o'clock now and the service starts at 10:00. You might want to move along. I know you don't want to miss any of my sermon."

I stood up and thanked Molly for the breakfast. Told Dub I looked forward to seeing him in the pulpit and headed for the front door. When I walked out of the house and down the steps toward my black Lincoln, I had the feeling that before the day was over; I might end up being a better person than I ever imagined it was possible for me to be.

"See you at church," Molly said, as she waved from the front porch.

I turned on the radio and pushed the scan button as I drove down the bumpy gravel road toward the river cabin that Grandpa Tom built in 1936, the year I was born. The first strong signal was 99 Country with Johnny Cash singing the old gospel tune *I'll Fly Away*. I hummed along and tapped my foot until Grandpa's place came into view. When I was a boy I rode there on my bike two or three times each week. When I stayed overnight my mother would tell me not to let grandpa tell scary stories before bedtime because I might have bad dreams. Even though I always agreed to such a plan, he would tell me at least one or two. Whatever bad dreams I had were worth it because he was such a great storyteller.

He had a horse barn and a pen where he raised a hog to be butchered when the weather turned cool in the fall each year. A chore I looked forward to helping him with more than anything else.

On this day, I had one primary mission and that was to scatter my father's ashes in the Oak River. When I pulled up in front of the cabin and stopped in front of a vine-covered rail fence, I felt the same slight pressure change I did when I came into contact with the spirits at the schoolhouse. It was as if the air around me had thinned out and I felt like I was moving in slow motion. I looked over my shoulder when I thought I heard the rumble of thunder, which did not seem possible, as it was a beautiful morning with the sun rising above the tops of the trees and not a cloud in the sky.

I walked to the back of the car and opened the trunk lid. I picked up the black metal container and trudged off toward the Oak River.

"Kack, kack, kack," the harsh rattling call of a Kingfisher winging its way downriver caught my attention when I walked up to the river's edge. It could not have been a more fitting welcome, as my father dearly loved the brightly colored birds. I watched him dip and dive above the surface of the water until he swooped up into a tree and perched on a low hanging branch.

I slipped off my shoes, rolled up my pant legs and waded out into the cool water where the early morning sun cut through a wispy layer of fog. I looked up the river at the still, deep hole where Sycamore and Cottonwood trees shaded the banks. A school of silver minnows swam along the edge of the swift current in front of me. When a soft warm breeze whispered through the tall pines behind me, I felt the presence of my father so strongly there was no doubt that he was close by.

When I unscrewed the cap on the black urn and scattered the grey-white ashes, the breeze spread his remains out into a cloud the shape of angel's wings. I watched in awe as the spiritual image hovered above the surface of the sparkling water, then slowly drifted down the river and finally came to rest.

"Today, Lord, I return to you the ashes of Dreaded Benson. He was a kind and gentle man whose life on earth made the world a better place." Until I heard myself speak the words, I had not been conscious of the fact that I was going to say anything.

Having put my father's ashes to rest and made peace with my brother, I thought about how life passes us by like a flowing river and we should appreciate every moment we are allowed to spend on earth. There is no reason to hurry. Life is about the journey and not the destination.

Chapter Nineteen

As I walked up the path from the river, I felt like I was floating on air. When I reached the car and looked at the cabin, I noticed the front door was standing open and smoke curled out of the chimney. I stared at the sagging tarpaper roof and got the awful feeling that if I walked inside, it might collapse. My heart beat faster when I saw an old man with a white beard shuffle past a broken window.

No doubt I would be better off waiting until my next trip to Lewiston when Dub and I could go inside the cabin together. The kids at the schoolhouse with a yellow glow of spirit energy in their eyes had made a haunting impression and I wanted to put off joining them as long as possible.

I started to open the car door and froze when I sensed someone was behind me. I slowly turned around. Standing in front of me holding the unopened package that had been on the floorboard since we left Kansas City was Buzzard Thompson.

He looked the same as the day Dub and I saw him drown in the river. Wearing ragged, dirty overalls, his face, arms and bare feet were bruised and bleeding. Pieces of leaves and even a dead horsefly were trapped in his scraggly, greying beard.

With tears in his eyes, Buzzard held out the package. The instant I took it from him, he disappeared, leaving behind a musty, dank odor that smelled like an underground root cellar.

I stared at the package unable to believe my eyes. Instead of having Dub's return address written in the left hand corner like when I picked it up at the post office, now it had Buzzard Thompson's name, crudely written in what appeared to be dried, dark brown blood. With trembling hands, I slowly unwrapped three layers of brown paper. Bang! The door to Grandpa's cabin slammed shut as I peeled back the last sheet of paper. There was no longer smoke rising from the chimney and the wooden shutters on the front windows were closed.

I took a deep breath and pulled out a note written to Sheriff Johnson, dated September 1, 1949. It told about the murder of Buzzard Thompson's family and the two dead men that Dub and I found. Milly Thompson—the wife of Buzzard's brother, a big talker they called Razzle Dazzle–signed it. The reason Milly gave for the horrific crimes that her late husband had committed was due to him being an evil spirit in a past life and that he drank so much moonshine whiskey it pickled his brain.

On a separate piece of paper, dated August 1, 2002, Milly wrote that she followed Razzle D to the Blue Hole, killed him for his crimes before he murdered anyone else and buried him in the gravel bar. She figured it was the least she could do, since he loved that spot more than any other place on earth. Milly signed off by saying she hoped the poor soul could find some peace there because he never had any while on this earth.

After reading the notes, I felt like I had stepped out of the darkness into the dawn. With the new information, surely Sheriff Johnson could get a sample of something that belonged to Razzle and DNA link it to the leg bone, which would make Nick and a whole town full of people happy for sure.

I looked at the clock on the dash when I got inside the car and saw that I only had fifteen minutes until Dub began to deliver his sermon. *What a great finish to the story Dub and I started over fifty years ago,* I thought. With my heart pounding and a smile on my face, I pushed on the gas pedal and sped down the gravel road.

RIVER'S EDGE

When I pulled up in front of the People's Good Faith Church, I saw my brother's name, Dub Benson, Pastor listed on the marquee. The Sheriff and one of the parishioners were standing under a big oak tree talking, I figured everyone else had gone inside. I got out of the car and looked at the Sheriff with the intent of telling him about my discovery. On second thought, I decided to tell Dub first, since he was there at the start of the incredible saga, he should be the first to know who was responsible for the killings.

I nodded my head at Sheriff Johnson as I walked past and went inside the white, wooden building with a steeple that housed a sliver church bell. I stopped and stared at the window at the end of the building behind the altar, which had an amber colored cross that ran from the floor to the ceiling of the church. The bright sunlight shining through the window cast a golden glow down the center aisle, creating a pure-of-heart mood. I looked on both sides of the aisle to see if any of the spirits had shown up, I was hopeful that Doodle would make an appearance so I could say goodbye.

The congregation seemed to be made up of only living souls, all of whom watched as I walked toward the front row where Nick and Jake had saved me a seat. I slumped my shoulder when I sat down, trying to make myself look smaller so I would be less conspicuous. I quickly realized I was too big for a simple body maneuver to make a difference in my appearance. So I straightened up before the congregation started to think I was either deformed or downright silly.

"You were almost late, Papa," Jake said. "We've been here quite a while."

"But I'm not late," I grumbled out the side of my mouth, loud enough that a young girl behind us muffled a giggle. "Sorry if I made you worry."

"We caught twenty Crawdads before church," Nick said. "We saved 'em to take home and cook."

I looked at Nick and frowned, thinking his announcement did not need an immediate answer.

Dub stood to one side of the lectern talking to a lady that played the piano. I figured there would be a lot of music when I noticed a banjo leaned up against the wall, next to a fiddle and a guitar.

When Dub looked around and noticed me, he walked across the room, stopped in front of us and stuck out his hand. When I grabbed hold of it, he turned toward the congregation and said, "This is my brother, Tommy. He was with me at the Blue Hole on the camping trip when we were kids." That was all he needed to say for people to give a low rumble of approval.

"Where's he been all this time," I thought I heard someone say. When I looked around the lady in the pew behind me smiled and I realized my mind was playing tricks on me, again.

"I'm blessed to have my brother and his grandsons, Nick and Jake, with us today. Hope to see them around these parts more often." I nodded my head when Dub looked at me and smiled. "Our Sunday mornings are a little different than most churches. Instead of bowing our heads to pray, we look into the sunshine as it lights up the cross."

Dub turned toward the golden rays shining through the stained glass window and with his palms held up toward the heavens, he said, "As the sunlight brightens our day, we open our hearts to all of God's creatures. Be kind to one another and help your fellow man." He paused for a moment to lay his hand on my shoulder. "Carry my kinfolks, Tommy, Nick and Jake home safe today. Thank you Lord for the blessings you have bestowed on our little river town."

An older man with a grey ponytail got up from his pew on the left side of the aisle, a young girl with long blond hair who was maybe sixteen stood up on the right and they walked toward the front of the room. Smiling at one another when they met at the podium, the man picked up a guitar and the girl lifted a flute. Dub joined them, put the fiddle up under his chin and the three of them began to play a soulful version of "Amazing Grace."

When the song was over the guitar player switched to of all things, a bagpipe for the next song and Dub sang the first verse of an Irish ballad called "Pine Wood Hills." "I'm a rambler and rover and a wanderer it seems. I've travelled all over, chasing after my dreams. But a dream should come true and a heart should be filled. And a life should be lived on the pine wood hills."

The Irish ballad made me think of Father Frank Hogan who brought a group of immigrants to the Ozarks in the mid-1800s and they all mysteriously disappeared. When the song was over, the musicians bowed and the congregation clapped loudly. Dub laid his fiddle down and stepped up to the podium.

He slowly scanned the congregation and stopped when he looked down at me. "Take time to say you're sorry so you will have no regrets. Tomorrow is not promised to anyone. If you wait for it and the day never comes, you'll surely regret the time you wasted today."

Jake laid his head on my shoulder and I thought about how those few words could have saved Dub and me so many years of being lost from one another. I looked up at the ceiling and swallowed deeply to hold back the tears.

"Until we meet again. Keep your mind free from hatred, live simply and give more than you receive. A small price to pay for God's blessing." That was the end of Dub's sermon. The musicians picked up their instruments and for the last song, they played a foot stomping tune called "Old Joe Clark." After that the service was over, people moved around, talking and shaking hands.

"I'm Bob Conner, grandson of Zeak Conner," a young man said as he walked up and shook my hand.

"The Conner brothers, oh yes," I said. "Remember 'em well. Zeak was the littler of the two, I believe?"

"He just looked littler because his brother, Lyle, was so big," Bob said. "The Blue Hole story is one of the best. Except some people still think the Conner brothers had something' to do with the murders. I'll tell you here and now they didn't."

"I never thought so," I said with a slow drawl, remembering how I actually used to figure they were the number one suspects. "Excuse me, I'll be right back." I turned around and headed out of the church toward the car. I picked up the package and hurried back inside. I walked down the aisle between the wooden pews, stopped at the podium and handed Dub what would probably be the most important parcel in his life.

"What ya' got here?" Dub asked. "Looks like an old scroll or something." He removed the brown wrapping paper and picked up the note from Milly Thompson. His eyes got bigger as he read each line, as he discovered that Milly's husband–Buzzard's brother, Razzle Dazzle–was the one who killed all the members of the Thompson family and the two guys that Dub and I found at the river.

"You'll be interested in this note," Dub said as he handed the letter to Bob Conner. "Proves your Pap and his brother had nothing to do with any of the unsolved murders."

"Thank you, Lord!" Bob said after he read the note. "Thank you, thank you."

"I'd never figured things could turn out this way," I said as I walked up beside Dub and put my arm around his shoulders. "I'm happy the innocent people under suspicion all these years have been cleared."

"Proves once and for all that truth really is stranger than fiction," Dub said.

I smiled. "You also proved a sermon doesn't need to be long winded to deliver a powerful message."

Sheriff Johnson said after everyone in the congregation had a chance to read what Milly wrote, he would use the notes as evidence. People gathered around under the shade of a big oak tree and talked about when murder invaded Lewiston and how the citizens had been held hostage for so many years. A couple of the men carried out two freezers of ice cream that had been churned in the basement while the service was going on and people lined up and got their treat.

"Moonshine will do that to a person," Bob Conner's wife Ruth said after she read the notes. "A bad batch of hooch caused my uncle Billy to go blind."

"Shame about Buzzard havin' to live in the wilderness when he did nothin' wrong. Hot in the summer. Cold in the winter. Fightin' off bugs and snakes. Mercy, it'd be sad and lonely," Frank Ivers said as he passed the note to a well-rounded older lady wearing a purple dress. Like everyone else, she shook her head after she read the confession.

"A lesser man never would have survived as long as Buzzard," Frank said as he spooned in a last bite of ice cream and headed to the freezer for one more dip.

"We need to think about heading back to Kansas City," I said to Nick and Jake. "I've got to get away from here before I eat more ice cream and blow myself up."

Sheriff Johnson walked up and laid his hand on Nick's shoulder. "I'll let you know what happens with the DNA results on the leg bone."

Nick looked at him and smiled.

"I want to know, too," Jake said as we walked toward the car. "This is like something on TV, only better."

"It's been the best time ever these last few days," Dub said.

The boys ran up to the car and climbed inside after chasing a yellow butterfly across the church lawn.

As I opened the car door and slid into the driver's seat, Dub poked his head in the back window and shook the boys' hands. "What about making this campin' trip an annual event?" he asked.

"If annual only means only once a year. We need to come more often," Jake said and everybody laughed.

The parishioners waved good-bye when I started the car and yelled for us to come back and see them soon.

Sheriff Johnson looked at Nick and tipped his hat. "Thanks for the help, young man. If you ever want to move to the country, I could use a good deputy."

I glanced in the rear view mirror as Nick grinned and waved back at the Sheriff. When I drove over the wooden bridge and looked down at the water, I saw my friends from days gone by, laughing and swimming in the river. In the distance, I heard the clanging of the school bell.

"What are you looking at, Papa?" Nick asked.

"Just taking one last peek at the river. Thinking about the nice weekend we've had."

As I passed the limestone corner post I looked at Grandpa Tom's name, inscribed at the top of the list along with the other men who helped build the bridge. I thought about when I was ten years old, Grandpa and me were standing in the barn lot behind his river cabin. The rising sun cast a golden glow on the sparkling frost-covered ground as it shone through the yellow leaves of a maple tree. Reddish flames lapped up the sides of a long black vat filled with bubbling, boiling water. I walked over beside Grandpa as he shouldered his .22

rifle and with the sound of the exploding shell ringing in my ears, the butchering of another hog signaled that one more year had come and gone.

The weekend journey that began as a celestial call from a spring-fed river had changed my life and I would soon be coming back home.

The End

Growing up in the in the Ozark Mountains during the 1940's and 1950's Love helped his uncle run a fishing camp on the Jacks Fork River during the summer—a spring fed stream named by life Magazine one of the most scenic float and fishing streams in the world.

The picture is of an old man named Art who lived downriver a couple of miles. I must say a few words about him because he was one of the best storytellers I've ever heard and influenced my writing a great deal. He lived a self-sufficient life growing all his own food and brewing moonshine whiskey he sold primarily to city slickers from St. Louis, Nashville and Kansas City for a buck a gallon. His claim to fame was he never poisoned anybody, which, with moonshine, was not always the case. He also raised hogs.

Art was a happy fella until the feds followed a flock of buzzards circling above his still and nabbed him for the third time one hot summer day. After that they decided to hire the good old boy as a tourist attraction to make denatured whiskey in Alley Springs State Park and demonstrate how the corn liquor brewing process was done. I'm pretty sure he'd run off a batch of 180 proof stuff now and then after the park closed for the day.

Art enjoyed his new life for many reasons, one being he didn't have to worry about being put in jail. He wore bib overalls, a red flannel shirt, a straw hat, smoked a pipe fueled by tobacco he grew in his garden and gathered a large crowd most days at the whiskey making exhibit. He always brought a black and tan hound dog to work for company. The old dog, who was named Trouser, got a fair share of pats on the head from the tourist and was treated like a king by little kids.

It was a sad day when Art died for many reasons—including he had never trained a replacement so there was no longer whiskey to be made. Trouser passed away a few days after Art and they were buried side by side on top of a bluff overlooking the Jacks Fork River.

Google The History of the Ozark Mountains if you want to get an inside look at what things were like back in the day.

Rolland Love's Bio

Rolland Love is the author of short stories, novels, plays, a best-selling computer book and a co-author of Homegrown in the Ozarks: Mountain Meals and Memories, a cookbook that was a finalist for best book of the year in Missouri.

He created and presents workshops on how to write your life story, which has been developed into an authoring website Imastory.com. Love as a speaker, has appeared on talk shows, been interviewed by numerous publications including the Kansas City Star, which has praised his *Mark Twain* writing style.

Rolland was a re-enactor with the Lewis and Clark bicentennial expedition and played the role of Silas Goodrich, expert fisherman. He created a workshop about the adventure, which he presents to schools, libraries, retirement centers, business and civic groups ...

To schedule Rolland as a speaker or present a workshop contact him Email: Storiesrus1@gmail.com

Other Books By Rolland Love

Eight novels and short story books are available in the OzarkStories.com Series.

My latest publication is a coming of age memoir Born Dead on a Winter's Night. Selected as one of the best reads by Amazon Kindle January 2018.

RIVER'S EDGE

In addition to a print version of Ozark Mountains Fishing Stories. An audio is available, which is based on the adventures of author Rolland Love who lived, wrote and reads the fun adventures. Here's what you can expect while listening to the (1) hour and (20) minutes recording. "Real fishing stories. You can even listen to them with your kids around the campfire, in the tent, at home in their beds to get 'em fired up for the big camping or fishing trip. OR, **download** and **burn** a CD to listen too on your next road trip."

The stories are enjoyed by fisherman and non-fisherman of all ages

Having been with me on this outdoor adventure and survived. I want to close with an important life saving tip. *Beware:* More people are killed by lightning each year than any other violent weather, including **hurricanes** and **tornadoes**. When thunder roars go in doors!

Rolland Love

I hope you enjoy reading my novels and short stories and listening to my fishing stories. Google me some time if you're looking for more down home information.